CW00428541

ABOUT THE AUTHOR

After many years as an actor in film and television Phil moved into writing and producing feature films, series and single dramas for TV, radio, documentary and animation.

He has written three psychological thrillers, Siena, Single Cell and Time*Slip*.

Through his company, Funky Medics, he produced, devised and wrote, animations and comic books for the UK, Europe and US on health education.

Originally from Pembrokeshire, West Wales, he now lives near Cardiff.

Visit: philrowlandswriter.com

Published in Great Britain in 2022
By Diamond Crime

ISBN 978–1–7397448-0-9

Copyright © 2022 Phil Rowlands

Diamond Crime is an imprint of Diamond Books Ltd.

Thanks to Steve, Greg, Jen and all at Diamond Crime

Book design: jacksonbone.co.uk
Cover photograph: iStock

Also by Phil Rowlands
Siena
Single Cell

For information about Diamond Crime authors
and their books, visit:
www.diamondbooks.co.uk

Time*Slip*

A story of time and place

PHIL ROWLANDS

CHAPTER ONE

March 1943
North Beach
Bridlington, Yorkshire

It was the worst night since the catastrophic storms over New Year.

Huge waves battered the shoreline, howling winds and icy rain whipped and twisted, and cracking thunder and jagged lightning echoed around the sides of the bay. It was not a night to brave the elements, but two policemen dressed in heavy capes and helmets, one shorter with a slight limp, were almost at the end of the deserted promenade, their bodies leaning into the ferocious gale, metal-toed-and-heeled boots clicking and sliding on the saturated surface.

They stopped at the top of the steep steps that led down to the beach, their heads coming together briefly, then the one with the limp moved carefully and slowly down onto the slippery wooden treads. He hesitated then, as the other turned and headed toward a hut that sat under an overhang leaning out from the high cliff behind it, shouted to him, his hands cupped around the sides of his mouth. It took a moment for the other to hear then he stopped, looked around, and, seeing the beckoning arm, went back. He listened, his ear close to the other's mouth, then nodded and followed him down to the sand. They struggled against the wind and rain as the sea pounded the beach. In the distance ahead of them, at the far edge of the cove, the outline of a Lookout post was just visible.

Suddenly, the taller man caught a brief flickering beam of yellow light bouncing close to it. He shook the wet out of his eyes. The light flashed again and lit up shadows and stones in the wall. He grabbed the other's arm, pointed towards the Lookout, and shouted "A light!" The two men stared, waiting for it to reappear, then, when it didn't, they hurried towards the building. It was exhausting pushing through the buffeting and blasting of the storm and the one with the limp found it hard to keep up and almost fell as he tried to match the other's speed.

When they got there, they paused for breath, then moved around, careful to keep below the long, narrow observation slit, until they reached a wooden door where the rock face behind gave some shelter. The one who'd stumbled reached inside his cape, took out a truncheon and held it at head height. He grasped the metal door handle, slippery in the wet, and with difficulty turned it and slowly pushed the door open. The other pulled out a torch and turned it on. The beam was dim, the batteries almost out, or damp. He shook his head and they stood there, listening for any sounds that weren't their own.

The light from the torch died suddenly and the darkness was absolute then a sudden zigzag explosion of lightning directly above them reflected on the long blade of a knife as it slammed through cape, uniform, and deep into flesh.

* * *

The Present
North Beach
Bridlington, Yorkshire

It was a rough, miserable, and grey day: the wind howling and the rain pelting. Ian Chambers, tall, rumpled, forty-nine, writer, wrapped in heavy coat and drop-eared cap against the drenching wet and bitter cold, battled the storm from the end of the deserted promenade to a small shelter overlooking North Beach. Maybe the sight and sound of nature's raw power would clear the shit out of his head and make space for a genius solution to gestate and grow. A solution that would give him an ending for his latest novel, an ending that made sense and would leave the reader, if not totally fulfilled, at least satisfied.

His mobile vibrated and rang. He turned his back to the sea and checked the caller id.

"Fuck!"

CHAPTER TWO

He hurtled out of South Kensington underground station and waited, jiggling with impatience and a sudden need to pee, for a red light to stop the mid-morning traffic, then dodged across the road, just missing a cyclist slinking on and off the pavement, and swerving around an old woman carrying a large box as she hesitated on the kerb. He looked at his watch. Shit! He was so late. He picked up speed and rounded a corner, then turned into a small mews between a flower shop and a coffee boutique. He reached the door of an elegant white town house and touched the video pad button for the Thane Literary Agency. A very young, very classy, but slightly sneering face looked out at him. "Yes?"

Two-way video. That was new since he'd been here last.

"It's Ian, I've got a meeting with Janey at ten thirty."

A pause as her eyes flicked away.

"It's nearly quarter to."

"I know. I'm late."

"You are." A condescending, tight-lipped little smile twitched and went.

He controlled himself. No point getting angry. He needed to get in now and antagonising her would get a negative reaction, make him even later and Janey even more tetchy. He smiled and hoped that calm and charm might work.

"Please, let me in, sweetheart."

It didn't!

"Is she expecting you?"

Of course she's fucking expecting me!

He took a breath. "Yes."

There was a pause as her eyes narrowed and she searched for something lost in the 'no reason to remember' bin.

"Er… Ian…?"

He felt a roar of response, the words bubbling behind his lips, ready to explode out and batter her into submission. *Don't!* You need her to let you in. Stop it! Keep calm!

"Chambers."

She looked blankly at him. For fuck's sake!

"Ian Chambers, I'm one of her writers." Jesus Christ. He'd been with Janey for nearly ten years; although this was his first trip down to London for months and he couldn't remember if this was the same dim door ward as last time. None of them stayed long but, male or female, they were all the same: rude, posh, and not very bright.

Ian knew today would be tricky. Usually, he was admonished on Zoom or FaceTime but, because he'd missed another deadline, this was going to be a very sharp slap, probably alongside the threat of having to pay back his miserable advance for the months-late draft of his book. And all that would be much more painful and effective administered in person by the Dragon, hence the summons.

"Just a minute."

He fought an urge to smash the video pad and splinter the face it held as the door opened and a woman came out.

He knew her. Jaz Stevens, a BAFTA-winning screenwriter, who also had Janey as her agent. She smiled at his obvious distress. "Did she forget you… again? Too old to be of interest!" She kissed him. "You're a bit sticky, darlin'."

"I know, I ran, I'm late…"

The face on the pad came into focus. "What was your last name again?"

Jaz moved quickly out of the way as Ian pounced towards the door. "Janey is in a foul mood. Best not to annoy her with your witty words."

"Perfect." He moved quickly past her. "Thanks, Jaz, let's grab a drink soon."

"I'll be in the Bell for a bit. I'm meeting Phil Gethin for a bitch about our exes."

Ian had just reached the stairs and turned his head towards her. "Can't today. I'll call you when I'm next coming down."

"Make sure you do. Have fun with the Dragon."

She went and the door shut, swift and silent. Ian, not looking where he was going, tripped on the third step and landed on his knee, avoiding a full body crash with his hand and elbow.

"Fuck!"

Janey Howell was scary at her worst but could be frivolous and flirty when one of her writers brought in a large wedge of bestseller or film rights cash. Today she was the former. Not a spark of fun or even empathy touched her cold green eyes. Her age was hard to judge but she was somewhere in her early forties. Her husband was an academic and she had four kids. She was one of the three directors of the Thane Literary Agency and knew every sensitive part of body and mind in those she was eviscerating.

She had rated Ian's writing highly and championed him when she first took him on, having been a driving force through a couple of critically acclaimed books, one a standalone psychological crime thriller and the other a coming-of-middle age journey that had touched hearts and brought in enough cash to earn an invite to the agency's annual bestselling authors' binge. However, for the last two years, Ian had struggled to write anything that hit the same mark, then he'd come up with this story. He thought he'd cracked it, until six weeks ago, when he'd dried up and knew he hadn't. But he persevered and a week ago he thought he might have finally come up with a good way to finish it. Now though, he had suddenly fallen into darkness and doubt and was still fifteen thousand words away from an ending. They were floating in the murky swamp of edified endings and remained just out of his reach.

Janey was sitting behind a cluttered desk and Ian, on an expensive, uncomfortable stretch sofa, was trying to look relaxed and untouched by her searing critical summary of his worth. He was failing, and wanted a cuddle, not another sabre cut. His mind had drifted to find a safe place when he suddenly became aware of a deafening silence. Hard and unblinking, she waited for his response.

He thought about the way his voice would sound

before he spoke and managed a normality he didn't feel. "How long?"

"Five weeks."

"Shit."

"Is that a problem?"

He tried not to hesitate but did. "No…"

"Sure?"

"Yes."

A long moment, and then she looked away as her mobile rang.

"Good!" She answered it. "Lara, just a minute sweetheart." She glanced at Ian. "I'm on your side. Don't let me down." She turned away. "I loved, *loved*, the NYT reviews. Should keep you near the top of the list for another couple of weeks."

She flicked her fingers towards Ian and blew him a kiss, her good humour restored by the touch of fame and fortune from the Big Apple.

CHAPTER THREE

Lucy Carroll, mid-thirties, small, dark, and quirky looking, sat at a corner table in La Puerta, a Spanish restaurant just off Sloane Square, reading *The Letters of Sylvia Plath*. She was disturbed by the beauty of the words and her own self-doubt surfaced and slipped easily into the well-worn list of her positive and negative traits. She was sometimes too pragmatic, occasionally fierce, and easily combative, but mostly her default was warm, generous, bright, witty and, on balance, it brought her more friends than detractors. She was a talented poet who had authored ten popular collections. Her day job was as senior lecturer in Verse, on the Literature course at Queen Mary University of London. She had also written two unpublished novels. Her favourite review of her poetry was about *Words of Hope,* a short anthology on the theme of loss.

The beautiful and lyrical poetry of Lucy Carroll resonates with a simplicity and truth that instils courage and hope in all those who fear they might never find a light to lead them out of the shadows of their grief.

Where the fuck was the little shit?

Despite the recognition of her past work soothing the pain of others, she had glanced at her watch and a sharp dart of anger surfaced. It was pathetic! She'd give it another ten minutes, then go. She forced herself to return to Plath.

Ian came into the restaurant, looked around, saw Lucy, and headed for her table. He decided that smiley with a hint of apology would work best.

However, for that to have a chance, she'd have to look at him.

She didn't.

"Sorry I'm late, a long battering from the Dragon." He sat down. There was no response or movement from Lucy. "I need a drink!"

A waiter approached the table with a bottle, showed Lucy the label. "It's the only Ribera del Duero we have. It is expensive."

She smiled at him. "That's fine, thank you." She went back to her book. Ian realised that this was going to be trickier than he'd hoped. He watched the waiter as he opened the bottle. He played the 'not looking at Ian' game too. He sniffed the cork and poured a small amount into the glass in front of Lucy. She took it and sipped.

"Lovely."

Her eyes met those of the waiter, and, for a brief moment, he fell in love, then feeling Ian's eyes on him filled first Lucy's glass then Ian's, still not looking at him. He left the bottle on the table.

Ian picked up his glass, touched it to Lucy's, and took a drink. He felt it warm its way down. He waited for the calm but as Lucy lifted her gaze away from the book to him, he knew it would probably be the opposite.

"What train are you getting back?"

It was the one question he didn't want to answer yet… but probably best to get it over with and then hopefully it would all be up from there on. "Six fifteen… it's the only…"

"You little shit!" For a moment he was stunned and although he saw her pick up her glass wasn't prepared for her to throw it over him. She did. He caught a drop on his tongue.

"Nice."

The waiter, hovering at another table, moved quickly towards them but stopped, not sure what to do. He didn't want to get punched or piss them off so they complained to his boss. In Spain this was nothing, but here, there could be mayhem. Then, as they both laughed and Lucy accepted Ian's kiss, he knew it would be all right… for now.

He'd never understand the Brits. They were all mad!

* * *

In Driffield the weather was foul. The small Yorkshire town looked drab and miserable in the torrential rain and the stinging wind. Nora Chambers had had enough. Her waterproof coat and hood weren't keeping the wet out, the heavy Waitrose bag was cutting into her hand, and her five-year-old son, George, wanting to stay at a bookshop window with a Winnie the Pooh display, had managed to pull away from her. She tried to grab him and the bag swung out, hitting the large window as an olive oil bottle slipped out and cracked on the pavement, the golden liquid seeping out

"Shit! Shit! Shit!"

She glared at the bottle, glanced around, saw a bin outside the next shop.

George looked hard at his mother. "That's a bad word, Mummy."

"I feel bad!" The words were louder, harsher, and angrier that she'd meant them to be. George started to cry.

"I'm sorry, sweetheart." She lifted him up and with difficulty managed both him and the bag. "Let's go for a hot chocolate."

The effect was instant, the tears stopped although the 'you frightened me' face was still there. After a moment, he kissed her cheek and smiled.

Nora ignored the looks of distaste for her using bribery from those close enough to see and hear what happened. Fuck 'em! She couldn't pick up the bottle as well, so she put George down. "Wait here, Georgie, I'm just putting this in the bin."

"Can I look in the window?"

"Yes, but don't move." She left the bag on the pavement next to him. George tried but it was hard to not move and look in the window behind him. He gave up and watched a little dog sniff at the bag until his mum came and snatched it away, grabbed George's hand and pulled him after her.

* * *

At La Puerta, a man in a chicken suit was arguing with a waitress who was trying to get him to leave; a middle-aged woman, beautifully dressed, with a large gin, was having a FaceTime chat with a younger version of herself, tanned, topless, with a blue Mediterranean Sea behind her; and another Ribera was being brought to Ian and Lucy's table by their wary-looking waiter, who realised that the atmosphere had changed again. They seemed to have lost any loving feeling and were even more spiky than they had been at the start of the first bottle.

"I don't see the point in us going on," Lucy said as her eyes bored into Ian's.

Ian hesitated, then decided that brief, honest, and direct would do it. "All right." He hoped for the best but tensed himself to roll with a shower of words or wine.

There was a dramatic freeze. Babies have been conceived in less time. Contracts signed. Lives taken. Then it ended. Lucy snapped into open-eyed disbelief and spat out, "All right?"

Ian glanced at the waiter, who was holding the opener like a weapon, then back to Lucy. "Yes, all right."

"What do you mean, all right?" The ice was spreading towards him.

"All right, I don't see the point in us going on." He almost hid the sharp breath of failing courage.

"You little twat!" Her voice rose. "When were you going to tell me? Over the coffee or after a fast and fumbled fuck at the flat?"

"Fumbled?"

"Fast and fruitless fuck better?" That was loud enough to turn heads, and for the waiter to take a step back and hold the bottle as a shield in front of him.

Ian almost threw back 'lazy', 'lecherous', and even 'loving', but chose the more dangerous truth. "Nora's pregnant."

Lucy froze. Her face was a death mask.

At the door of the restaurant the chicken was being held back from the waitress by a large rabbit in a green coat.

Ian slowly moved his chair back and stood. "I'm really sorry, sweetheart."

Lucy shot up. Ian, reaching out to touch her, stopped at the look in her eyes. The waiter touched her on the shoulder. She turned quickly and glared at him. He moved away. She looked around the restaurant. Everything was still, locked in the moment. Then she turned back to Ian, tilted her head to one side, and punched him, her arm moving like a piston, her fist sinking into the soft flesh of his stomach. Not quite a knockout blow but enough to drop him to the floor. She looked at him for a moment then walked away, smiling at the waiter as he scuttled backwards.

"He'll pay!" She made her way towards the entrance between the quiet tables and as she went out, the chicken and the rabbit applauded and did a little pecking and bobbing dance.

The waiter watched her leave. His love was now in full bloom and he looked disdainfully at Ian as he pulled himself up off the floor, and almost successfully hid his sneer as he spoke.

"Would you like anything else, sir?"

"The bill!" Ian sat heavily in his seat and wished he could start again and do it differently.

CHAPTER FOUR

Ian arrived in York an hour late with the anodyne and confusing announcement of the delay being caused by 'unusually heavy rain and a broken-down train.' Even the train manager had to contain his derision.

The weather had deteriorated as they'd travelled north from London, as had Ian's spirit.

The train was crowded and as they'd moved from station to station the crush in the corridor between seats allowed little chance of making it to the loo in time if you put it off for too long. He had just managed to push his way through when a barely dressed woman came out.

"I wouldn't go in there, pet, shit all over the floor and the seat just cracked. Would have cut my arse if I hadn't fucking flown off it."

The thought of this gargantuan young woman, squeezed into a couple of yards of distressed satin, taking bare-arsed flight almost gave him hysterics but the need for a pee was greater and took him through the door. Without looking around him he used the small basin.

It had taken him twenty minutes and a challenge for his place to get back to his window seat. Not that there was any comfort when he managed to elbow his way in ahead of a small man with a leather jacket and a face like a ready to burst balloon. He was surrounded by five bored, restless, and pissed off kids slowly taking the sanity away from their exhausted mum. She was almost invisible under the youngest two, one a wriggling and crying two-year-old and the other a venom-spitting baby that screamed for milk. Ian's hangover threatened to explode as the cacophony took his self-inflicted headache from manageable to near mortal.

When he'd eventually got to York, the relief of getting off the train displaced the guilt and fear of his being found out, not only for his now-ended affair with Lucy, but for spending money on a meal with her when he and Nora were struggling to keep their heads above water. At least he'd have a week or so until the credit card statement landed, and he had to find a reason good enough to placate her.

Nora flashed the lights as Ian looked around the car park. She had to do it three times and give a loud burst on the horn before he found her. He ran over, threw himself through the door, and slammed it. Nora closed her eyes.

"Don't slam the door... please."

"Sorry." He leaned across, kissed her, and looked behind him. "Where's George?"

"At Daniel's." Nora looked tight and tired. She briefly dropped her head then sighed, started the car, and slowly moved off. Ian had a moment of panic over the bum-tightening thought that Lucy had called her. He tried to push it away, but it stuck hard and festered. He took a breath and summoned up a sympathetic and calm tone.

"Bad day?"

"You could say that." Sharp with a quick eye-flick towards him!

"Me too!"

The wipers struggled to clear the pounding rain on the windscreen as the worn rubbers scratched and squeaked.

"What happened?"

"Not now, I need to concentrate."

"All right."

As they battled their way out of the city and onto the A166 that took them home, Ian panicked and tried to read Nora's mind. As usual it was a pointless exercise.

"Is George on a sleepover?"

"No!"

"Right."

They picked George up from his friend Daniel's in the next village to theirs. Daniel had an older brother and a six-month-old sister and his mum, Rose, carried the baby and shouted at the brother. It was obvious that she was pissed off with them for being late. It took ten minutes to get George out of the house and by the time Ian had strapped him, struggling and not happy to have to go home, into his seat, they were both soaking wet and George was crying because Ian had shouted at him.

Nora leaned over the seat.

"Stop it, now, or you can walk home."

George took that in. "It's wet," he said with a sob he hoped would work. It didn't.

She started the car and moved off as Ian scrabbled into the front seat and slammed the door again. Nora glared at him.

"Sorry."

She accelerated, skidded, and then shot off.

"Did you give Aunty Lucy a kiss from me?" said George quietly after a long pause.

* * *

After leaving the restaurant Lucy had to keep the rage from bursting out at the innocent males who smiled at her or let their eyes settle briefly on her face or body. One tall and stooping hipster hesitated in front of her and asked if she was all right. Lucy snapped at him to get the fuck out of her way, which he did, shocked and hurt.

She powered on to Piccadilly, through Green Park and slowly the heat of anger eased to a dull ache as she passed the Circus, Leicester Square, and then followed the early rush hour crowds through Charing Cross station and over the bridge across the Thames.

The South Bank was one of her favourite places and the tables of second-hand books always calmed her as she searched for those rare magical finds that lifted her spirit, Emily Dickinson, Rumer Godden, Christina Rossetti, and of course Sylvia Plath. She had once found an almost perfect copy of Plath's volume of short stories, *Johnny Panic and the Bible of Dreams,* that had thrilled and excited her until she got home, started to flick through, and found that two pages had been ripped out of the middle of one of the stories. She'd tried to fill in the missing words with her own, but it was a miserable attempt. She was not Sylvia Plath. Another time she had found a poem, 'I like that you are crazy not with me', by Marina Tsvetaeva, a Russian poet who looked a bit like Victoria Wood. The last verse seemed to mirror her and Ian's relationship.

'I thank you with my hand and all my heart, For loving me (that you don't even know!), For the sweet peace, I own in the night, For the scarce meeting in the eve's fast flow, For our not-walking under the moonlight, For our not-standing under the sun's glow – That not with me – alas – you lose your mind, That not with you – alas – I lose my own.'

Today, however, there was nothing that would divert the approaching collapse into self-pity and regret. So, she went home, took the battery out of her mobile and put it in the bathroom so she wouldn't be tempted to do anything stupid, then slowly worked her way through one of the last two bottles of champagne that Ian had, when his last advance had come through, given her to celebrate her next book launch, a launch that was now a month away. He couldn't be there because it was Nora's birthday.

She finished the bottle, screamed 'Fuck you!', then felt the pain as the claws of her usually gentle tabby cat, Plath, dug in. Plath, who had been purring on Lucy's lap, had yowled, reared up in shock and gone into immediate attack mode.

* * *

George was so worked up that it had taken Ian an hour to settle him down. He had read two stories and made up one about a little dog that found a lost child before the boy finally dropped off to sleep. Then he and Nora sat down to eat. She told him about her shit day and shouting at George and he moaned about Janey and drank his way through almost a bottle of wine.

The cottage was low-ceilinged and a mix of old and new. The living/dining room had a cluttered and cosy feel. There was a large open fire, a deep old comfortable sofa, and pictures covered the walls. The alcoves either side of the slate fire surround were shelved, stuffed and overflowing with books. George's play box, an old ship's trunk, was open and the floor around it was littered with toys, books, pencils, crayons, and paper. In the corner of the room, a narrow wooden staircase wound up to the bedrooms, Ian's writing room, and a large family bathroom. On the table there was a wok with the remains of a risotto and a wooden board with chunks of crusty bread.

Nora rubbed her neck and yawned. She felt exhausted.

Ian picked up the wine bottle and was surprised to find it empty. He got up, holding it.

"Haven't you had enough?" She tried to sound reasonable, not snarky, but didn't quite manage it.

Ian looked at her for a moment. "No." He headed towards the kitchen, a new, almost paid for, extension that had seemed like a good idea before Nora became pregnant again. Now it was an extravagance they could have done without. It was a large L-shape, classy, contemporary, and light, with a set of sliding doors that opened out on to a terrace and the steeply rising garden that ran into a field with a small cluster of trees. Out of sight of the table there was a large cooking range, pale wood cupboards with brushed steel handles, and a double sink.

Nora felt really cross with Ian. She picked up some bread and slammed it onto the board. It didn't make her feel better. Suddenly there was a loud "Shit!" from Ian and a bottle exploded as it hit the floor.

Nora closed her eyes then slowly opened them and waited.

Ian appeared, his hand wrapped in a bloody dishcloth.

"Sorry, I'm pissed. I cut my hand picking up the glass."

Nora got up. "Let me see."

She unwrapped the dishcloth carefully and wiped the blood away. There was a deep cut in the fleshy bit of his thumb and blood was welling out.

"Hold your arm up."

He did what he was told. "Let's go somewhere tomorrow, the three of us."

Nora started to clear the table.

"You've got to finish your book, George has to go to school, and I've got a clinic appointment." She took the plates and the wok into the kitchen.

Upstairs George cried out loudly, then shouted, "Mummy!" Then again, louder: "Mummy!" A pause then a scream: "Mummy!"

Ian looked towards the stairs. "I'll go."

Nora came from the kitchen. "No. You'll drip blood all over him. I'm going to bed anyway. I'm shattered."

"Mummy!"

"How long have I got to stay like this?"

"As long as it takes."

She disappeared up the stairs. Ian lowered his arm and the blood started again. He threw his arm back up and sat at the table.

Eventually the blood stopped. Ian found a plaster to cover the cut, then went upstairs and looked into George's room. Nora was asleep and he was cuddled tightly into her.

He closed George's door quietly and went into his and Nora's room, undressed, and got into bed, thinking he would lie awake in turmoil all night but the amount he had drunk during the day kicked in and he was in a deep sleep within five minutes.

The next morning, he felt terrible. He tried to work but his stomach lurched and cramped and the half-gallon of coffee he'd drunk brought on a pounding headache as he tried to make sense of the jumble of words he'd blindly thrown on to the screen. He deleted them all. His thumb hurt but wasn't bleeding. He'd covered it with a fresh plaster and was trying to keep it out of the way. It was stuffy and hot in his small writing space. He realised that he needed air even if it was cold and wet.

He heard muffled shouts from outside and opened the window. It was freezing but helped make his sense of being able to stay alive a bit stronger than it had been an hour ago.

Nora was struggling to get George into the car.

"George, get into your seat."

"Don't push, Mummy."

"Sit down then."

Ian leaned out of the window. 'Do what Mummy says, George.'

George looked up, waved, and sat in his seat.

Nora glared up at Ian.

"What?"

She shook her head, walked around to the driver's side, and got in.

George opened his window. "Bye, Daddy."

"Bye, sweetheart, have fun at school."

"Can we go to the beach tomorrow?"

"We'll see."

"Please, Daddy."

Nora turned round to George.

"Shut the window."

There was a slight pause before George said, 'You didn't say please, Mummy.'

"Now!"

George watched Ian as the window closed.

Then the front passenger one opened and Nora leaned across and shouted, "Don't forget the logs."

"I won't."

The window closed and, as she started the car, George opened his again.

"George!" Ian could just hear the edge to Nora's voice through the open window

"You opened yours, Mummy." George smiled up at Ian.

The car stopped and Nora started to get out, but the window closed. She slammed her door and drove off.

"Don't slam the door…" Even though she was out of sight, Ian said it almost under his breath.

He sighed heavily, sat at his desk and looked at the screen. At the top of the page was a heading: *Chapter Twenty-three*.

He glanced at his hand, waggled his thumb, then looked back at the almost blank page. 'Fuck it!'

He saved the document in several different folders and on his My Passport drive, then put the MacBook to sleep, rotated his head, and closed his eyes. He snapped them open again as an image of a cold and acid Lucy shot in.

George was singing and Nora distracted as they pulled up in the crush of cars outside the school.

George stopped abruptly. 'Mummy?'

"Yes."

"Why did Daddy shout at you last night? It woke me up."

Nora touched his cheek. "He didn't, sweetie, he'd hurt his hand."

She got out and went round to George's side. He'd already undone his belt and opened the door. He jumped down. Nora bent over to kiss him. He threw his arms around her neck. "I love you, Mummy."

Nora's stress slipped away for a moment.

"I love you too, gorgeous."

He put his ear on her tummy.

"I can't hear anything."

"It's too small yet..." She glanced across at the school. Most of the children had gone in, only a few stragglers were left. "Quickly, or you'll be late."

George kissed her again, ran through the gate, then stopped and turned around. "Will I have a baby sister?"

She laughed. "You'll have to wait and see."

George nodded then galloped to the teacher who was waiting at the school entrance.

Nora watched the door for a moment after they disappeared, then checked her watch. "Bugger."

She rushed into the car, slammed the door, and turned on the ignition. Nothing happened. She tried again. It just turned over.

"Don't you bloody dare!"

Then she gently touched the key and kissed the steering wheel. "I'm sorry I shouted. Please, baby, for me." She took a deep breath and tried again. It started. "Thank you." She put the car in gear, waited for an SUV to pass, then pulled out quickly in front of a large van… and stalled. The van just managed to swerve round her. The driver gave the finger and mouthed, "Stupid cow."

Nora breathed deeply and turned the key. The car started. She checked there was nothing coming and moved off.

* * *

The room was dark and shadowy, a broken shaft of sunlight edged through the not quite closed curtains and touched the back of Lucy's head as she lay, naked and face down on a large 1960s sofa, her hand hanging limply over the side, her fingers bent where they touched the light wood floor. Nearby there was a mobile phone and further away a glass and two empty champagne bottles. There was a scrabbling noise against a door and suddenly the mobile rang with a series of piercingly loud

screams from the shower scene in *Psycho* – a ringtone
that had once seemed funny but was soon unbearable.
She had changed it to an actual telephone bell only for
Psycho to return frighteningly when the battery was
taken out or recharged from empty. Somehow it had
become the default and she hadn't been able to delete
it.

Lucy's head jerked violently as she tried to open her
eyes. After a moment of pain, confusion and panic, she
realised what it was; she must have put the battery back
in her phone. Then a wave of panic washed over her.
Had she rung anyone? The screams drove the thought
away. She had to stop it before her head split open. Her
hand twitched and touched the vibrating and screeching
phone. With a huge effort she grasped it and fumbled for
the 'call accept' button, almost impossible when your
eyes refused to focus. At last she found and pressed it
and the noise stopped.

"Yes." Her voice was ragged and harsh.

"Are you alright?" Ian said quietly. He was trying to
be calm but concerned. "I was worried about you."

"Fuck off!" Lucy threw the phone onto the sofa then
turned over and lay back again, this time face up. Slowly
she felt the cold seep over her then realised that she had
no clothes on and was going to throw up. She struggled
from the sofa and lurched towards the door, dragged it
open, and tripped over Plath as she rushed to the
bathroom. Somehow, she kept her balance and just got
her head over the toilet bowl before her stomach
exploded. The spasms emptied her until there was only
retching left. She held onto the toilet as she stood and

tried to make her legs stop shaking. She gulped mouthfuls of water from the tap in the basin, until the foul taste and dryness eased. Slowly she came out of the bathroom but as she went through into the living room again to find her clothes, she stepped on something that oozed up between her toes. She looked down, horrified. It was cat shit!

"Fuuuuuuck!"

Plath, with a sense of impending doom, rushed past her, crashed through the kitchen door, and flung herself through the cat flap.

CHAPTER FIVE

Ian was on his second pint of Old Peculiar at the Spoon and Cup, the small pub a quarter of a mile from his home. He sat at the bar trying to do the Guardian crossword. *Unpunctual but brilliant police helper keeps in time.* Nine letters. The first *o* and the last e. Suddenly it was crystal clear. He said it quietly, "Oscellate." He wrote it in pleased with his cryptic skills.

"I, not e. Osc*i*llate."

He glanced round. Nora was standing close behind him. He should have felt a presence. He hadn't!

"Damn!" It didn't make sense now but he changed the *e* to *i*, got off the stool, and gave her a gentle kiss. "Smartarse! Drink?"

"Tonic." There was a clock over the bar; her eyes flicked towards it. 11.30. "Didn't you have enough yesterday?"

He couldn't think of the right words so didn't answer.

"I'll be outside." She smiled, warm, but knowing and tired.

Josh, the landlord, young, just getting to know everyone in the village after taking over six months ago, smiled. "I'll bring it out."

"No, it's OK. I'll have a top-up half, please."

"Sure?"

"Yes … no… just the tonic."

"Good move."

"I've just had one, if she asks, not that she will… I hope."

Josh laughed and handed him the tonic, in a glass with ice, lime, and mint. He was trying to add a bit of style to the pub. Ian left the Guardian on the bar.

It was sunny now but cold and wintry. Nora didn't seem to feel the chill but Ian did. Not only the weather but a sliver of ice from Nora too, and it was that made him shiver. He did up his jacket so she wouldn't know.

She did. She was far too sensitive and all-seeing.

"George thought you'd shouted at me when you cut yourself. It woke him up."

He reached over the table and took her hand. "I'm sorry, I'll explain to him tonight." She tried to pull her hand away. He held on to it, hoped she'd smile. She did. He let go.

"It's all right, I told him. So why aren't you working?"

Ian looked at her for a long moment. She drank her tonic then held his gaze.

"I'm not going to finish the book."

"Don't be so bloody negative."

"I'm not. Just realistic."

"You've got five weeks. Plenty of time, if you don't keep slipping off to the pub when you get a bit lost for words."

Ian drank half of what was left of his beer. "It was just today. Bit hungover, needed a drink to get me centred." He took a breath. "After today I'm going to limit myself to a glass of wine with dinner until it's done."

"How was Lucy?"

Ian's heart skipped and he was sure his face twitched. "Lucy?"

"You said you were meeting her for lunch to talk about the latest "little shit" in her life."

Fuck, he could hardly breathe. Easy. Just answer.

"Yes, I did…" he struggled for a name, "Mark. It's good at the moment."

"You said she was in a state."

He thought, quickly but not too quickly. Pause was better than panic.

"She's a bit of a trauma tart."

"So, it's still going on?"

"Yes, he's up for age and experience. Probably got an Oedipus complex."

Nora gave him a look and took another drink. "Is she going to get up here for George's birthday?"

"What?" He'd forgotten that little poison dart.

"She was going to bring him up, so we could check him out. How old is he, twenty-two? Lucky girl, I wouldn't mind a bit of young meat…"

That was a shock Ian couldn't hide.

"But I suppose I can make do with you: older, flabbier, more wrinkled, but still with a few tricks a girl can enjoy."

She stood up, leaned down and gave him a kiss.

"Get back to work and I might be nice to you after George is in bed."

"Where are you going?"

"Meeting Hattie for lunch."

"She all right now?"

"No, Jo's still being a prick about her going back to work."

"Is he?"

"You don't think so?"

Wrong answer! "Sorry, I wasn't really listening."

Nora waited.

"Yes, he's a prick!"

"Good." She gave him another quick kiss. "Work!"

He watched her as she walked away, turned round briefly, the 'now' in her eyes friendly but clear. He hoped that the jumps and twists in his gyrating stomach weren't visible.

* * *

Lucy reached for her phone for the third time. As her hand touched it, it rang. It was the normal tone again. She didn't recognize the number. She frowned, hesitated then answered it. "Hello?"

"It's Tamsin…" One of her Masters' students. "I'm really sorry but I'm not going to be able to meet you today…" Shit, she'd completely forgotten the tutorial! "I've got a bad period."

She turned her relief into a thoughtful and caring tone. "That's fine, don't worry, we'll catch up. Hope it eases soon."

"Usually takes a couple of days! Monday?"

"I'll text you."

Lucy didn't like messing up her tutorials but doing one today would have been a nightmare. She looked at the phone then searched for Ian's contacts and tapped 'house phone'. It rang and she prepared herself.

* * *

Ian didn't want to go home just to fester and look at a blank screen, so he decided to go for a walk and try and plan the next chapter. He knew what it had to say but not the way to do it. Walking sometimes helped, particularly if he had other stuff tangling him up. And it was a great way of blowing out overindulgence too.

The Yorkshire Wolds were at the end of the lane they lived in. It was one of the reasons they'd bought the house. Before George came along, they'd have flurries of foreplay in the dusk and once made love behind a sheep shelter, thinking they were alone but exciting six old walkers as they slowly passed at the top of the Dale.

Usually, he'd walk through the steep-sided valley to the village on the other side of the Wold and have a pint there before coming back, but today he didn't go all the way to the top of the dale. Halfway up his legs had started to complain so he'd stood and looked back along the valley. There was always something stark, dangerous, and beautiful about this perfectly sculpted landscape and he felt he shared space with all those who over millennia had experienced its strange and timeless power.

On his way back he stopped and sat on top of a sheep shelter at the bottom of the valley and tried to clear his mind of all but time and place and just let its rhythms help stimulate his creativity into finding a solution for the final chapter of his book. Slowly the first faint shadows of the end of the story appeared and he felt more optimistic about finishing it by the deadline. He didn't know how long he sat there but it was starting to get dark by the time he left. The wind was louder and stronger and the clouds rolled thick and black. Lucy and London seemed too far away for Nora and George to be tainted by his betrayal. But it was still so fucking wrong! He was pathetic. Talk about Hattie's Jo being a prick, Ian's prickishness was a mammoth to Jo's mouse.

He sat at the kitchen table making notes. He always did this with pen and paper, seemed to need the physical connection between hand, head and blank page that was more sensitive and less distanced than with a keyboard.

He set out the next chapter in his own style of shorthand. Sometimes, when he did that and worked too quickly the sense of what he was trying to say was lost and he had to go back and start again. But this time it was good and after an hour he was ready to put it into the book.

Nora and George had come back as he was making coffee to take up with him and he persuaded them to have hot chocolate and marshmallows. It was their favourite and he'd planned it on his walk, as a treat. It worked with George, who hugged him before he took his plastic mug and sat on the floor in front of the sofa to watch TV. Nora was not such an easy sell. She was happy to have the treat but knew it was because he'd been an arse and that made it less caring and selfless.

"How did you get on?"

"Good, got the next chapter mapped out. Just going up to do it now."

"Great, knew you'd get there."

She sat and dipped her marshmallow into the chocolate.

"I almost forgive you for being a drunk."

"Almost?"

"Yes,"

As he went into his study, he heard George's angry little voice. "It's not working, Mummy, it's all funny." Then there was a noise, a crash, and another angry cry.

Nora's voice, calm but firm, sounded like she was next to him. He didn't know how she did that! Her projection was amazing. She should have been a stage actor. "George, don't kick the DVD player."

Ian shut the door behind him and turned on the desk lamp. Next to it the landline was flashing. There were messages. Hardly anyone called that phone, only family and Janey, who always wanted to give him time to consider what she'd said before he responded. Sometimes she'd leave a message on his mobile asking him to phone her or tell him to listen to the message she'd left on the landline. If the slap needed to be sharp and speedy, she'd call both until she spoke to him.

He pressed play.

Janey's voice was clear and controlled. "Hello, darling! Had a chat with Tim today and he was a bit spiky about you missing the last deadline. He's definitely in pruning mood, so you need to get your finger out. Three weeks would be good…"

The bastard, hadn't she told him she'd said five? No, of course she hadn't.

"I did fight your corner and said I'd given you five but he wasn't in listening mode. Tony Sparks has just been poached by Frasers…"

That's not down to me…

"I know that's not down to you, darling, but it focused him to sharpen the knife on those who he perceives not to be pulling their weight…"

Not getting him shitloads of cash!

"Or bringing in the money…" A brief pause for his heart to stutter. "Anyway, sweetie, do your best. I know I've been a bit sharp but I wouldn't want you to be tossed out with the tea leaves." Another pause. "I talked him into taking you on in the first place so don't make me regret that little slip. Love to Nora and little George."

So good to know she had his back. The next message started.

"This is a message for George…"

It was Lucy. Ian froze. He wanted to switch it off but knew he had to listen.

"…from Aunty Lucy. I'll be coming to your party with Mark, sweetie. Tell Mummy, will you? Big hugs and kisses to her and you…" A long beat with a little breath, "And Daddy. Tell him not to worry about putting us up at home, we'll book an AirBnb. Can't wait to see you!" A couple of kissing sounds before she finished and 'that was your last message' came on.

He put his hand over his mouth, muttering "Shit, shit, shit, shit!" and tried to stop the panic as the door opened.

"Who was that?"

"What?"

"Sounded like Lucy."

Ian took a quick silent breath, turning away to the window then back again.

"It was. She's coming to George's party, sends her

love, bringing Mark and doesn't need to stay with us."

Thank fuck!

"Who was the other one from?"

Jesus, talk about bat ears!

"Just a do it or die threat from Janey, but in three weeks not five."

"Just as well you've got a plan then. But not now, you can put George to bed while I make tea. He had his at Hattie's."

* * *

It had taken a while for Lucy to forgive Plath the cat shit crime, but they had eventually made it up and now sat together on the sofa as she FaceTimed one of her closest friends, Tolly, short for Bartholomew. It was a name he hated: his evangelical Baptist Jamaican mum's attempt to tie him to Jesus. It had failed, and Tolly was a humanist, a pragmatist, a psychologist, and above all a passionate believer of finding good in all things… except when it came to Ian, and to his own partner of twelve years, who had left him one morning to live with a BA pilot who was younger and more attractive than Tolly, and an Eton-educated Tory. He wasn't sure which was worse.

Tolly appeared on the screen: mixed race, purple spiky hair, grey eyes, and orange glasses. "So, what has the shitbag done now?"

She told him what had happened in the restaurant, then her walk through London and falling into the champagne at the flat, and about the message she'd left and then this morning's throwing up and the cat shit through her toes. Tolly tried hard not to laugh but failed.

"I'm fucking over the moon that it's ended. You knew he was never going to leave her."

"I never wanted that!"

"Of course you did!"

"No, I didn't! It was only ever supposed to be best mates with bed thrown in… where I was just an old pal … Except down here, where it was different, safe but with no commitment on either side."

"You knew there was always a chance that she would get pregnant again and he would realise what a shitbag he really was and give it up it on a flush of guilt." He paused. "Get into that gorgeous blue McCartney rich Lizzie passed on to you, call an Uber, and I'll meet you in the Soho at nine."

He disappeared and Lucy looked down at Plath. "What do you think?"

Plath stared at her for a long moment then stretched and jumped off her lap. Lucy laughed.

CHAPTER SIX

After two hours of trying to focus without slipping into terrifying Lucy and Nora scenarios, Ian had only managed one pathetic, miserable, shit-awful sentence. It glared at him from the screen. *Forcing himself into the seeping and foul corners of his conscious thoughts, Ivan tried to contain the cry of ecstasy as the exquisite pain tore through him then slowly subsided leaving him longing for the next searing moment as the red-hot tip of the lash…*

Ian pounded the delete key and the words disappeared. Fuck it, he couldn't do this now.

He ejected his back-up drive, put the MacBook to sleep, turned the dim light off. Suddenly he remembered the messages on the landline, deleted them and went out leaving the door open. As he left there was a loud boom of thunder, a crack of lightning, and the rain started hammering against the window.

Nora was almost asleep when Ian came into the dark bedroom.

"I'm going for a walk."

Nora turned towards him. "What?" She looked out of the window. "You're out of your mind."

"I won't be long."

"Take your phone."

"Yes."

"Are you all right?"

"Just need to clear my head." he said too quickly

She noticed but was too exhausted to say anything. "Be careful. Don't wake me."

"I won't." He gave her a kiss.

He left the door open enough for her to hear George if he cried, then went downstairs and through the kitchen into the hall, found his fur-lined boots, put them on, pulled a thick woolly jumper from a cupboard, grabbed his coat and a drop-eared cap, then, quietly shutting the front door, went out.

He drove to Bridlington. After he'd parked, he walked along North Beach, holding a large rubber torch. Its strong beam lit up the saturated sand in front of him. Some way out, crashing waves rampaged and rattled onto the shore. There was no one but Ian there on this wild night. No one else disturbed enough to be out in it. The wind and the rain, like needles, swirled and slapped into his face. The cold and discomfort though, was cathartic. There was nothing but the raw power of nature as it stormed and roared. Ian stopped and turned his head away for a moment's respite then forced himself on. Battling against something he couldn't control had always been a way of avoiding or balancing problems that were of his own making and this edge of the land, this place, was perfect for that.

He raised the torch, explored the darkness ahead, and saw a World War Two Lookout post, broken and crumbling but still standing. He moved the light around it, then, as he changed the direction of the beam, it touched the high and rugged cliffs beyond. There was a sudden loud crack of thunder. He switched off the torch and waited to see the flash and sizzle of lightning. It lit up the sky then splintered and died. In the darkness that followed, on the periphery of his vision, he caught a flicker of light from the Lookout. It was there briefly then stuttered and disappeared. Ian walked towards it, shone his torch onto the walls, and lit up a small opening that once had been a doorway. He stood outside it for a moment, listened for sounds that weren't his own or of the night, almost impossible with the cacophony of the storm, then walked around it and came back to where he had started. There was no one else there.

The doorway was filled with rubble. Ian shone the torch inside. There was nothing he could see from that angle, so he leaned in and moved the beam around the small space. It was empty and stank of piss and shit and a mixture of other foul smells. Where the fuck had the light come from? Was it the remains of the lightning flash that lingered in his sight? He clambered over the rubble and edged himself through the doorway. He stood in the centre of the circular shell and looked around at the rubbish that had been dumped there. He didn't want to know what it all was. He crossed to a small lookout slit in the wall and stretched up to see the sea breaking the darkness as the foam rose and slammed down again. It felt colder in here than outside and it was slowly freezing his face. Then he felt a moment of terror at a shocking feeling that he wasn't alone. But there couldn't be anyone there. He'd looked. There was nobody in or outside.

Suddenly the torch went out. He held it in front of him to use as a weapon. What the fuck was happening now? There were new heavy-duty batteries in it. He'd put them in when he got to the beach. But it didn't matter because he was in a black impenetrable space. He tried to move but nothing worked. He shouted but nothing came out of his open mouth. Then without warning there was a violent wrenching blow to his stomach and an intense pain shot up into his chest. He screamed, but again there was no sound. An internal blackness joined the outer and he fell heavily to the sandy, littered floor, unmoving, still, no breath, no sign of life.

* * *

In the Domino club in Battersea, a home for punters across the LGBTQ spectrum, it was brash, flashing, loud, sweaty, and dimly lit. The dance floor was packed with combinations of twos and threes, deep into the music or each other in a maelstrom of movement and mating.

Lucy and Tolly sat on a purple sofa and watched the action from a mezzanine above the pounding, strobing mass of drink and drug-fuelled fun. Tolly was high fashion in Galliano and Lucy classy and stylish in her blue designer hand-me-down. A red-haired waiter came over. He was wearing tight mini shorts and was tall, bare-chested, and gym toned. He picked up the empty bottle of white Rioja.

"Another of these, girls?" His voice was deep and full of Louisiana camp.

Tolly looked up at him, held the gaze for a moment too long, then leaned towards Lucy. "Luce?"

Lucy shook her head. "No, I'll die."

Tolly kissed her then touched the waiter gently on the hip. "A Sunrise with a twist of gin, please, heart."

The waiter moved his hand. "Sure thing, hon, but no touching."

Tolly lusted as he walked away. Lucy hit him on the arm.

"Stop it!"

"Got a breakfast meeting with Bible belt money, wouldn't do to go in smelling of bedded southern boy."

"You're disgusting."

Tolly laughed and pulled her to her feet as the music changed to slow and smoky. "Let's have a smooch."

"No, I need to get home."

"It's either you or Red. Your choice."

Lucy looked hard at him. "All right, but after that I'm leaving."

"Boring old tart."

He hugged and kissed her then took her hand as they moved towards the stairs.

* * *

Inside the Lookout, the sound of the storm and sea battering the shore was muted by the thick walls but some wind and rain slipped through the slit window, dappling the sand and ruffling some shreds of newspaper caught in the mess in the doorway. Then a roar of thunder, a jagged flash of lightning, a huge gust and a torrential sheet of horizontal rain. Sharp, heavy drops hit Ian's face as he lay with his head facing the crumbling doorway, his body twisted to one side, his legs bent under him. His torch was lying by his head, its beam lighting up a mess of faeces, needles, cans, condoms, and bits of food.

He slowly started to come round with the rain on his face. He opened his eyes and for a moment lay there as the memory returned. What had happened to him? He moved his arms first and then his legs. They all worked. He turned onto his side, rolled on to his knees and carefully stood up. He knew he was alone now. He remembered the blow and the searing pain in his abdomen. He touched the place then took his hand away and looked at it. He glanced around for the torch, found it, picked it up, shone it on his hand and then his stomach. There was nothing there, no blood, nothing hurt, no sign of any attack at all. He rolled the light around the lookout. It was empty.

Then fear and panic came in equal measure as he tried to make sense of it. He had to get out of there. He scrambled through the doorway and out into the full force of the storm. It almost threw him over but he held his balance, ran and stumbled back along the deserted beach. His mind could only follow one thought. He had to get away from there.

He reached the steps that led up to where he parked his car, slowed, inhaled deeply and by the time he got to the door his breathing was almost back to normal. He took his keys out, opened the car, pulled off the coat and hat and dropped them in the back, slid onto his seat and locked the doors. Leaning his head back against the headrest he tried to make sense of what had just happened. But there was no sense in it. There was no one there, then there was. He was attacked and had fallen into a black hole. It felt real. But none of that could have really happened, could it? It must have been a manic moment brought on by stress. A sort of psychological torture for his betrayal of Nora and George. One that he had manufactured as a punishment. A masochistic suggestion of what should happen to him for what he'd done.

Suddenly he felt a weight of exhaustion and his eyes lost focus. He wasn't sure he would be able to drive. He shook his head hard, rubbed his eyes, and moved off, turning on the radio, finding the BBC World Service as the pips ended for the three am local time world news. That would help. The normality of it would centre him on the present, not the recent past.

He got home intact. There were a few hairy moments of falling asleep and jerking awake before he pulled off the lane and through the gateway to the cottage. He stopped close to the door. For a moment, after he turned off the lights and engine, he sat staring out of the windscreen then looked down, placed his hand gently on his stomach and slowly pressed it. He waited for the pain. There wasn't any. All he felt was an overpowering tiredness. He tried to force his eyes to stay open but the light over the porch door was too bright and he had to close them again. He knew that if he didn't move now, it would be too late, and he'd be asleep. With a huge effort he dragged himself out of the car, pulled the keys out of the ignition, fumbled around the lock in the cottage door, finally opened it and went inside.

In the bedroom, Nora was snoring softly. Ian took off his clothes as though they were great weights and dropped his body heavily onto the bed. Nora moved as she felt the weight on the mattress but didn't wake, just turned, and rolled away from him. On the edge of consciousness, Ian looked out at the room. He seemed to be in a kitchen. Not the one in the cottage, one more basic, more like his grandmother's when he was very small but even older.

He tried to rationalise what he was seeing, but it was too surreal… and then suddenly he was deeply asleep.

CHAPTER SEVEN

February 1943

In the small, warm, and cosy kitchen, Catherine Robbins was making sandwiches on a round breadboard next to a wooden drainer and spotless enamel sink. The radio, a ten-year-old brown Bakelite Ferguson, set on a dresser that was filled with knick-knacks, china cups, jugs, and saucers, was playing the Ivy Benson Band, and a kettle on the small stove was starting to boil. Her clothes were drab and well-used, her hair tightly drawn into a bun. Exhaustion had filled in dark rings around her sad and tired eyes. She looked older than thirty-three.

On one of the chairs, two set either side of a small table, her husband, Walter, a hard-looking man with short hair and a tight moustache, just turned thirty-five, was polishing a well-worn black boot, sleeves rolled up. He spat on the leather and brushed it again until it shone. He was finally satisfied and placed it alongside the other shining boot, looked at them, then put them on. Always the right one first. He pulled the laces tight, making sure they were equal lengths, then tied them in a double bow.

Catherine cut the sandwiches into fours and put them into a tin box with two plain biscuits and a small slice of cheese. She turned off the kettle and filled a flask with the boiling water, added a little bit of milk from a jug, made sure the screw top was tight, then fitted the cup over it. She put them both into the black canvas bag that hung on the door handle. It had a gas mask tied on to the carrying strap. She watched Walter stretch out his legs and look at his boots. "They'll be covered in muck by the time you get there, and, in this weather, they'll start leaking again. You should ask them for a new pair."

Walter looked at her for a moment. There was a flicker of irritation in his eyes and then it went.

"They'll do for another few months if I look after them."

He stood up and rolled down his sleeves, did up the buttons on the cuffs, then took a police uniform jacket off the back of the chair and put it on. There were sergeant's stripes on the arm. Catherine held out the bag.

"There's an extra pair of socks in there. You'll need them if the rain mithers on."

Walter, limping slightly, went to her and put his arms around her. She tensed when he touched her. He kissed her cheek. She didn't flinch but her eyes showed her unease. "You're a good wife, Cate." He took the bag and put it on the table.

Catherine moved back to the sink and started to wash the knife she'd used for the sandwiches. "It's little enough!"

Walter sighed and buttoned his jacket. He stood in front of the mirror on the wall above the range with its flaming coals, straightened his tie, took a comb and brush from the mantelpiece, and 'did' his hair. It was a ritual, once with brush, twice with the comb. Satisfied, he put them back and for a moment looked at his reflection, then watched Catherine through the mirror. There was a sadness in his eyes.

"Perhaps it's time we thought about what Dr Clarke suggested… the adoption."

"No!"

Walter sighed, picked up his bag, and put the strap across his chest. "All right, love.'

Catherine turned around on the edge of tears. 'I'm sorry."

Walter smiled at her. "I shouldn't have brought it up."

Catherine looked away. Walter lifted his helmet from a hook on the door.

"Look, why don't you pack tonight, then we can get off as soon as I get home. I'll sleep in the train.

'I don't know if I want to go. It's…"

"Come on, love, you'll enjoy it once we're there."

There was a pause. Walter glanced at the clock on the dresser. "I've got to go."

He opened the door.

"Be careful," she said quietly. He smiled and winked at her then went out closing the door behind him. "You're all I've got." She said it to herself as her eyes filled with tears.

The music on the radio stopped and was replaced by the warm, safe, and steady voice of a newsreader. "This is the BBC Home Service. Here is the news at eight p.m. on Friday, the fifth of February 1943."

Walter walked quickly along the pitch-black deserted street towards the hazy unlit shape that marked the blue lamp of the police station. His limp didn't seem to slow him down. His steel toe-and-heel-capped boots clacked on the pavement. His head was down against the strong wind and the driving rain rolled off his helmet and cape. It was a pig of a night and he'd be out again in an hour. He reached the station, hurried up the steps and through the door.

Inside, behind the counter, Sergeant Dan Pilkington, a solid, kindly bear of a man in his mid-fifties, was on the telephone. His voice was calm and reassuring. "Now, don't worry, Mrs Bott, if we find him, you'll be the first to know." He put the telephone down. "That woman sees spies everywhere." He looked Walter up and down and grinned. "Bloody hell, Walt, you look a bit damp."

Walter took off his cape and helmet. "It's pissing down out there."

"You'd better dry off a bit." A slight beat, then the punch line. "Before you go out again!"

Walter hung up his cape on a rack by the door and it dripped into the steel tray underneath it.

"You're all heart, Sarge."

He lifted the counter flap and went through.

"Get yourself a brew and bring me one with a couple of ginger nuts." He held out a large tea-stained white mug. Walter took it. "How's Catherine?"

He hesitated a moment. "Not so good! She was doing all right then Elsie Sparks, next door to us, got pregnant again. It'll be her fifth. They must be at it cats and dogs when Bert gets home on leave. Cate feels it's not fair," he smiled wryly, "but then, life's not, is it? Still, it could be worse. I could be out in the thick of it…" He stopped. "Sorry, Sarge, been a bit of a bugger of a day. I'll get that tea."

Pilkington felt for Walter, they'd known each other a long time and he valued him both as a copper and a friend. "Perhaps the change of air will do her a bit of good. You been up there before?"

"Aye, our honeymoon." He smiled. "That was a happy time. Let's hope it works its magic again."

"Don't forget to change into civvies before you go out."

"Lucky I left them here after the last lot then. The big coat still in the cupboard?"

"It is. Arthur's going straight from home to relieve you. He'll pick up Billy on the way. Got your weapon signed off. I'll give it to you on the way out."

"I'll remember the ammo this time too. You sure it's on for tonight?"

Pilkington laughed. "So the boss says. Now get my bloody tea, I'm parched."

In the neat and tidy bedroom, dimly lit despite the blackout curtains, Catherine folded up a dress and jumper and laid them carefully in an open case on the bed. She looked around the room, saw a necklace on the dressing table, picked it up, put it around her neck and glanced in the mirror. It was a small ruby cross in a circular setting. She smiled then put it down, looked back at the case, and thought for a moment. She opened a drawer and started to take out a couple of Walter's shirts but felt something behind them at the back. It was wrapped in tissue paper. She took it out, put it on the bed and carefully and tentatively unwrapped it. It was a tiny white woollen baby's cardigan. She started and her eyes locked onto it for a long moment then filled with tears. She touched it lightly with her fingers then gently, reverently, picked it up and held it against her face. The wind rattled the small window and the rain pounded against the glass.

CHAPTER EIGHT

Outside the closed bedroom curtains, the rain drummed against the glass, and the wind shook the old frame that needed replacing. They had done the one in George's room first but would have to do this one soon. It had started letting the rain in, leaving damp patches on the carpet under the window. The cold seeped through the gaps too.

The room was in semi-darkness. Ian was lying face down on the bed, the duvet covering him from the waist down. He was dead to the world. Suddenly he started and his eyes snapped open.

"Jesus."

Disorientated he looked around and, after a moment, realised where he was and slowly relaxed. He turned his head to look at the bright numbers on the digital clock on the chest of drawers across the room. It was ten thirty. Through a small gap between the curtains, he could see the grey wet day. "Shit." He'd wanted to start early this morning.

He pushed the duvet off and sat up. Pain shot through his stomach, and he cried out.

It hurt like hell. He touched it and looked down. There was a large bruise and redness covering and around his belly button. Where the hell had that come from? Had Nora found out about Lucy and pummelled him in the night? No, that would have woken him up. Then the marks started to fade. He was really confused. Then he remembered what had happened to him last night.

In the bathroom, Ian pulled faces in the mirror. Nothing was different. His face was what it was. He looked closely into his eyes and the face in front of him started to change. A hard-looking man with short hair and a tight moustache appeared.

Ian spun round. There was nobody behind him. He shook his head, looked back to the mirror and the face was his own again. What was going on? First, last night, and now he was seeing things. Did he know the face? No, of course he didn't. He mustn't give in to this. There will be an explanation. Perhaps he should tell Nora, but she wasn't here and even if she had been, she would have said that he was losing it and if he didn't throw so much alcohol down his throat and focused, instead of butterflying from one thing to an unconnected other, then he might not imagine things. So probably just as well she was out.

Sat on the toilet, he closed his eyes, took a deep breath, and went over what had happened when he was on the beach. It was unreal. He had gone there in the raging storm and climbed into the old Lookout post. It was after that it became impossible to understand. Had somebody attacked him? Had he fainted for some reason and landed on something hard and sharp, on his stomach? He could remember coming round and the struggle across the beach to the car, the drive home, and falling into bed. But none of it made sense. Perhaps he had finally slipped the bounds of sanity into the world that lived inside his head. A writer's descent into the made-up lives he created and inhabited.

It was bloody freezing in the bathroom. As he dressed, he thought out a plan, He'd have something to eat, then drive over to the beach again and see what the lookout in daylight told him.

Nora arrived back at twelve. As always, the morning had been a rush. Check-up at the dentist, pharmacy, and then a big food shop at Lidl. She'd spent eighty-five pounds, but it meant they had enough to last two weeks, possibly three if they planned meals well. She was fed up always checking what was cheapest, which wasn't necessarily the best despite their promise. She would have loved to go mad in Waitrose. But she couldn't. They were on a really tight budget and if Ian had to pay back the advance they'd given him, they'd be in even more of a mess. Her mum had helped them out, but she couldn't ask her again and face the 'bit of reality now you have one child and another on the way' lecture. On top of that she was feeling sick, not all the time, but when it came it was rough and made her feel like shit. She'd had a clear run with George, just a couple of weeks, but this was worse. All this swirled around her head as she parked the car. She dropped her head, closed her eyes. God, she was exhausted too. She got out of the car and went to the door and opened it.

"Ian, will you help?"

There was no answer. She went inside and headed for the stairs.

"Ian?"

There was still no answer. She couldn't hear any music and he usually worked with it playing. He might have gone out for a walk. She was getting cross now as well. He knew she was doing the shop. She went back into the kitchen and saw a note on the table. It was on a big sheet of paper, so she'd see it. But she hadn't.

Gone to the beach to try and clear my head. I've borrowed Josh's pickup. I love you. Grumpy xx

On the table there was a mug, a couple of ends of burnt toast, and a jar of peanut butter. She sat down, unscrewed the top of the jar, took a big dollop and stuffed it in her mouth. She suddenly realised he'd left the door unlocked. She was really pissed off with him now.

On the drive to the beach the rain had eased off and Ian tried to focus on last night in the Lookout. He felt the shadows shifting with the smell and sights slowly slipping in, but then his mind suddenly flipped into a cold wash of shame and trepidation. It was Lucy with her threats of coming up for George's birthday. Shit! That was going to be tricky. *Tricky?* It was going to be fucking cataclysmic! He tried to force out that awful scenario, but it wouldn't go. His mental twists and turns took him from wrenching guilt to an agony of consequence and then, in another mad spin, to the time he had first met Lucy.

He was thirty-five then and had been, amongst many other things, a teacher, a delivery driver, and an unpublished author. He'd just come out of a three-year relationship and was still smarting. He was offered a job through an old university friend who edited a local newspaper and needed someone to cover all the 'shit stuff' that no one else wanted to do. The job was desperately boring, but he stayed because he'd been promised a feature spot when it came up. Then his friend moved to a national daily and the new broom was heading his way. It paid practically nothing anyway and he'd had to work in a bar to get by. He'd also sold a few short stories and poems to anthologies that had little creative credibility and were published from a tiny shop in Covent Garden called Voice. What that 'voice' was however stayed a mystery. The guy who'd run it, Theo, had no literary awareness or discernment and too much money. Basically, he didn't give a fuck, but, if he liked you, he'd pay, publish, and display whatever crap you produced. But at least it had made Ian a published author and covered a couple of his smaller monthly outgoings. Theo had even talked of putting up some development cash for a short film after Ian had pitched him an idea. It hadn't happened.

It was at his other place of work that Lucy had come into his life. It was a small and atmospheric café bar, called the Shed, a bit too hipster for its time, but slowly finding a growing punter base that liked the smartarse wit, irreverence, and rudeness of the staff. Ian had fitted in perfectly. Most nights at six a trio of regulars came in: Stan, a Marxist photojournalist, Stumpy, a very small but perfectly formed successful architect with a slight lisp, and Rob, a music teacher, dedicated trombonist, and evangelical Salvation Army band member. Each had quirks and tacky traits and had little success with the opposite sex.

One night Stumpy surprised them all by arriving with

Lucy, a potential client. She was in her early twenties and a bit taller than him, which at least put her over bar height. She had spiky hair and an attitude to match, giving as good as she got, particularly to the tarnished trio. She and Ian had slipped into an easy bounce of wit and wisecracks and when the others left, she'd stayed for something to eat, and later Ian had joined her on his break. They had got on well and talked about meeting up again, but not at the Shed. They'd finally settled on a trip to Brighton the following Saturday.

It had been a bit wild, each trying to out crazy the other, but a lot of fun. They'd drunk too much, been to the funfair, had several ice creams, walked along the promenade, and told stories of starts and stops in their lives and relationships. On the train back to London they had kissed and by the time they reached Battersea Park Station they knew they were going to spend the night together at Lucy's flat. It was fun and they both loved the silliness and sex but by the time Ian left two days later, they had fallen for each other as friends. She said he was probably a bit too old for them to be lovers. He'd soon want kids and things and she wasn't ready for that sort of commitment. She was doing a Masters' in Literature at Queen Mary's and had self-published a book of poetry. Friendship was probably best. Ian agreed. Even after such a short time, they could both see that as a long-term thing.

It had been like that for years. Lucy had been a part of Ian's life and welcomed, albeit sometimes warily, by all the important women he had loved and lost. Then Nora arrived, and Lucy had accepted her as a constant in his life. They had, after a couple of spats when one of them felt that the other was being unfair to him, become good friends and often joined forces to keep him focused.

It had stayed like that until eighteen months ago, when everything had changed and the boundaries of 'just friends' faded and became fuzzy. Ian had gone down to London on his own for a 'Best British psychological crime thriller debut of the last ten years' awards ceremony, which included his first book, *Heartbeat,* in the short list. He hadn't won, didn't really mind, accepted the Dragon's 'Next time, sweetie' platitudes and then gone to eat and drink with Lucy. He was staying at her place that night. They were both plastered and suddenly something clicked, and they kissed, did it again, and then it was too late to stop. It was uncontrollable, carnal and messy, and afterwards they were both wiped out and fell into a deep drunken sleep. The next morning Ian had woken with a struggle and found Lucy, naked and near, her eyes locked on his.

"Shit, what happened?"

Lucy almost smiled. "We did." Then she kissed him again. "Friends with a fuck thrown in." Then they kissed again and that was it. It had happened and couldn't be undone. They should have left it there, but they didn't. It was exciting and somehow, despite the guilt about Nora, they managed to create a normality that balanced between strict emotional safety lines. If there were a chance of being found out, it would stop. It was their decision and their responsibility to keep it hidden. It wasn't a regular thing, just when time and place were right, and should have worked with the manageable morality they thought they controlled.

And it did!

Until it didn't.

* * *

In London, Lucy had been doing almost the same, flipping the blame between them and going over and over what had happened and why… fucking *why*? Of course, she accepted that it had taken the two of them and she had many sharp and punchy moments of chilling guilt and remorse. However, deep down, it was really Ian she blamed. He should have stopped it or told her he couldn't do it. She would have backed off and they would never have been in this mess. It could have been put into the 'never mention it again' drawer. Since that first little foray after the day at the beach, she hadn't had any feelings about him in that way again. Ever. He was like an older brother. But there must have been something lurking in her that did want it to happen and, once it had started, it became a bit out of control, although she knew it wouldn't change her life or last for ever. It was just for now. Why was she so angry with him? It was a two-way thing, not one hand clapping! But he was the one with the wife and child. It was down to him to be the grown-up here. It wasn't like it was something they hadn't done before Nora, even if it was only several times over a couple of days nearly fifteen years ago. Only a step beyond a cuddle! She'd had plenty of lovers and she'd shared the stories of the good and the bad with Ian. He always made her laugh and see that she was worth better, but as long as she enjoyed the sex and didn't take it all seriously, it was fine; even if over the last few years most of them had been of an age that made it just possible for her to be their - very young - mother. He'd always been on her side and there whenever she needed him to soak up her anxiety or anger and find a way to lift her out of it. They'd shared bathrooms and beds with no problem and no fumbles, drunken or otherwise. But that all changed when their relationship did.

She still had younger men and it didn't bother him at all. It was just that she had begun to see what he was like in this different relationship. The lack of thought and consideration, the fitting in the fucks around his timetable, were his not hers. She could cope with the hot flushes of embarrassment and anger. It was this last hurt that was the hardest to bear. Was it losing that excitement of the forbidden? Or, and this was deeply disturbing, was it the fact that Nora was pregnant that made it such an excruciating ache this time? She could just about handle being a selfish betraying bitch but not that, after her last miscarriage had damaged her womb, she would never have the same as Nora. She was always going to be a real or substitute aunty, but never ever a mum. That was difficult to handle on her own. It would have been Ian's baby, but he knew nothing about it, couldn't ever know, it was her weight to carry. Did she see this as punishment for what they were doing? Sometimes... but mostly the pain of the reality was enough to make her not care about the cause. It wouldn't change anything, make her feel better, able to treat it as one of those unexpected things life just threw at you, to show how inconsequential and small you really were in the vast confusion between being and then not being. She had never been a great believer in an all-powerful force that, if you had faith, would always protect, and enrich you. Once she had tried Buddhism to find a way through a problem and had liked the focus on the internal control that let you see clearly and follow the path of least harm to you and those around you... and to be honest, it had worked that time. Maybe this was a time to revisit.

All this had been going on in her head as she'd been walking from a meeting at St Paul's. She had reached Holborn tube station, stepped off the pavement and almost landed in front of a bus. The guy from the paper stall had leapt in and pulled her back.

"You all right, love?"

He was about the same age as her dad would have been and it brought tears to her eyes. Her dad had died of a heart attack two years ago. Low moments when raw emotions ruled always brought his loss back. Ian had been wonderful and had even come to stay with her for a week after the funeral. And they hadn't slept together then! She was slipping back into her thoughts when she realised her saviour had said something.

"Yes, thank you. I was miles away."

He smiled and went back to his stall. She carried on walking and finally came to Covent Garden. She wandered through the stalls, looking but not really seeing anything as she thought about leaving that message on the landline. She'd wanted to scare the shit out of him, but did she really mean to go to George's party? It might do the job on Ian but it could be a disaster, and not only ruin the day but Nora and George's lives. It wasn't them she wanted to hurt!

She was distracted then by a couple of street performers in front of the church in Covent Garden. One was spinning on his head and the other was carrying a large water jug on a tray balanced on his chin as he rode a high monocycle in ever decreasing circles. She didn't notice the large chicken from the restaurant follow in her footsteps as she walked away but she heard the laughter and saw the focus of people watching what was happening. She stopped and the chicken, looking away and waving at a group of young children, bumped into her. She looked at it in surprise then suddenly realised where she'd seen it before and laughed.

"Where's the rabbit?"

"Gone for a burger." He hopped uncomfortably from foot to foot.

"What do you want?" She didn't have time for this even if it had cheered her up.

"You're wonderful, I think I love you!"

"I'm not and you don't."

"Can I talk to you?"

That's it! She'd had enough of the talking bird. "No!"

The chicken flapped its wings, tried to look sad.

"Buy you a coffee then?"

"No."

"I thought I'd never see you again."

She gave him a hard look.

"Fuck off!"

* * *

Ian stood at the top of the steps leading down to the beach, looking towards the small dark shapes of coast-hopping carrier boats as they crawled along the horizon. In his head he was working hard to see everything for what it was and not what his over-fertile mind tried to rack up. Today there was a normality here that was trying to force the dark memories of last night to an explainable reality. But it was a battle. It was blustery, cold and bright, the sea grey and wild with white breakers that cracked and diminished as they reached the shore. There was a scattering of walkers on the wet sand; some with dogs that obediently trotted at their feet or spun in tail chases, darting and barking at the birds or finding friendships with sniffs and snaps. Some couples, their closeness or distance from each other suggesting a myriad of stories; some holding tight to small hands as toddlers tried to escape and run into the water or chase the seagulls too.

Ian's hands were cold, so he pulled on gloves from his pocket and went down onto the sand. After a moment, he glanced towards the concrete Lookout, old and crumbling in the clear light. He hesitated for a moment. Did he want to do this? Really? What would it achieve to go in there again and if he did, then what? See if he sensed anything unreal or got punched again or passed out or realised that it was all a fantasy he'd conjured up with one of his involuntary leaps into make believe!

But he knew that he was going to do it.

Had to do it!

Had to find out if it was insane to believe the truth of what happened or madness not to think it possible. The strangest things had happened to the most pragmatic and centred of people. He was way off that spectrum and his mind had often taken him where decent, normal people wouldn't dare look, let alone explore. Perhaps this was payback for not pulling in the reins of his vigorous imagination.

He walked quickly towards the Lookout. Up close it was more solid than it looked from a distance. He was sure that he must have seen it before yesterday, but it hadn't stuck in his mind. It was just one of those things you took in and dismissed as not essential to remember but that somehow hung on some hook in your memory, ready to be used if needed.

He circled the small building, leaving a moat of distance between him and it, to allow his mind to assess the danger and his ears and eyes to see and hear if there were any signs of life, natural or not. There were none, and by his third circuit he was ready. If anyone was watching him from the beach, they'd wonder at his strangeness but not want to find out more in case he engaged with them. The one 'barker' on the beach and they had to come across him. So, they'd turn away and carry on with whatever had brought them to this wintry spot.

Ian couldn't remember the last time he felt this scared of taking the next step, apart, of course, from the heart-stopping effect of the news of Lucy's coming visit and what to do about it. He tried deep breathing but it didn't help. Yogic calm didn't come naturally to him.

Just do it!

He scrambled over the rubble and bits of fallen wall that partially blocked the doorway. It was easier to do this time because it wasn't dark and there wasn't a raging maelstrom as the heavens crackled and the wind hurled the rain at him.

Inside, the light from the small slit window threw shadows around the walls and the detritus built up over years of neglect and misuse. And the smell was even worse than he remembered, foul, faecal, and filled with a taste of the stale saltiness of high tides, rotting and rancid scraps of food. He stood in the middle of the small space and tried to block it out. Outside, dogs were barking and there was the muted sound of the sea but in here it was silent. Suddenly the light faded to black, and the temperature dropped from bearable to icy cold.

Shit, what was going on now?

Panic shot through him, sharp and acid, and he had to get out.

He tried to move but he couldn't. Only his eyes had motion and they reacted in horror. His heart pounded and a scream bubbled up but made no sound then faded away.

In front of him there was the outline of a man in the darkness, his arm raised, something pointed in his hand. It was a large knife. He was still, very still. In front of him there was a wooden door in the wall. Slowly the handle turned and as it opened a dim torch beam shone briefly and revealed a dripping silhouette behind it.

"Thought you lads said you were leaving it to the boys in blue to scare off Adolf's mob?"

The light went out and the man with the knife lunged and thrust it upwards into the centre of the figure in the doorway.

It groaned and slumped to the ground. The man quickly pulled out the knife, looked down for a moment then stepped over it.

Ian felt nothing as he lay on the sand and mess. There was no pain, just a sense of not being in his body. His eyes were wide open. He heard the crash of the door being kicked open and three strong beams of light pierced his eyes.

"Who is it?" A man's voice and a face loomed in front of him. "Oh Christ, it's Walter!" A hand crossed Ian's eyes and touched his neck "Taff, call the Station. He's dead."

The torches and voices faded, the light changed, and Ian stood in the centre of the Lookout. Outside there were dogs barking and the sound of sea and wind. A bark closer than before, followed by a scrabble and a yelp. A small dog was trying to get over the rubble at the door.

"Thomas, come here!"

A pissed-off woman's voice turned the dog away and it ran off.

Ian tried to get his head around what had just happened and struggled out of the door and, exhausted, slumped on the sand. The dog, a small terrier, came back, followed by a tall woman in a red raincoat with a large hood almost covering her face. She was brandishing her dog lead like a whip and although giving Ian a wide berth was ready to strike if he attacked.

"Thomas, come here! Now!" The dog stopped, sensed that she wasn't happy, and ran back to her as she quickly moved away from Ian. He watched them abstract as they drifted amongst other shapes on the beach. He tried to focus but his senses didn't want clarity. They needed time to process what had happened. His eyes cleared and the beach, sea, people, and dogs were real again. Then his body reacted to the cold and wet with shivers and spasms, and his stomach twisted, a breath-stopping leap that pounded into his chest. Jesus, he was having a heart attack!

But he wasn't. The pain stopped. He managed to control his breathing and slowly got to his feet. He stood, facing into the wind as the rain eased and stopped. He glanced towards the Lookout. What the sweet fuck was going on? What had happened just now didn't have any explanation or reason either. He felt what he felt, heard what he heard, and saw what he saw. It was incredible but, unless his sanity had already gone, something had happened to him in that shithole on the beach. It was like a nightmare except he was awake and aware of what was happening. Why had it stopped when it did? Was it like that dream of falling where you never hit the ground because if you were to reach an end point, it would be real and you would be dead?

He wasn't sure what to do now. Going back for a rerun wasn't going to happen. Perhaps if he ran it past Nora and made her realise that it wasn't just one of his skips into a world that only he could access, she would help him find a way to explain it. But he knew as he walked back along the beach that it wouldn't happen like that. She'd never believe the story. He didn't even have the bruises of yesterday to show as evidence. Or did he? Suddenly there was hope in his heart and he ran back to the car. He stripped off his coat, threw it in the back, and lifted his thick sweater and T-shirt, willing the bruise to still be there.

It wasn't.

"Fuck, fuck, fuck!"

He must have said it louder than he thought because Thomas and his red-macked friend both jumped as they passed him and rushed towards the safety of the promenade.

The journey home was a blur as his mind scattered impossibilities and tried to create reason or discard reality. Every suggestion that pierced the implausibility of what happened, even a descent into dementia, seemed a better option than accepting it as an unbelievable truth.

He dropped off the pick-up at the pub and walked home. What had happened was becoming less clear but with moments, sharp and harsh, that snapped in and out. He had to control it. It would be better at home. Nora brought a safe and secure reality. He would find a way to talk to her.

The car wasn't there so Nora had gone out. He tried the door but it was locked. He searched the pockets of his coat. He didn't have the key with him so he must have left the door unlocked when he'd gone out. That would have pissed off Nora when she got back. A ray of hope that perhaps she hadn't, glowed and died. No car and the door locked. She must have done that, unless the house had been ransacked and the thoughtful thief had made sure it wouldn't happen again and had even left the spare under the usual tile at the bottom of the drainpipe putting the leaves back on top of it. Inside though there was no more disruption than usual except that Nora had drawn a downward mouth under his note and left all the stuff that didn't need the fridge on the table and written, *Back after I pick up George. Put away things NOW or I WILL be cross and unreasonable!!*

Whenever problems were presented that seemed insurmountable, Ian found that writing it all down as simply as possible allowed him to focus on what was on the page, not in his head. Not trying to make the words flow in clever and sometimes convoluted prose provided an uncluttered picture. If only he could do that all the time in his books, it might make them more accessible, certainly trimmer and less hard work to read. His editor's sharp verbal slap of 'Just tell the sodding story… not what it had for breakfast!' was stuck on the wall, behind his desk.

So, when he'd put everything away and tidied up, he glanced at the half-full bottle of Rioja on the worktop. It would be nice but might lead to more wine than work. And, although he could qualify it by telling himself it was not creative skill that was needed and one glass would just take off the edge and lead to focus, he went for coffee instead.

It had taken him an hour, removing what was indecipherable splatter and just leaving the bare facts. Some of what he wrote surprised him. His mind cleared of its creative function threw out things it had stored that had failed to make it to his important to remember inbox.

He read it out loud to create a distance and make the

words sound real.

There is nothing logical in this.

I was there.

I was taking part.

I was the victim.

It was in the past.

During WW2!

How do I know that?

It was what was said.

'Adolf's mob!'

Walter was a cop!

He was killed.

He's dead, they said.

How could it happen?

It was real.

It happened.

Walter was killed, not me.

I had bruises from the attack, but they didn't stay nor did the pain.

How could I have become part of that world?

Are all times parallels of other times?

Does the present and past exist side by side?

If they do, are they accessible?

Has some fiction I read or saw become a reality as a punishment for being such a twat with Lucy?

My grandfather lived in a world he made up.

He was barking mad!

Is that my genetic gift?

I need to stop this now!

This isn't helping!

SHIT!

He got up from the table and went upstairs, taking his cold coffee with him, to hide his scribblings in his secret place, an old CD box of the Fureys. He'd lost the disc years ago.

He was about to leave the room when a huge clap of thunder made him jump.

"Jesus!"

He went across to the window, counting, 'One, two, three, four.' The thunder exploded again. Four miles away! As he got close to the window a huge, jagged streak of lightning cracked and burned and darkness closed in on him with the sound of crashing waves and winds.

CHAPTER NINE

The foaming white and violent waves slammed into the sea wall, throwing sheets of spray over the top of the stones and railings onto the promenade. It was freezing and the howling wind swirled the torrential rain and sleet into sharp spikes.

Walter, hand cupped around a cigarette, wearing a long heavy raincoat and a black sou'wester, was in a narrow alley opposite the beach, at the side of a long decrepit two-storey building with blacked-out windows and a large, padlocked door. It was the Starlight Club and has been closed for the last twelve months since its owner, a local villain, Jimmy Douglas, had been put away for laundering cash through an illegal betting operation. Sadly, they couldn't keep him inside. He'd got some high-ups on the payroll and had walked after three months. Walter had done his first bit of undercover on that one. He hoped it might lead to full-time CID attachment, but he was still waiting. Tonight's job was another fill-in for someone on the sick.

He was watching an old van parked a hundred yards away to his left in a small car park near the end of the promenade. The van had arrived half an hour ago and the driver had thrown a cigarette out, turned the thin slit of headlights and the engine off, then sat there unmoving, slowly disappearing into the darkness inside the van. Walter could just see the misting on the windows and a hand clearing a spot on the side one. A sudden loud crack of thunder turned Walter away to face into the alley as a huge fizzle of lightning flashed briefly over the promenade. He wasn't visible from the van but didn't want to risk even a momentary glimpse of his face in the sudden spark of light. He pulled up the collar of his coat as he turned back. It didn't do much. This sort of driving rain always found a way in.

He looked at his watch, took a last drag on his cigarette, dropped it and crushed it with his foot. Through the barrelling noise of the storm and the sea, he heard something, sharp and clacking, coming towards him from the other end of the alley. He turned as a figure, wrapped up like him in rain gear but with a trilby, stopped and looked around.

"Walt, where are you?"

Walter came out of the shadows towards him. "You're early, Arthur."

"Had a bit of a do with the missus. Anything happened?"

"Sod all yet. Van's been there for half an hour but no sight of the truck yet." They both looked towards the van.

"Right, why don't you nip off… "

At the sound of an engine Arthur pulled Walter back into the alley as a lorry, its lights out, passed them. "Bugger me… talk about bad timing!"

Walter grinned. "Who for, you or me?"

Arthur looked out. The lorry had pulled up behind the van, engine still running. "Both of us! I'm not chancing it on my own and Billy isn't going to get here in time."

"Thought he was coming with you?"

"I gave him ten minutes to say goodbye to Doris, she's off to Morecambe for a couple of weeks.

"She hoping for better weather over there?"

"Yes, forecast says lots of sun." He laughed. "No, her gran's ill. The hospital won't let her out without someone at home and as Doris is a nurse, seemed like the right thing to do. Hey up!"

The van pulled around to the other side of the lorry so that the doors faced the back of the wagon. The lorry driver came around the truck and opened the doors as the man in the van joined him. They moved inside the lorry.

Walter ran past the Starlight towards the car park, tucking himself into the cliff that edged it. Arthur followed in his footsteps.

"They won't see us with the door open. You nip round the front and grab the key and I'll give the lads in the back a bounce. Billy should be here soon, but we'd better get a move on."

"Sure?" Arthur sounded wary.

Walter glanced at him. "It'll be fine. Don't think they'll be up for any heroics on a night like this." He looked across at the lorry. "Right, let's get it done."

Walter ran to the back and Arthur to the driver's door.

Walter waited until the engine stopped and then dipped quickly around to the back of the truck. The two men stood by a large crate, the van driver working on it with a crowbar. He looked up. "Bloody thing's cut out. I told Reggie I needed a new one."

"Waste of fuel that, lads, hate to think you'll run out on the way home." Walter switched on his torch and the powerful beam caught them like a spotlight. In his other hand was a gun.

The man with the crowbar span round.

"Who the fuck are you?" He was a Geordie.

Walter smiled. "I'll give you a clue. You're nicked!"

Arthur came round the other side of the lorry as the man with the crowbar charged towards Walter. Walter dropped the torch, grabbed the man, and used his weight and momentum to throw him down but got caught in his legs and went down too. They struggled and suddenly the gun went off.

Arthur had the other one up against the side of the lorry and butted him hard in the face, held him upright, punched him, threw him down and gave him a hard kick in the ribs. He looked over at Walter, grabbed the torch from the road and shone it on him. "You all right, Walt? You're covered in blood!"

"Just about, but he's not. Caught him in the gut. Need to get him to hospital." Walter was pressing his hands down hard on the man's stomach.

"Jesus, that hurts!"

"Just trying to keep some blood inside you. Lie still!"

There was a pounding of feet and Billy, overweight and short for a policeman, appeared and almost went over as he skidded to a stop

"Jesus Christ, it looks like a bloody abattoir! What happened?"

"Billy, nip down to the box on the corner of St Mary's Street and call in. Need an ambulance now and a car to take this other little bugger in. Mind, after what Arthur did to him, he might need a bit of putting back together too."

Billy looked around, white-faced, eyes wide and scared.

"Now, son, or the bugger will bleed out and it'll be on you."

CHAPTER TEN

Slowly the pictures and sounds faded and their reality was no more than a shadow of a memory. Ian felt exhausted. What the hell was happening to him? He sat down at his desk and opened his laptop. He decided to research Bridlington during WW2 and see if there was anything about the Lookout. Perhaps that would help him find some context. Without thinking he typed *Starlight Club, Bridlington, 1940s* into the search box. It made him start. Where the fuck had that name come from? It wasn't what he was going to type in. But he checked out the results anyway. There was a lot of stuff about clubs all over the UK called the Starlight or similar. As he scrolled through, something caught his eye and he stopped. It was a picture of a club on a seafront. He clicked on it and there was a brief description. It had been opened in 1930 and demolished after a suspicious fire in 1948. It was a place that he almost recognised…

He took a breath and decided to stop then and try and clear his head before delving deeper into the web. He deleted the browsing data and went into Netflix to look for *Call My Agent*. It was his recent go to for distraction and time-wasting. He'd been told about it by Jaz Stevens and was halfway through the third series. It helped to settle his churning stomach, and he took masochistic delight in the similarities between the cold-blooded lead agent and Janey.

Nora hated driving at the best of times, but in this weather, it was torture. George was playing up. It was her fault for being ratty and unreasonable. She'd shouted at him! He was now whimpering and refusing to talk to her. She took a deep breath and hoped her voice was warm and loving.

"Nearly home, sweetheart!"

She indicated and pulled into the lane leading to the cottage.

George wasn't going to let her off that easily. "I'll tell Daddy you were horrible." Horrible had become one of his new favourite words and seemed to be exclusively used for her.

"I'm not horrible." She was almost in tears but too cross to cry. "I'm just tired and have a headache. I'm sorry, I shouldn't have shouted at you." She glanced briefly to see George glaring at her and poking out his tongue. She just managed to keep the explosion in but as she turned back, she scraped the side of the gate as she pulled into the drive.

"Fuck." It was out before she could stop it.

"Mummy, you hurt the car."

"It's nothing, I hardly touched it." God, she felt pathetic. She didn't at that moment give a shit whether it was a little scratch or a write-off.

"You said a bad word."

"I know, I'm sorry."

"Daddy'll be cross with you."

Nora took a deep breath again. Ignore it!

"I want him to get me out."

"Do you?"

"Yes, because you're horrible, horrible and..." George paused, thought hard, then remembered, "...nasty"

That was the final straw. "Right."

She got out. "Where are you going?" George knew he'd gone too far.

"To get Daddy!" She slammed the door and stepped into a large puddle. "Shit!"

"Mummy!" George crumpled and screamed.

Ian jumped as the door slammed open and Nora stood there, dripping and angry, snorting like a wet dragon.

He hadn't heard her come up the stairs. He was engrossed in bitchiness and betrayal. He pressed the pause button.

"What's the matter?"

"Why didn't you answer?"

"Didn't hear you. I was watching *Call My Agent*."

"Really?"

"Yes, I'm sorry."

She softened. "Will you get George out of the car, please."

"Why didn't you do it?"

"He thinks I'm horrible and nasty."

Ian smiled. "Nasty Nora!"

"Don't." She tried to stay calm. "Just get him out... please."

"All right."

Nora went. Ian got up and looked through the

window. He could just about see George's face through the rain pounding against his window. He was screaming.

George had taken an hour to get to sleep. He'd eventually forgiven Nora. He'd let her use his favourite boat and Gaz the gorilla during bath time. When he'd got into bed, he didn't want her to read a story, so she sang 'Puff the Magic Dragon' to him. He loved it. She had too when her dad had sung it to her. She didn't know why, he was a lovely, warm, and caring man but he had a shit voice.

She felt calmer as she sat and watched George's sleep-innocent face and felt a great surge of love, then withering guilt at the way she'd been with him. She would really try not to be so grumpy from now on. She couldn't blame it all on being pregnant. Could she? Difficult not to when she was so tired, although, on the plus side, she'd only been sick a couple of times today, which was a first.

She touched her tummy. "Don't listen to me. I'm not going to be a shouty mummy again to your big brother or you, when you get here, I promise!"

She was exhausted though. Ian was making dinner. He'd found a great recipe for nut roast about a year ago and had gone mad for it for about a month, made a load, put it in the freezer, and hadn't touched it since. He'd decided tonight was the night to try it again with a salad. Good for them both, nuts and greens. She wasn't sure. She hadn't been a great fan when she'd first had it, but he'd persuaded her to have another go. Everyone else had seemed to like it that first time.

Beans on toast would have been her top pick, with a

can of Guinness, joined-up cravings that she had both with George and the bump. She felt her eyes closing and could have easily tucked up against George and slept. But she wouldn't. She needed to spend a bit of time with Ian. He was even more distracted than normal! It felt like his presence was wonky and distant. Like he was somewhere else. He often slipped into a land that lived in his mosh pit of a mind, but she knew the signs and signals for that and just ignored it. This was different though. She had to find out what it was, exorcise it, and get him back on track, for book and family. And he was drinking too much... again. That was going to have to stop too. She'd wait until he'd got the book out of the way before she had a go at him. He was always edgy when he wasn't sure what he was doing creatively and had a deadline forced on him. He needed focus, not fear, to get it right. She loved his writing but getting him to do it was as painful as piles sometimes. That stopped her mid-thought. Jesus. Why did she think about them? She'd had the worst bouts ever with George and couldn't bear the thought of that happening again. And her head was all over the place. There was something buzzing in there that needed to get out.

Suddenly it came with a cold flush of apprehension. It was George's party the day after tomorrow and although nearly everything was organized there were a few things left to do. She didn't have time! Ian would have to do them. She'd talk him through the list tonight. It wasn't hard. Check on who hadn't replied to her 'let me know that you're still good to come' messages, make sure there were enough party bags and ring the rink and confirm they had the right number of shoes and that they were the sizes that she'd sent them in an email. She dragged herself up, leaned over and kissed George.

Ian stuck his head round the door. "It's on the table."

"Just need a pee first."

Ian looked across at George. "He's so beautiful." He went over and kissed him on the head then leaned down and kissed Nora's tummy. "And you are too, bumpy." Nora pushed him away gently." And Mummy, of course."

"Piss off… but thank you!" she said with a laugh and a kiss.

"Guinness?"

"Of course! You weren't going to drink tonight, were you?"

"Too late! Forgot I'd said that, sorry."

Nora had to take it back: the nut roast was really good. Obviously her taste buds had become deranged with the hormone buzz… she had seconds too.

They talked about the birthday to-do list. Most of the things Ian could do tomorrow but, on the day, he had to pick up the cake from the bakery on his way to the party. So, he had to make sure it was going to be ready in time and that he left early enough. She'd had perfect mum dreams of doing it herself but ran out of time and enthusiasm. She had another thought then. Extra woollies in case it was colder than she remembered at the rink. There were always a couple of parents who hadn't thought through the ice-cold-warm-clothes equation, and she wanted to have spare jumpers on hand. A bit of crossness crept in. Why had she let herself be talked into having the party at the ice rink? It had seemed like a good idea at the time, but she hadn't been pregnant then. It was after George's friend Ben's party there six months ago, and George had loved it so much that he wanted his there too. The only way to be able to guarantee it was to book then and pay half up front as a deposit and the rest on the day. If they had to cancel, they'd lose the hundred and fifty pounds and George would never have forgiven her.

After letting that all out she fell asleep when Ian was telling her his ice rink story when he was a bit older than George. It took him a while to notice but then he gently woke her up and led her to the stairs.

"I'll be there soon." She didn't hear and was halfway up. "Just have another glass first."

He poured the wine, threw a log on the fire, then sat on the sofa and stared into the flames.

He'd really fucked it up with Lucy. Why had he ever thought that it was a good idea? He should tell Nora. Stop… where the fuck did that come from? That would finish everything. She'd take George away and the new baby and probably stick a knife in him too… No, she wouldn't do that, she'd be smarter, more subtle, more deadly. Perhaps she'd put some sort of poison into his eye drops, something that couldn't be traced but would stop his heart and shut everything down. He'd researched it once for a book that never got beyond page two of a treatment. It was from a rare Japanese plant that only grew in the Chichibu Mountains and had been used by Samurai spies to kill traitors. Perfect for him then. Had he told Nora about it? She never listened when he droned on about how clever he was at finding oddball things, but perhaps this was something that had caught her attention.

He had to stop Lucy coming to George's party. That scenario was too terrifying. Fear of her saying anything, and disgust with himself for being in that position in the first place. All while he was trying to be the fun father of the birthday boy!

Perhaps he should go down to the Lookout again. This time it might be taken out of his hands and whatever it was that had attacked him would get it right this time and finish him off. God, this was a nightmare. Perhaps he had slipped into insanity already and nothing real had happened at all. But Lucy was real! And so was what happened on the beach…

"Daddy!" George sounded fully revved up. "Daddy, there's a big spider!"

Oh God! He hated spiders but had forced himself to be brave for George's sake. He didn't want him to grow up afraid of them like he had. So, he said they were just a bit ugly and harmless and really friendly and didn't mind when he picked them up. He tried to keep the scream from bubbling out if they moved against his fingers. It hadn't worked, George was still scared but now thought that Daddy really liked spiders and was happy to take them outside to play with their friends, even the imaginary huge monster ones that followed him from a bad dream and sat on the edge of his bed.

"Daddy, please."

Ian shook his head and tried to find his hero voice.

"I don't want to wake Mummy up, she's very tired."

"Daddy!"

'All right, I'm coming, sweetheart.'

Ian was halfway up the stairs… when he stood on a small plastic car which cracked open. A sharp end cut into his foot. "Shit."

"That's a bad word, Daddy."

Where had the spider fear gone? His voice was closer and when Ian looked up, his hand still rubbing his foot, he saw George at the top of the stairs, looking at him crossly. Oh, Jesus, there was a large spider on his shoulder, but he obviously hadn't noticed it. He'd have to try and grab it quickly. What if it started chewing on his hand? It looked big enough to devour at least a finger before Nora came to the rescue. George was just standing there as Ian shot up and lunged for the spider, which was miles ahead of him, throwing itself across Ian's hand to the floor with a sway of quick time silk and disappearing into a hidden hole in the skirting board. George screamed and fell over and just as Ian picked him up, Nora rushed out of their bedroom. George scrabbled out of Ian's arms and ran to her. She picked him up, turned around and took him into the bedroom.

"You can sleep in his room."

She shut the door and Ian realised that the spider must have caught him with its fangs. There was a red mark. Great, he was probably going to turn into Spiderman and be terrified of himself.

He sighed at the injustice and crawled on his hands and knees into George's room.

Strangely, he slept long and well and George and Nora

had gone by the time he got up. He hadn't heard them come in to get George's clothes and she must have decided to let him sleep in.

There wasn't a chance of any creative brilliance scraping though his deep sense of impending doom, so working on the book was not an option that would divert him or produce anything that he wouldn't have to bin later.

The one burning need was to find a way to stop Lucy creating an unmanageable shitstorm, that was not just fantasy but a realistic solution.

If he was to achieve that, he had to come up with a way to manipulate things so that Fate dipped the balance of probability his way for once. But that wasn't really fair on Fate and its tricks and treats. It had given him moments of success and a few accolades that would generate envy in some equally talented and probably more worthy recipients of cash, book festival gigs, and options for films and TV. A couple of options for TV on his books still had a bit of time to run and if he could get this next novel out and into the lower end of the best sellers list, it might stimulate movement and another payment.

Just then his phone pinged. It was a long WhatsApp from Nora reminding him about checking that he did everything on his list, and to ring the bakery to make sure the cake would be ready for him to pick up, and to get the right sizes of woollies for the kids with some bigger ones needing the hand-me-downs that George hadn't grown into yet, and to pull out some of theirs too for the parents who hadn't thought it through for themselves.

She finished with a love you and a kiss. He sent a 'thumbs up', 'hug' and a 'smiley face with kissy hearts'. As it disappeared, he had a moment of panic. The kissy face was too much. Nora would think he'd done something that would piss her off. He'd have to deal with that. Then he got cross with the parents who mightn't have realised that ice is cold. Fuck them! If they were that stupid, then they deserved to freeze their bits off! He wouldn't do it!

But he knew he would. Couldn't risk a row, get caught on the back foot and start talking, get confused, particularly if he'd been drinking, start fudging why Lucy might not come up. Nora would smell a huge rat and his pathetic selfish little world would collapse. Perhaps it might be better to get it over with?

He quickly poured a glass of wine and drank it. God! It tasted foul. Then he realised it was the wrong bottle. This was one that was corked when he'd opened it. He must have thrown away the good one he started last night.

That bit of reasoning was quickly driven out by the next sharp jab of thought. Lucy! What was he going to do? A wisp of hope blew in briefly. She mightn't come anyway. Not fancy three hours in the cold and a noise level approaching agony. But that was just wishful thinking. In the real world he knew that wasn't going to happen. She'd come to cause him pain and fondle her fresh meat man when the kids weren't looking. But she'd make sure *he* was! Why wouldn't she come? And she'd have a woolly to wear. Always thought ahead! No, not always… Wish she'd done that when it all started and had told him to 'fuck off' because she didn't want to ruin the friendship and betray a wife!

He had to do something to take his mind off it. He found the list of names of parents and sent an email reminder, rang the rink and checked that all was as it should be, and the people in the bakery, who said it was all fine and they'd even throw in a special little honey pot cake, just for the birthday boy. Probably best to save that one for home where there was no risk of others wanting it. Or perhaps he could stuff it down his own throat and let Pooh's favourite food give him a choking pass.

He played with his phone and then in a moment of madness rang Lucy then frantically cut the call and sent her a text saying it was a pocket pop. Sorry, he did it by mistake. Almost instantly, he got a 'thumbs down' back, followed by 'PRICK'. Why did he do that? Did he have some weird kind of Munchausen's, where rather than an illness, he created a world where all was simple and sweet and where Lucy wasn't going to cut off his balls, ruin his son's birthday, end his marriage and possibly his life?

* * *

In London Lucy watched the tight arse and toned back as Mark stretched, legs apart, bits dangling, and slid seamlessly into 'downward dog', trying to see himself in the wall-length mirror behind him.

"This right?"

"Yep." Twenty minutes before she'd pretended to come as he bounced against her bum and with a final thrust released his 'power pump'. It hadn't been that pleasant the second time and she was now just sore, not satiated. The first time was fun and fulfilling but then they'd tried the talking bit as he curled into her back. Her need for a deeper sense in the shadows of the sex always left her ashamed too after these sessions. It was her fault though, not his. He was what he was! Sweet, generous, loving, sexy, caring, and still youthful enough to make her feel uncomfortable at the years between them. He was twenty-two but looked eighteen. He was also not the sharpest knife… anywhere. So, their talks were about daily life; his job as a driver for a minor villain who had pubs and restaurants, and football. Tottenham was his team! But then it ran out and he started another bout, terrier-fashion. At least it stopped the struggle of saying something. She wanted more than this. Warmth and words, love and literature, politics, poetry, and people, and someone who stretched her mind and made her explore other worlds. She wanted someone like the little shit who had just cracked and broken her heart. Fuck, fuck, fuck! She struggled to stop the anger but it was too late.

"I've got to go back to work." She threw herself off the bed.

Mark stood up, turned. "Thought you had the rest of the day?"

"Just remembered I've got a tutorial with a student who's struggling with her thesis on Pushkin and his women."

"Who?"

"Doesn't matter! Can't let her down. Sorry."

"Shall I wait here?'"

"I'll call you later."

She suddenly felt bad and kissed him. He pulled her down to his erection. 'Can it wait five minutes?'

She dragged herself away. "No."

"Why not?" He was hurt.

"Fuck off Mark, it's not all about you!"

There was a long moment then he moved away. He looked hurt and surprised. "I know. Sorry."

Shit. None of this was down to him "It's not you, Marky. It's me who should be sorry. I'll call you later. OK?"

It was. It didn't take much.

It was a bright, fresh, cleansing afternoon with a shimmer of sunshine and a chill bite of wind. Lucy was on her yellow bike with the basket under the handlebars.

She was crossing Hyde Park on the way to Piccadilly to treat herself to tea at Fortnum and Mason's. It was something that she did occasionally. And no one knew. Not Ian, Tolly, or any of her group of close friends. It was just for her. Most of them would have been horrified but it had become a sanctuary that helped lift her mood and motivate her when she needed it most.

She usually had a mix of Earl Grey and Assam tea and a cake. Her first choice was the mango and guava cheesecake, with the Colombian espresso brownie a close second. She had thought about book therapy on the South Bank but decided that tea and a treat was what she needed most. Her magic library could wait until the next time.

She came out of the gates on to the Hyde Park

roundabout, dodged through the traffic, and walked the bike to the stands outside Green Park station. They were all taken so she chained it to the railings of St James's Park and walked up past the Ritz. She and Ian had gone there for tea once, just after they had slipped into sex and deception. Ian had to wear a Ritz green jacket and tie that was forced on him by the waiter when his old suede coat and expensive but tieless linen shirt were regarded with disgust. There were a few other green-jacketed interlopers scattered among the disdaining faces of the regulars and they decided to leave before Lucy punched any of the smug little shits and got thrown out or even arrested for assault. Ian had suggested going to Fortnum's. But her special place was not to be shared even in the first flushes of their passion! She said it was too full of old farts, crumbling scones and fondant fancies. So they had gone to the World Café in Neal's Yard where he could have worn a *Shit happens* T-shirt and a banana leaf thong and nobody would have noticed.

She started getting angry that he'd invaded her thoughts and so she forced him out in a power strut to the food hall of Fortnum's. She wandered around gorgeous goodies that she would never afford before queuing for tea behind a very beautiful young man. He was being touched and teased by a woman who had dressed for her forty-years-ago self and obviously didn't give a fuck! Not that she had any right to sneer, with Marky, who used the mirror more than her, providing the same service. She felt a flush of fear as she watched them. In thirty years, that could be her unless she pulled it together. Having a child would make a difference but that wasn't possible. Perhaps she could adopt. She pulled herself back from this random thought as the beautiful young man stepped back and she felt his bum against her crotch. For a moment it was exciting but then he spoke.

"Sorry, babe!"

He had a voice like a twelve-year-old smoker from the Black Country! She started to laugh, and he looked surprised, then confused, then turned away and back to what he knew. The woman with him kissed his cheek, glanced at her with a withering sneer of wealth, and was about to say something but, luckily, got interrupted by the 'seater,' as he ushered them in. Lucy had time to calm herself before being led to a sad place for one in a corner, almost hidden behind a table of four large Canadian women who'd just been to Buckingham Palace and adored the busbies and red tunics that were just like those the Mounties wore. They weren't, but Lucy didn't care about that or her single spot. She took out one of Sylvia Plath's short pieces while she waited to be served. It was called *Mary Ventura and the Ninth Kingdom*. She hadn't known of its existence until she found a battered copy a couple of months ago in the clutter of one of her go-to book stalls near the Festival Hall. She opened it and started to read.

* * *

Ian-decided to walk to the village on the other side of the Wolds, have a couple of pints, then head back and see if the mercurial magic of the glacial drops and rises around him would stimulate and suggest some sort of solution.

Of course, it didn't! The pub was shut for a refit and as he turned to go back, he got a call from the Dragon, direct and dart-like, to get moving and not fuck about.

"If you need some inspiration, talk to your mate, Lucy. She has a good sense of endings."

Fuck's sake, where had that come from? But he couldn't blame Janey, it was he who had instigated it. She had with a lot of persuasion and promises from him eventually read Lucy's second novel, *The Songbird*, and although she was unable to take her, or it, on, had loved the story, structure, and shape of her writing. Ian had a growing paranoia that if he was dropped then Lucy might well fill his place.

To make the day worse, it started raining on the way back from the pointless trip to the pub. As he sat in the sheep shelter at the bottom of the deep cut and waited for it to stop, he realised that he would just have to live with whatever happened tomorrow and hope that Fate unleashed a good fairy instead of a furious and vindictive one. He had to let this go for now or he'd either have a seizure or admit everything and watch his world collapse and crumble tonight instead of giving it another couple of hours respite until the new day broke and… so did he!

Eventually the rain stopped and as he crawled out of the shelter; the sun shone through in one of those 'see, I was here all the time' moments that nature throws at you. But it didn't last. When Ian reached home and saw that Nora and George were back, any feeling of optimism oozed out and he had to force his face into a focus that would hide what was in his heart. He could sometimes fool Nora but not often. This would be the test of tests. He took a deep breath and vowing not to drink or panic and try to make sense when he spoke, opened the door and went in.

There was an unusual silence as he came into the empty kitchen. He looked up at the clock. It was teatime or should have been. He glanced into the living room, that was empty too.

"George, Nora, where are you?"

There was no answer, no sound of shuffling or movement or giggles from George. Perhaps they'd gone out. No, the door wasn't locked. Nora wouldn't have left it open, even if they'd just popped next door. This was weird and his worry started weaving a worst-case. What if something had happened to them? Maybe they'd come home and there was someone waiting inside? He pushed that little horror out of his head but ran up the stairs, loudly, just in case, and shouted, 'George!' Though what that would do apart from alert and provoke an attack, if there was anyone there, he hadn't thought through. At the top, he stopped and listened but there was nothing. Moving slowly and quietly he looked in their bedroom, George's room, the bathroom and finally, as he opened the door to his writing room and reached for the light, there was a shattering harmony of screams, and a blanket was thrown over him. Ian screamed too but it was muffled by a mouthful of musty old wool. He struggled and shouted, tripped and tried to fling it off, his heart beating so hard he thought it would burst. Then the light came on and a small hysterical face pushed up under the blanket.

"It's only me and Mummy, Daddy, don't be scared."

The blanket was pulled off and Nora, helpless with laughter, stood over him. Ian tried to speak or smile but he had to get his breath back first. Nora knelt down beside George who was now cuddling and patting his dad and saying he was sorry for frightening him. She gave Ian a kiss.

"It was George's idea. He wanted to make you jump."

* * *

Lucy got home about seven after cycling round Hyde Park and the Lake. She'd switched off her phone before going into Fortnum's and forgot about it until she got back to the flat. There were three missed calls and a message from Mark.

Sorry babe, won't be able to make the early train with you, got to take the boss to a meeting in Richmond. I'll have to meet you there. Will let you know what time I get in. Keep in touch. Love you.

She felt a sudden guilt about Mark and wondered if she should tell him not to come and she'd just go to the birthday, stay in a hotel, and then come back the next day. Enough time there to make a point and the little shit squirm. She knew that she wasn't going to say anything to Nora. It was George's day, and she wasn't going to spoil it. But that wasn't fair on Mark. He'd been looking forward to this and she owed it to him. And it would really piss Ian off to see her with someone younger and firmer and more fuckable, and imagine the muckiness she'd get up to with him.

She ran the bath and while she was waiting packed carefully to look casual but classy. She also threw in a couple of warm woolly tops that would do for the ice rink too. Just as she was about to get into the bath, Tolly rang, and so she put the phone on speaker, and lowered herself into the rose and jasmine foam that had cost a fortune but was worth it.

"So, what you're going to do to the shitbag, then?"

Just for a moment, before she answered Tolly, she had the numbing thought that maybe it was her who made these things happen and she was just a selfish, grabbing little bitch who deserved all the crap and confusion that came into her life.

* * *

Ian had finally persuaded George that frightening him like that was very funny, and a really good trick. Nora had to leave the room because the bubbling memory of Ian's frantic face made her splutter with suppressed giggles, which didn't help as George kept being distracted and telling her not to laugh at Daddy. Eventually George had been persuaded that Daddy was fine now and without that worry, he realised how hungry he was and wanted his tea. Ian said he'd do bath duty and later, when they got into Shark and Dinosaur battles in the water, he ended up as wet as George was and together, they soaked the bathroom.

In the kitchen Nora heard the bangs, stamps on the floor, squeals and laughter. She came up, looked around the door, saw the state the bathroom was in, and told them to grow up and clean it now! After she stormed out, and a brief pause, there was more laughter. When they'd both calmed down, they dried up all the wet bits using three towels, two of which were clean and, as George said, would mean more shouting when Mummy found out.

"Don't worry, Georgie, I'll say it was my fault!"

George wasn't sure but by the time the bathroom was almost back to normal, he'd moved on to his birthday and was asking questions about things that Ian didn't want to think about now... or ever. Would Aunty Lucy be there for the beginning of the party? Was she bringing her boyfriend with her? Could she stay with them for a week? And, most important of all, had she bought him the bright red and yellow roller skates? She'd promised them to George after they'd seen someone wearing a pair in the park when she'd come up for a visit. George had loved the colours and wanted a pair that were the same. Aunty Lucy had said that he was too little then but that when he was six, she'd buy them for his birthday. Despite it being eighteen months ago, he still remembered it and as his birthday got closer went on and on about them, how he'd show Daniel and might even let him try them out. He'd drawn at least ten pictures of him wearing them, or of him and Aunty Lucy, where they both were.

Ian didn't tell him that Nora had told Lucy not to do

it. She thought six was too young for roller skates, particularly as George had no sense of danger and went at things full tilt from a standing start, to collide and crash in seconds. If George carried as many of his genetic blips as it sometimes seemed, then it was probably the best thing for him too.

As George got ready for bed, he chattered away about Aunty Lucy, how great she was and how much he loved her and how he wanted Daddy to read *Lenny the Lobster Can't Stay for Dinner*, a choose-your-own-ending storybook she had given him last Christmas, in which you could decide what happened to Lenny. Ian didn't think Lenny would do it for him tonight. Not a strong enough distraction. He needed to still his fluttering mind and drive out thoughts of the horrors Lucy's visit might - not might, would - generate, so he said he was going to make up a story about a hoverfly called Henry.

He wanted to create a story that would exclude any other messy thoughts entering his head. The creative process was going to be interactive, with George adding characters and scenarios and interrupting the flow if he wanted it to take the story in another direction. They'd done this sort of thing before with other stories, and of course, up to a point, with Lenny, and they both had fun doing it and giggled, sometimes uncontrollably. It was great for George's creative growth too, and his teacher had said that he was one of the best in his class at telling stories. The last story they'd invented was about a sad donkey called Daniel who thought nobody cared about him so had run away in the middle of a cold and snowy

winter. It had gone on for an hour
fallen asleep in the middle of the
finish it off the next day. Sadly, wi⌐
had lost some of its energy and st⌐
them were satisfied with the ending w⌐
managed, after many adventures, to find his way home.
This time Ian would make sure that he finished it
properly.

"Henry was a young hoverfly, who lived in a small
garden that was stuffed with flowers, an apple tree and
gooseberry bushes."

"And strawberries and chocolate ones too," said
George.

The story was halted to discuss the difficulty of
growing chocolate on bushes.

"Some of the ingredients of chocolate do come from
plants but they don't grow on the bush into a fully
formed chocolate bar, even without the wrapper."

George didn't let him get away with that. "It's a
made-up story, Daddy, and if I want a bush that grows
chocolate and Henry is happy about it then it's all right.
And my birthday is nearly here, so it's up to me!"

Ian conceded that it was a well thought out point and
they carried on with the story. As they got more deeply
into Henry and his pals and their very strange and surreal
world, any lingering thoughts of Lucy slipped silently
away.

Later, after they ate, Nora and Ian talked through the
next day and made sure that everything was as ready as
it could be and that nothing had been forgotten.

"What time is Lucy arriving?" she asked.

…an had just managed not to twitch as he said, "She's …oing to text which train she's getting, but she'll be here by the time it starts." Unless I can find a way to stop her.

"Good."

They were both exhausted and by the time they'd watched an episode of an Icelandic TV detective drama they'd recorded, Nora was asleep. He woke her up and they both went up to bed. Ian, probably because of the activity he'd expended with the bath, Henry's swirling story, and keeping Lucy scenarios at bay, fell asleep as soon as he hit the pillow and it was Nora, wide awake and ready to worry about George's birthday, who had to distract herself. She read until the words went woozy and her eyes started to close. Just before she put out the light, she kissed Ian and felt a surge of love for him. Asleep and gently snoring, he looked like the Ian she'd met and fallen in love with and who made her laugh even if the conflict in their personalities made life *interesting* at times, and not always in the way she would have chosen. But she wouldn't change him. Would she?

CHAPTER ELEVEN

Lucy had nearly missed the train to York. She arrived at Kings Cross with only a short time left to buy her ticket and make it through the barrier on to the platform before they stopped letting people on to the train.

She was getting hotter and crosser as each carriage she walked through increasingly seethed with grumbling travellers. There were no free seats, apart from a quarter of one next to a very large man who was eating a hamburger and had another two on his lap. By the time he'd finished them too he would have oozed over the rest of it. As she was caught up in the moving mass trying to find a seat and pushed into the café and bar area, she just caught the sliver of seat being taken by a woman the size of a small stick insect wearing headphones and a scarf that covered her mouth and nose.

She jostled in the mostly male crush at the bar, but, just as she finally pushed her way to the counter, a bit of sisterly bias managed to get her the attention of the woman who came to help the harassed attendant already serving. It pissed off several of the men who had been there longer than she had, but she ignored them, as did the woman.

"What can I get you, pet?"

"Cappuccino and two croissants, please."

"Sure." She glared at a man in a Liverpool FC beanie hat who touched her arm to get her attention. "Don't."

"Why is it so packed?" Lucy was getting crushed into the counter.

"Nightmare, last two trains were cancelled because of a driver shortage. Don't think you'll get a seat, pet. The train manager just locked himself in one of the staff toilets after being threatened by someone who'd booked seats a month ago and it's taken because no one put the reservations out." She laughed and went to get Lucy's order.

Lucy pushed her way through and just wanted to sit down, cool off, and get her head around the shit storm she was heading into, decided to pay the twenty pounds to upgrade to First Class. With a bit of luck, because the train was heaving and the train manager in hiding, she might get away with not having to pay the extra amount. She struggled her way to the front of the train and its peace and space for the privileged and wealthy.

* * *

About the same time Lucy left home, Ian jerked awake and struggled to understand what had brought him to the surface and where, or even who, he was. This alien world he'd been snatched into was loud and fuzzy and he seemed to be in the middle of strange and warm gusting winds. Slowly the mist in front of his eyes cleared. George, so close his features were distorted, was blowing hard on to his face and, looking past him, Ian saw Nora doing some sort of dance, her arms waving over her head and a featureless mask stretched across her face. Was it some sort of pagan ritual for mother and child that she usually practiced in private but had now decided to let him see? Then he realised, as her face was thrust out of the mask, that she was pulling a sweater over her head. He closed his eyes to try and reboot his day.

"It's my birthday, Daddy!"

His head almost exploded as George screeched the unintelligible jangle of words into his ear, again and again. He then pulled the duvet off him and tried to drag him out of bed. Ian looked to Nora for help, but she darted forward and joined in to complete the task of hauling him on to his knees and then pulling and pushing him upright.

"Two onto one! That's not fair!"

He was now fully awake but not in a happy way. Why was all this happening to him? Then in a flash he knew. It was George's birthday! George's birthday, George's birthday! That silent but urgent mantra seemed to work. He pulled himself free of them, pulled joggers and fleece over his naked and cold body, then grabbed George, threw him up in the air, blew a raspberry on his neck, draped him, laughing and shouting, around his shoulders and ran out of the door and down the stairs. They were quickly followed by a concerned Nora who could see a crashing fall, broken bodies, screams of pain, and a buggered birthday. But, somehow, more by luck than care, they all reached the bottom safely. Ian ran around the kitchen with George wriggling and twisting around his neck, made two circuits of the table, then sprinted into the living room bit, threw him onto the sofa and tried to tickle him. But that wasn't going to work on a little boy who was six years old today and wanted his present.

"Stop it, Daddy!" he said fiercely. Nora, calm again now and smiling, came in pushing a red and yellow bike with stabilisers. She had a red helmet balanced like a pimple on her head and knee and elbow pads in the same colour under her arm. George stopped struggling and his eyes opened wide, and in one lunge he was off the sofa and stumble-running towards the bike. Nora and Ian started to sing 'Happy Birthday' but George, with a quick, "Thank you. It's so sick, Mummy and Daddy," turned the bike around, pushed it into the kitchen and made for the door as the helmet fell off Nora's head.

"Sick?"

"Daniel's new favourite word. Means it's the best," explained Nora.

"Oh, right, of course."

George was just going outside. "We need to get to school. You'll have to tell George and get him ready. Perhaps we should have left the bike 'til later. But I couldn't wait. He's been on about his present since he got me up at six and it was either give in or lock him in the larder."

"Why me?"

Nora just looked at him. He went after George.

"Text Lucy and see if she's on her way."

Ian just avoided the doorframe as his nemesis came at him like a tsunami.

"Yes, I will." Hoping he had kept any negative inflections out of his voice.

"Is that a problem?" Obviously not!

"No."

Then he saw George ride his bike into the water butt. There was a crash as a pot fell off the top and broke and George followed it onto the gravel.

Something more important than Lucy took over as Nora pushed him out of the way to get to her little boy who was howling and holding his knee, blood seeping through his fingers.

For a brief moment, before the added guilt came, he was pleased George had come off his bike and distracted Nora from the boiling and acid anticipation of Lucy and her destruction of all he knew and loved.

* * *

In First Class, there were, apart from Lucy, five passengers, all of whom looked like they'd paid the full fare and not just topped up their 'cheapest they could buy' tickets. She'd found an empty table seat and sat by the window. With a bit of luck there would be enough seats without anyone having to sit with her. In this cool and relaxed space, the world of crushing cattle class seemed distant and those sharing it with her, self-satisfied, superior, and smug. And, you know what, it didn't bother her at all. She even smiled at a deeply stylish couple as she passed on her way to the empty table she'd spotted from the door. They glanced at her then went back to their newspapers and complimentary toast and tea. They obviously didn't think of her as one of them. Might have been the whiff of common or just the way she looked, hot and crumpled with no privileged bearing or arrogance. At another time she might have been hacked off with that but now that she could move her mind away from the battle through the bodies, there were more important things to think about. The other three people in the carriage were a cleric with the purple top of high office, reading a holy book and making notes, perhaps looking for loopholes, and two men sitting opposite each other, both on laptops with spreadsheets showing, talking in whispers. She just heard the words 'merger' and 'unseat the bastard' before, sensing her presence, they froze like a bad Zoom connection and waited until she had moved far enough away to carry on unheard with their plotting.

She drank her coffee and ate the surprisingly tasty croissants while she looked at the news on her phone. Not much happening except political stupidity and arrogance. She read her emails. She ignored a handful of work ones that didn't need a quick response and was just about to close her mail when a new one dropped in. It was from Greta, a woman she'd met at a seminar, who was, like her, on a panel, 'Women in Verse', and who had flatteringly said she'd love to look at Lucy's novel *The Songbird* because she'd read all her poems and was a huge fan. She had a close friend who was a publisher of new women writers and, if she felt she might be interested, she'd pass it on. Today's mail was good news. The publisher loved it and was going to discuss it at their next emerging writers meeting. *Songbird* was one of six to be discussed and if chosen would be published early next year. Lucy was thrilled and daydreamed about the possibilities for a moment then sent an email to Greta thanking her and saying that she'd buy her a meal when she was next in London. Then there was another ping as a WhatsApp message came in. She ignored it for a moment, taking out her new copy of *Johnny Panic and the Bible of Dreams* from her backpack. Last week she'd been going to try and find the story with the missing pages, online, but gave up after an hour's fruitless search and decided to buy another copy from Amazon. She started to read the weird and wonderful story but couldn't get into it. She put the book down, watched the landscape flash past for a while, then sighed and picked up her phone and opened WhatsApp.

Nora wanted to know if you were on the way. Are you?

Did *Nora* really want to know? Maybe for numbers, but she could sense his overriding anxiety.

Her reply was brief and sharp. *Yes.*

She waited, looking at the phone then as she put it down, it pinged. It wasn't the little shit again. It was Mark.

Should get there about five/five thirty. Can't w8 to cu.

Was this such a good idea? Should she get off at the next stop, text Mark and go back to London? She could come up with a good reason. It was a dangerous game she was playing. Nora was very smart and knew her well. She might feel the tension that was bound to be there whatever she did. The friendship with Nora had become close over the years and they shared a lot. How could she have let it all happen? What would Nora feel like if she found out? Bitter, battered, hurt, humiliated, abused... and angry. Really fucking angry! It would destroy her and her family and nothing would heal that wound. Ever! She was beginning to feel an uncontrollable panic, her stomach twisting and fluttering, her mind spinning scenarios of screaming accusations, searing shock filled faces and monstrous misery.

The train had stopped at a station and people were getting on. One man, middle-aged, well-dressed, good-looking in a slightly ravaged way but with hair too long and lank, thought he caught her eye as he passed the window. He smiled and looked hopeful as he nodded towards the seat opposite her, but Lucy, still in the chaos of her thoughts, didn't notice or hear the whistle or was even aware that the train had stopped and was now moving again.

Lucy heard sounds, muffled words, turned and saw the same man standing next to her table, smiling down at her.

"Hi, I'm Sam. Mind if I join you."

His voice was neither high nor low but had a breathiness, the delivery practiced. He expected the response to be a positive one. Everything about him said that he knew she would be interested in him and would accept his presence. Lucy looked past him and saw that only this jerk had joined the six of them already there. There were other seats for him. She held his look as he slowly saw what was in her cold and unblinking eyes and his cockiness slipped. He laughed uncomfortably. He had to find the obvious retort to regain control and come out without any loss of credibility. It finally struggled through.

"Fuck you!" he growled in a way that he thought was threatening and final.

"Really?" Her tone was derisive, contemptuous. It took him a moment to work through it then he bristled but it didn't last more than a flicker and he walked off with an eloquent "Cunt" thrown towards her. It was louder than he thought or meant it to be. The cleric raised his eyes briefly and the two plotters, for a moment, acknowledged a fellow alpha male, then smiled at his failure and went back to changing the fates of the 'bastard' of the spreadsheet. Lucy watched him go to the end and sit with his back towards her, then dismissed him.

She thought for a moment then smiled. It was one of resolve and not one of fun. She had to go! She couldn't pull out now. She had to face it, make it as all right as it could be. It was all for George. She loved him. She couldn't let him down. She thought about the red and yellow roller skates she'd bought him and for a moment imagined his face then she suddenly recalled a text from Ian about them. It was something Nora had said about the skates. It had completely gone out of her mind because she'd already bought them. She went into WhatsApp and searched back until she found it.

"Fuck, fuck!"

Nora said not to buy them.

That's all Ian had written. Just not to buy them, not why she didn't want him to have them. She'd got him a bunch of other things, but they were the special present. That would not be a good start. She'd tell Nora as soon as she got there. Perhaps she'd changed her mind and was now happy for him to have them. It wasn't a terrible thing to do anyway. The really terrible thing was what she'd been doing with his daddy. A carelessly ignored text was pretty much at the bottom of the scale of those sins. She'd worry about the skates when the time came if she was still breathing and there was no carnage. For now, she had to plan her escape.

It couldn't be too involved. Simple was always best. She would do the party then leave with Mark as soon as possible. The ice rink would be chilly so there wouldn't be a lot of standing around chatting. She'd spend as much time on the ice with George as she could and try to hold it together with Nora so it all seemed normal.

She saw the train manager come into the carriage, look around checking for new passengers, then head towards her, passing the others, without a look. She took out her ticket and credit card and smiled at him.

"The twenty pounds upgrade, please."

Thin, balding, red-faced, and an unhealthy forty, he wasn't a happy and contented soul. He looked at her ticket for a long moment. "Can't do that…"

He paused as the tannoy crackled and a panicky female voice broke through.

"Train manager to the café, straight away, please."

The man jerked, closed his eyes, breathed a shaky "Fuck," and glanced at Lucy. He looked like he was going to cry. "Have this one on me, I mightn't make it back here again." Then he turned and hurried off. Lucy almost felt sorry for him. He was having a pretty shit day too!

* * *

Earlier that morning Nora and George had been picked up by Rose and Daniel so Ian could have the car. Rose was a part-time teaching assistant at the boys' school and so would bring them and a couple of friends to the party.

George had still been cross with Ian for being dragged away from his bike but proud of the war wound he was able to show Daniel. He waved in a 'bored royal' sort of way as they drove off. Distracted but still cross with him was Ian's take on the look his son gave him. After they'd gone, Ian finished making up the party bags and added a few extra ones just in case the count was wrong or someone else turned up. He put them on the kitchen table with the selection of woollies, including one for him. His was an expensive cashmere and wool roll neck that he'd bought from TK Maxx in Manchester. It had been reduced from three hundred pounds to fifty and fitted perfectly. He loved it. Nora was with him to approve it and she'd bought a bag that cost five pounds more than his jumper. Fair and equal treats for the both of them!

That had been just before they knew about the bump and the possible repayment of his advance. Now their dwindling cash flow, particularly after what they'd paid out for the party, was in a very sad state. Still, the jumper was perfect for today, classy, warm, and stylish. He'd feel good and, if life as he knew it was going to go into freefall, at least he'd pass muster for the short time he had left. He cleaned up the kitchen then went to the Spoon, where he sat outside and sent Lucy a text as Nora had told him to. It took him half an hour to get the words right and another ten minutes before he found the courage to send it. Josh had come out and asked him if he wanted anything. He'd broken the spell and Ian said he was just working something out and he'd be in for a cappuccino.

Ian was sitting at the bar of the Spoon with a large mug. The pub was empty apart from Josh, who was leaning on the bar opposite him doing a crossword. He groaned, looked up, puzzled. "Untidy little man, freezes, and hits last covering of family group?" Jesus!'

Ian looked at him, repeated the clue. "Is Jesus part of it?"

"What?"

"The clue."

"No."

Ian took a gulp of coffee then smiled.

"Got it?"

"I have."

Ian smiled again at the waiting Josh who was now looking impatient. " What is it then, smartarse?"

"Pint on the house?"

"No, might ban you if you don't give it to me though."

"You wouldn't do that."

"Get me a gold star from Nora."

Ian looked at him for a long moment, then sighed.

"OK. Rumplestiltskin."

"What?"

"Rumplestiltskin."

"Why?"

"Easy. Untidy, rumple. Freezes, still. Hits last covering of family group, ts-kin."

"For God's sake!"

A mobile rang somewhere close and muffled. Ian realised it was his, reached into his pocket took it out, saw that it was Nora. He checked the time.

"Shit!"

"What?"

"The cake!" The phone stopped and another phone rang. It was Josh's and Nora again. "I'm supposed to pick the cake up… now. Don't say I'm here." He rushed out. Josh waited until he was out of the door then answered.

"Hi, Nora."

"Is Ian there?"

Josh left just enough of a pause.

"No."

"Was he?"

"Came in for a coffee about eleven…"

"Is that all?"

"Yes."

"Sure?"

"Yes, he went to get the cake."

"Good."

"All set for it?"

"Just about."

"George will have a great time, he's a lucky boy. Wish I'd had a skating party."

A delivery driver came into the bar with a wine order

"Sorry. Got to go. Delivery. Have fun."

Ian was stuck at roadworks lights a couple of miles from the village where the cake waited for him. He'd already called them once and apologised for being late. They were fine. Probably used to it. Particularly from dads who are given instructions to be there on time and don't make it. Suddenly he remembered the party bags and jumpers. They were still on the kitchen table. He'd have to go back for them before heading to the party. Shit! Shit! The traffic started to move then stopped as the lights changed again.

"For fuck's sake, what's the point of that!"

Only four cars had gone through. He tried to stay calm; traffic from the other direction just kept coming and even when the lights changed his end, they still flowed through. This time the two cars in front of him managed it. He was tempted to jump with them and follow through but didn't. He was convinced this was all just for him. There was probably a drone spying on him, changing the timing of the lights as he got to the front of the line. Then in a numbing flash he got it. It would have been manifested by Lucy as part of the pre-evisceration to wear him down. He went cold at the reality of that possibility. It was a stretch, even for him. Wasn't it?

He tried to push down the panic but all he managed was to pull up pathetic and whining taunts about his weakness. Why had she suddenly come back into his head now? He'd managed not to think about her since he'd left the pub. But here she was rampaging through and filling the space. Where was she now? Suddenly his hopeful fairy threw him a lifeline. She might have decided it was bad idea to come after all and had turned around and gone back to London. She would do something like that. Change her mind quickly then act on it without dithering. Or if that didn't happen perhaps something else would so that she wouldn't make it. Not that he'd want it to be fatal for her or even debilitating. Perhaps a broken-down train that took hours to clear from the line so that by the time she arrived, the party would have been over, and they'd have left the ice rink and gone home. She and Mark wouldn't come out there. They probably needed to go straight to their AirBnb to rip the clothes off each other...

Thankfully he didn't have to follow that thought through because the lights turned to green. He was determined to make it through this time. He started to move but had to stop as the last three cars came through from the other side. He saw the green flicker, thought 'Fuck that!' and charged through before he missed his chance again. The adrenalin rush was enough to distract him... and Lucy slipped away.

The road works weren't long, two hundred metres or so, and he was picking up speed again when a tractor pulled out in front of him. He nearly ran into the back of it.

"You bastard!"

But shouting at it didn't help and, because it was a narrow single-lane road, he had to follow it all the way into the village. It stopped outside the bakery too and a woman got out, waved a 'sorry' at him, and went past the bakery and into a small butcher's shop.

The cake was amazing. It was a large 'hunny' pot with Pooh standing at the side, his paw stuffed into the top, honey dripping down the sides, under a tree with bees attached to the leaves and Piglet and the gang looking on, tongues hanging out.

It cost eighty pounds, which was a bit of a shock, but worth it for the look that would be on George's face when he saw it. The small cake would be great for George tomorrow on the come-down after his big day. They packed the big cake carefully in a wooden box to protect the architecture of the delicate bits of their creation. They wanted it back after it was finished with, for the next complex design delivery. Gilly and Trish, the confectionary magicians, had joined forces with Ned, an artisan baker, two years before, and had become popular because of these specialised fantasy creations. But they deserved it. The bakery also supplied bread and cakes to shops within a radius of thirty miles. Ian had ordered a sandwich too when he was stuck in the traffic and realised he was starving. He sat in the car and ate it, then found another way to get home that avoided the road works, to pick up the party bags and extra jumpers that he'd forgotten. Nora was going to the rink about half two to make sure everything was good to go. He'd promised her that he'd be there by three at the latest. The party kicked off at half past. Rose was bringing George, with Daniel and a couple of other kids, so he didn't have to pick him up from school. He had an hour and half to get there.

He made it back to the cottage with time for a tea and the espresso brownie he bought from the bakery. As he was about to leave, a darkness descended, and he started scrolling through a series of terrifying images of what Lucy might do. Suddenly his mind spun off and he was back in the Lookout. He felt the piercing agony as something tore through his stomach and travelled to his chest. It felt like a knife but could not have been a real one. He didn't bleed and the marks and pain went. But then he saw the face of the man and heard, 'Oh, Christ, it's Walter!'

Walter? Fuck! Not again!

His phone rang and dragged him back to here and now. It was Nora.

Ian spoke first. "Got everything. I should make it by a quarter to three. Cake is wonderful."

"Don't drop it." She sounded tense. "Did you hear from Lucy?"

He took a quick breath. "Yes, she's on the way. Everything all right there?"

"Yes. They hadn't sorted out where we'd eat but it's done now and in a better place, nearer the ice. Got to go, food's arriving. I need to check it's all there."

He picked up the stuff from the table and went out, loaded everything into the car, came back in, checked everything was off and that he'd put the small cake at the back of the fridge, then grabbed his jacket.

* * *

The rain was torrential when Lucy came out of the station concourse at York and just beat the guy who'd tried to sit with her to the only taxi. She sat back in the seat and tried to do some yoga breathing to calm her down. It didn't work and she remembered that the way it had worked before was that she had spent so long concentrating on trying to get the single nostril breathing right that she'd forgotten what was stressing her out. There wouldn't be time for that. So, she let her head fill and hoped it would have some positive effect. A sort of cleansing by chaos.

She was now sure that she hadn't done the clever thing by coming. It was really, really, fucking stupid. It was as much her fault as his, except his betrayal was greater because of Nora and George. But she came a close second. What did she think she was going to achieve? Suddenly she realised that the driver was talking to her.

"Sorry, what?"

"I said where to? It's how it works with a cab. You tell me where you want to go… and I take you there." He sounded bored and angry. Sarcastic little shit! She thought that she'd told him as she got in but obviously hadn't.

"Sorry, the ice rink, please."

"There you go. Easy, wasn't it?"

He turned back, started the meter, and drove off. She looked at her phone to see what time it was. Three thirty. She'd get there just after it all kicked off. That would be good, she could get lost in the mayhem, probably not have to speak to Nora until they'd got the kids to sit down for the party food. She'd just let Ian's panic peak before she told him that he was safe but that she didn't want to see him again. They'd have to find a way that they could seriously fall out, one that would be acceptable to Nora, but not serious enough for her to lose touch with George, even if it was just Christmas and birthdays. This would have to be one of those painful lessons that in the distant future she would see as a positive. She tried to write a script in her head but that didn't work. She'd just have to let instinct take over. Her sense of self-preservation was strong and Ian, once he knew that she wasn't going to ruin his life, would play along. It was only three hours at the most and then she'd be with Mark and could get away without difficult explanations. Nora would get it. She'd always been a little envious of her last few choices in men. Mind you, she didn't have to find common ground for those moments when sex wasn't the only stimulation she wanted on the menu. Mark's scope for laughter and learning was quite basic and mostly banal. And that was what she missed. Ian certainly kept her on her intellectual and emotional toes. She tried to shake that out. "For fuck's sake, stop it!"

"What?"

She realised she must have said it out loud. "Nothing, just talking to myself."

"Jesus!"

Ahead of them she saw the ice rink and tried to keep calm. Ice World loomed over the edge of the out-of-town shopping park. Its golden domed roof sparkled in the sunshine. It was on its own site but scattered around it were a variety of superstores, a go-kart track, a velodrome, and a huge multiplex cinema. The car park was full and as they pulled up outside the entrance to the rink, a torrent of schoolchildren poured out and across the road to where a dozen buses were parked.

"That's fourteen pounds fifty."

He was loud and aggressive. Lucy wasn't going to rise to it. She gave him a five and a ten pounds note and waited as he sighed and dug some change out of a cotton bag and thrust it at her.

"Will you give me a receipt, please."

He made a big deal of looking for a receipt book then scribbled on the top sheet, tore it off, and gave it to her, turned straight back and started to edge forward then stopped. Lucy tried to open the door, but it was locked. She glared at him. What was wrong with this moron?

"Oops." He smiled and unlocked it and she dragged her case and bag out and slammed the door hard. Childish but it made her feel better.

He stopped the car again, enraged, and looked as if he was going to get out until a bus came up behind him and hooted loudly. He shouted soundlessly at Lucy and the bus driver, gave them both the finger, and shot off, just missing a car pulling out. An ambulance, siren blaring, stopped outside the Velodrome.

Inside the ice rink Ian had just picked up his skates and was heading towards the ice when he felt dizzy and had to sit down. Jesus, the strain had got to him and he was going to faint. The lights around him seemed to dim and a blackness enveloped him.

CHAPTER TWELVE

Walter looked around the deserted waiting room at the hospital, drank the last of the tea in his cup, then screwed it back on the flask and looked up at the clock. It was five past three. He'd just about dried off in the two hours he'd been there. Arthur was in a treatment room with the thug he'd laid out and Walter was waiting for the doctor to give him an update on the one with the bullet wound. He'd sent Billy back to the station, to brief the duty inspector and to send Taff Davies to keep an eye on their man overnight. The goods and the vehicles were impounded in the police yard. Walter and Arthur would interview the walking wounded back at the station. He saw the doctor come down the corridor and went to meet him.

"How is he, Les?"

Leslie Herbert was past retirement age and had been Walter's GP before going back to the hospital to cover those who'd joined up. He looked exhausted.

"He'll live. It was more of a deep flesh wound and the bullet went in the belly and out of his side. It's why there was so much blood. Couldn't find it anywhere, probably been washed away by now. We've stitched him up but best to keep him in, see how he is tomorrow. I'll send the report round as soon as I've done it. I've been on call for twenty-four hours and out on my feet.

I'm getting too old for all this." He pointed back the way he'd come. "He's on ward four."

"Thanks, Doc, you're a hero."

Leslie checked to see if he was taking the piss then smiled and walked off as Arthur approached with the battered and bandaged man walking slowly behind him. "Nothing permanent, unfortunately. Got a bloody thick bonce, haven't you, mate." Arthur winked at him.

"Fuck off!"

Walter looked over at the man then turned back to Arthur. "We've just got to wait for Taff to get here and then we'll see what this one has to say before...." He stopped as he caught sight of another policeman coming in: fiftyish, very tall, and thin as a rake, with a long miserable face, carrying a dripping cape and helmet. "Here he is now. All right, Taff?

Davies nodded but his face didn't change. It never did.

"He's out for the count. Keep your eyes open though. I've organized some tea and sandwiches in a couple of hours." He pointed the way. "Ward four. You armed?"

"Yes, Sarge.' He tapped his pocket.

"OK, I'll get someone to relieve you at eight." He nodded at Arthur. "Let's go."

They'd left him in a small, dark oppressive interview room for half an hour to fester and try to keep warm while they decided which way to play it. The duty inspector, Sid Barnes, who'd lived in the same street as Walter until he got married, was a bit concerned at the state of their prisoner. 'Bit of a mess, isn't he, Walt?'

"Looks worse than it is, Sid. Arthur only gave him a little tap, did most of the damage as he hit the back of the lorry." Arthur nodded, not sure whether Barnes believed it as he clocked the sceptical look the inspector gave him.

"Did he?" He turned back to Walter. "I talked to the super. He wants a full report on his desk by first thing tomorrow. Make sure you do it before you go off shift. It shouldn't stop you going off with Cate though, unless our friend with the bullet takes a turn for the worse and we've got a death on our hands."

"It won't happen, and if anyone pops in to try and top him, one look at that miserable Welsh sod's face should make him think again. And if it doesn't, his gun will. Talking of guns, the bullet wasn't in him, doc thinks it went straight through. Arthur can pop over on his way home, see if he can find it. Is that all right with you, Arthur?"

Arthur didn't look thrilled but nodded.

"How long are you away?" Barnes asked Walter.

"Four days."

"All right. I can cover for you and, if necessary, stick Arthur on the front line and he can take the flak."

He smiled at Arthur.

"Thank you, sir, you're all heart."

"You're welcome." Walter laughed. "Well done though, lads, it was a good collar. Should upset the apple cart a bit."

Walter nodded." It'll certainly dent their pot of gold." He glanced at Arthur. "Ready to have a go?"

Just as they were going into the interview room, Barnes touched Walter's arm.

"Think it could be anything to do with Jimmy Douglas?"

"I certainly hope so." He had a sudden thought. "What happened to Billy?"

Barnes smiled. "Sent him home. He wasn't in any sort of state to go out again. Might as well be there as in the rest room. No use to anyone after your little escapade."

"He'll learn," said Walter. "Took me a while to shut everything out." He opened the door and they went in.

"Full name." Walter and Arthur sat opposite the man; Arthur ready to write it up.

The man looked hard at Walter. "Fuck off!"

Walter glanced at Arthur, who slapped the man on the un-bandaged side of his face. It was hard and stinging.

"Fuck was that for?"

"Better. We'll have a whole sentence soon. Name?" He tried to look tough but as Arthur reached over towards him again, he held up his hands.

"All right. Donald Stanley Keyes."

Walter looked at Arthur who spluttered loudly, "All right if I call you Don."

"It's Stan," Keyes said quickly.

Arthur looked at him innocently. "Why not Don? Don Keyes, that's good." He laughed loudly. "Donkey. Get it? Hope you can match up."' He pointed at his crotch. "Make you popular with the ladies if you could."

Keyes slowly worked it out. "Fucking hilarious!"

"What were your mum and dad thinking?"

"It's me grandad's name, on me mum's side.

"What was his surname?" Arthur was having fun. "Nutt."

This time it was Walter who exploded a laugh. "Nutt. Don Nutt, doughnut?"

"Yes, what's funny about that?"

Walter shook his head. "Didn't have much of a chance in life with your brain, did you, Donkey?" Keyes was really confused now. "So, you work for Jimmy Douglas?"

"Yes." He suddenly realised what he'd said. "Don't know who you mean."

"Too late, chum."

"Fuck off!"

Walter sighed. "I'm happy to give Jimmy a call and say you grassed him up."

Keyes twitched. "He wouldn't believe you."

"How do you know, you just said you didn't know him?"

"I don't."

For a moment Walter just looked at him then glanced at his watch. It was four fifteen a.m. "The Geordie lad is in a bad way." Keyes looked confused. "Your mate from tonight, the one who got shot, blood everywhere."

Keyes tried a smile. It didn't improve anything about him. "I could drop you right in the shit. Say I saw you shoot him."

"Was that before or after your little scrap with Arthur? Bit busy to have seen anything."

Keyes was thrown again.

"In the hospital before Geordie pegged out, he said it was all down to you. That you said it was a job for Jimmy."

"He's dead?" Keyes looked scared.

"Who is?"

"Geordie, you said he pegged out."

"Yes, Donkey, with the anaesthetic! He had to be put under so the doc could see what damage had been done."

"Don't call me Donkey."

Walter glanced at Arthur. "This is going to be a long night." He smiled at Keyes. "I'll give you another fifteen minutes then wake Jimmy from his beauty sleep. I can promise you he won't be a happy bunny."

They'd finished with Stan Keyes by six. It was difficult to join up all of his rambling, but Arthur managed to get the gist of it down and, after a bit of bluster, Keyes signed the statement. He'd admitted it was Douglas's van and lorry and that his boss had brought in Geordie because the rest of his boys were on another job. Stan wasn't meant to be there. He was just a run-around, never trusted for any of the heavy work. His sister was one of Jimmy's 'tarts' and she'd persuaded Jimmy to let him do odds and sods for a couple of quid. She'd warned him not to tell Stan anything that could be used against him. He wasn't good at keeping quiet. Not his fault, he just wasn't that bright. It should have been an easy and quick job tonight and he was the only one left after the regular driver had been pulled in for desertion and faced a court martial and a prison term.

Once he'd started talking, he couldn't stop. They'd had to lock him in a cell just to shut him up. He knew he'd do time, but he didn't seem worried. Save him having to look after himself for a bit. Only thing was they had to promise not to say it was him who grassed. As if that would help him!

Barnes thought they had enough to pull Douglas in and although his brief would have him out of there sharpish, it would unsettle him. Barnes had a personal grudge to settle. No one knew what it was, but with Walter away he would lead the raid on Jimmy's to check for stolen goods. They'd not find anything of course but eventually he'd take a fall. They all did when they got too cocky, and Jimmy Douglas was getting close.

Walter finished his report and was just going off duty when Taff Davies came back.

"Still with us?"

"Yes, came round about an hour ago and said he was going to have your balls for shooting him. I pointed out he'd attacked you, but he wouldn't have it. Dave Lee took over. Is it all right if I go off now, guv, promised the missus I'd be home before she goes to work, to look after the granddaughter? She'll throw a spit if I'm late."

"Sure. Enjoy."

The quick smile surprised Walter but it soon went and Taff's face returned to its usual morbid-looking state. But it showed that perhaps there was a bit more to Taff than misery and moodiness. He'd have to dig down and see what he could find.

"I will." Taff sounded different, softer and warmer.

"Good. Anyway, thanks for tonight. I'm off now too."

The two of them went out together.

As he walked home, Walter thought about Cate and their honeymoon at Robin Hood's Bay. They'd stayed at the Bay Hotel in Bay Town. Overlooking the harbour, the old hotel must have rattled and shaken in winter storms, but when Cate and Walter had stayed there it was summer and just a bit creaky with the strange noises of all old buildings. It was the first time that either of them had stayed in a hotel. The room was big with its own small bathroom. The bridal suite, the owner had called it and laughed.

On their first day, after arriving at the train station, they had dropped their bags off at the hotel and wandered around the small town. Everybody seemed so friendly. They'd had the best ice cream they'd ever tasted and ate mussels at a small café on the harbour, and then had a couple of drinks in the bar before going to their room and that longed-for first night. The first time was awkward for them both but by the time they dropped off to sleep, contented and satiated, they'd found their way.

It was before Walter's accident and they enjoyed long walks around the coastal path, days at the beach, the treat of eating out and the joy of then slipping into bed together, making love and talking about the family they would one day have and how they'd bring them here. It was a wonderful week and they'd known that whatever happened they'd be together for the rest of their lives. Walter's accident had happened late one night. It was a year after they'd married. By then he'd been a policeman for six years and was riding his motorbike home when he was hit by a car driven by a drunk. He'd almost lost his leg and had been out of action for months, but they'd let him come back when the final medical report said that he would lose only ten per cent of his mobility. They were right and, apart from a slight limp and an ache when he overdid things, he managed.

He was put on station duties at first but eventually went back on the beat. Cate had been wonderful and was caring and understanding when he got angry at the world. Over the years, life had its ups and downs. The children they so wanted never came. Cate lost two babies during early pregnancy. Then there was the terrible day when Dr Clarke said they should face the fact that she might not get pregnant again. Seeing the effect his diagnosis had on her, he had tried to soften it by saying that perhaps it might not be so black and white.

"Never say never. It's always possible. The body has its own rules and sometimes things happen when you least expect them."

He also suggested adoption, but Cate wouldn't consider it. She clung on to the doctor's 'never say never' but as time went on it seemed less likely that she would ever conceive again, and she became withdrawn and distant. Walter tried his best to comfort her. He loved her and if it was only going to be the two of them, that was fine by him. But he knew it would never be enough for her.

Walter had had his own dark moments too. He tried to enlist after war broke out but was turned down. Even though he knew that he could do his bit in the police, he still felt guilty as hell that his mates were putting their lives on the line while he was on a cushy number at home, keeping the villains and black marketeers in check.

Over the last year Cate had become increasingly depressed and was finding it difficult to do any more than what she considered her main duties. Keep the house tidy and make sure that Walter's clothes and uniform were clean and ironed and that his food was either packed and ready or on the table when he got home. He told her that they were a team and he didn't want her to wait on him, but it was too set in her mind. She hardly spoke to him and although he chattered away about his day she rarely responded. Occasionally there would be the flash of the old Cate and, for the most part, that was just enough to keep him going. They hadn't made love for months and he felt that, sometimes, she couldn't bear him to touch her. The last time they had sex it was not making love he had felt terrible when she just lay there impassively and said "as long as he was satisfied that was all that mattered". He'd gone into the bathroom and for the first time since he thought he might lose his leg, he'd cried. She must have heard him but didn't say anything. He never thought about giving up though. He loved her too much for that and deep down he knew that she felt the same way. He was willing to wait for as long as it took. He had to believe it would get better. He thought that it might be good for them to get away from their everyday life and go back, just for a few days, to where they spent their honeymoon. It had been one of the best times of their lives and perhaps it would work its magic again. Cate had been difficult to persuade but he had finally worn her down and she'd agreed to go.

When Walter had rung the Bay Hotel, George, the owner, said that they weren't officially taking 'paying guests' but when Walter explained that they'd stayed there eight years ago on their honeymoon and the reason he wanted to bring Cate here now, not going into it in detail, but just saying she was depressed and that she needed something to give her a lift, he was happy to take them in.

CHAPTER THIRTEEN

Lucy, wearing one of the thick but stylish sweaters she'd brought with her, waited at the pay desk for the woman to finish with a swearing old man who wanted his money back because it was too noisy in the rink. She was explaining to him that they had a couple of birthday parties in today and it was busy with after-school trade too. It was much quieter in the mornings. She glanced over at a security guard watching from behind a pillar. He came over and, after a bit of a struggle, led the man out. The woman looked towards Lucy. "Same every time he comes in. He's on his own and gets lonely, and a bit of a scuffle helps make it feel like someone notices if he's around or not." Lucy was surprised at her caring dip into the old man's psyche. Why? Just because she worked on reception at an ice rink didn't mean she was insensitive or not too bright. God, please don't let her turn into one of those bitchy cynics that she hated. She felt herself go hot. Great start to Armageddon!

"I'm here for a party, George Chambers…"

The woman looked at the screen, clicked her mouse, then pointed towards a corridor. "Down to the bottom, second set of doors and then turn right and that will take you to the right side of the rink. The party area is at the end. It's the best one, nearest the ice. Not good though if you have sensitive ears or don't enjoy an extra level of chill."

"Great, thanks, I can't wait." Lucy smiled and followed her directions, but her heart and head were trying to slip back the way she'd come and escape. Lucy took a deep breath and opened the double doors. Now she was here, she didn't have a clue what she was going to do, apart from stutter and say sorry, she shouldn't have come. She stopped and seriously thought of turning around and going back but the security guy from the front was behind her.

"I'll show you where they are."

Should she push past him and just run out? But by the time she'd thought that through they were inside, and he was pointing. "Down there."

"Thank you."

"No problem, pet," he threw back as he walked off the other way.

She could see them at the side of an area of the ice closed off with party ribbons. There was a gaggle of adults around a large table being loaded with party food, and a huge cake was being taken out of sight behind a counter. It was impressive. Directing operations was Nora, in amongst helpers and ice rink staff. She looked organised, a bit tense, and gorgeously dishevelled. She couldn't see Ian there. She looked over to where the kids were skating around with a couple of clowns and saw him sitting on the floor near the ice, putting on skates and wearing that bloody jumper she hated. What the hell was he doing? He couldn't skate. She'd taken him once and he was hopeless, fell over continuously, hurt his neck, and was a pain in the arse all day, moaning until they left and went for a drink. That was before the sex.

Not that that had anything to do with his skating ability. A quick fuck wouldn't have turned him into Torvill... or Dean. She couldn't remember which one was male, but they were the only two famous skaters she could think of.

The struggle stopped when she saw that Nora was waving at her. Shit! Smile and wave back. She did and headed towards the cabal of mums, trying to focus on what she was going to do next. As she got nearer, she saw there were a few dads there too, looking awkward and uncomfortable in old sweaters in odd colours that clashed with the designer jeans or suit trousers they were wearing. Some of the women wore woollies that didn't fit. She guessed that Nora had brought spares for those who forgot that it was going to be really cold if you weren't six. The clue was in the description on the invitation: *Ice Rink Party*. It was bloody freezing. She was bloody freezing, although how much of that was the fear of being found out creeping like mercury through her veins, and how much was the cold seeping off the ice, was difficult to quantify. Probably sixty-forty in favour of fear! She stopped herself following that through before it was obvious that she had slipped into a manic moment. She tried to judge from the inside what her face felt like it looked on the outside. But, by this time, she'd reached the table and Nora was in front of her, arms open for a hug. She looked pleased to see her.

"Thought you'd never get here. George has been worried that you weren't coming."

"Sorry, should have come up last night but I had a tutorial at six thirty." What was the point of lying about what she was doing yesterday? Nerves, or just the instinct of the conniving and duplicitous little cow she'd become.

Over her shoulder Lucy saw Ian take a few steps, turn around proudly, see that she was there and what she and Nora were doing, panic, crash into a small girl who was just coming off the ice, and go flying. Lucy felt laughter bubble. Nora pulled back and looked at her. Lucy pointed towards Ian trying to stand up and failing but managing to scrabble himself to the side and hold on to the barrier. Nora wasn't that amused. George and his friends were hysterical as the clowns glared and tried to outdo him.

"I told him to take some lessons before today, but you know what he's like."

Lucy hoped that Nora didn't sense the treacherous depth of her intimate knowledge.

"I do." She laughed and Nora smiled.

"Where's the boy? Mark? Can't wait to check him out."

Thanks, Marky! Neat diversion for her. "He had to get a later train and, sadly, won't get here until after the party. He's good with kids. Not far off one himself, I suppose. Still, he makes up for it in other ways."

"I'm sure he does. Lucky girl." Nora saw one of the staff drop some small cakes then pick them off the floor and put them back on the plate. "No, you can't do that!" She looked at Lucy. "Sorry, I'd better supervise. We'll catch up later."

"Anything you want me to do?"

"Sort Ian out. Tell him they've got half an hour before he needs to round them up."

"Will do! Where do I get skates?" She dumped her case, backpack, and coat on a chair. Nora pointed and then hurried off. The rest of the mums and dads just seemed to be chatting, drinking mulled wine and ignoring the preparations. Only Daniel's mum, Rose, the only one she'd met before, was in the thick of it. Good old Nora! She thought of everything. She'd never have come up with mulled wine.

Right, she couldn't hold off any longer. She headed for the attendant standing guard over the skates. She deliberately didn't look at Ian. Didn't want to see the fear. Wanted him to feel but not show it. He'd build up the maximum pressure and just as he reached overload, she'd let him know that it was going to be all right and he wasn't going to lose it all. She just hoped he'd manage to control all of that so it just looked like his normal behaviour at times of stress. Stress with George's party was fine and probably expected by everybody there who knew him well.

"What size are you, love?"

"Five, please."

He searched through a pile of skates and found one then, after a struggle, the other.

Ian thought he might die. He hoped not literally because that would mess up George's party too and one of them having a seriously fucked up day was enough, although, even at six, George would probably cope in a better way than he would. He fell over again. "Fuck." He hoped he'd said that quietly but the look from the large security woman patrolling the edges of the ice he knew that he hadn't.

"Less of the language, you prick," she spat at him. Her slipstream, as she passed close enough for him to be enveloped in her cigarette-and-meat breath, threw him off balance again.

Why couldn't he stand up without holding on? He didn't have long to search for wisdom. One of the clowns suddenly appeared like a swirling rainbow, grabbed both of his hands and rocketed off backwards with Ian trying to hide the scream as he was dragged, like a glider to take off speed, into the midst of the hysterical mass of tiny people, boys and girls, who had all stopped their expert movements to watch as the clown spun Ian around and let him go. For one moment a demented Ian thought he'd found his balance then, as the kids circled him, he felt he'd risen, levitating above the ice, before crashing down on his front and lying still, trying to work out which bits were going to hurt most or freeze and drop off.

He felt himself being lifted by hands under his shoulders and as he came up the painted sad face of the clown, eyes full of concern, was almost touching his as he held him tightly, front to front, until he had some sort of balance. "I'm so sorry, mate, didn't think I'd done it that hard. You alright?" He didn't sound like he meant it. Clown's revenge!

"Yes, I'll be fine." He tried to say it in a big voice, but it came out more as a squeak. The kids laughed and gathered around him then moved off when they saw there was no blood to entertain them. Even George, who for a moment looked worried, went to where the other clown was starting off a skating train.

"I'll sort him out. You get back to the kids." Lucy smiled at the clown who bowed to the ice then skated off, one leg raised in the air as he pirouetted, and joined the back of the train.

Ian felt her arms around him and her breath on the back of his neck. It was the only warm part of him. "Hello, shitbag!" He started to wobble. Lucy moved around him and took his hands. "Don't do anything, just let me pull you." Slowly they headed for the gap in the barrier. "Enjoying the party?"

Ian wasn't sure he would be able to speak but he had to try. He could see Nora watching from the table and shaking her head. He managed it in a whisper. "What are you going to do?" He sat down and started to take the skates off.

"What do you suggest? Have a word with Nora now or wait until we're alone?"

"Please…"

"Shut up." She stood over him, turned and waved at George who'd seen her, broken from the train, and was skating confidently towards them. The panic was spreading across Ian's face like a rash "I'm not going to say anything at all. Not for you, but because it's not fair on George and, although you are a selfish and inconsiderate twat, you're his dad, and me seeing your family shatter just to show you how bad I feel, isn't a good enough reason. I betrayed Nora's friendship. I'll never be able to change that, whatever happens!" George was almost there. "I'll stay for the party. You'll have to make everything look like it's always been with us. If I can do it, you can too. Mark's coming at six and we're going off to the Lakes." She turned away jumped onto the ice and spun George around. "Hello, sweetheart, happy birthday! Sorry I was late." She grabbed his hand and they sped off.

"Have you got my present?"

"Yes."

Ian watched them join his friends who were being paired off by the clowns to have races.

He wasn't sure how he felt. Relieved but not convinced that she would keep her word. Could he manage to pretend it had never happened and not do or say anything that would make Nora suspicious? Jesus, he hoped so. As he reached the guy with the skates, he saw Nora hold up both hands and Lucy waving back. Ten minutes before the meal madness started. He got his shoes back, put them on, and headed for the table, determined that he wasn't going to drink.

With horror he realised he was jealous. What the fuck was the matter with him? He glanced across and saw that Lucy was herding the kids towards the edge of the ice. He jumped as Nora appeared in front of him.

"What's the matter with you?"

"Sorry, thought you were going to hit me." He hoped it was light enough to sound like he was joking.

"Why would I do that? Because you made a dick of yourself on the ice? Left Lucy to sort out the kids? Because you sometimes piss me off by being stupid? Or that you left me to organise this all on my own?"

"All of them. But I'm up for it now and you can leave the rest to me."

"Just help, that's all I want." She saw the first of the

kids coming back. She'd bought them all slip-on shoes as a job lot from the market in Driffield, so they could carry their skates and keep them for the final session on the ice before the party wrapped up. "You can get them all sat down and check with Sean," she pointed to a young guy with an Ice World T-shirt and baseball cap, "and tell him that he needs to get the cake ready with the candles."

Ian suddenly had a horrible thought. "Was I supposed to get those?" He tried to keep the panic out of his voice.

"No, I sorted it weeks ago, had to get them made."

"Oh, right." She went back to check the mass of food that was arriving at the table.

He saw George holding Lucy's hand, coming towards him, so he quickly started organising those kids that had already got there and were hovering. "I asked Aunty Lucy if she would stay with us tonight because it's my birthday and she said she'd think about it."

Ian gave George a kiss on the head to hide his flutter of fear. "That would be nice," he muffled through George's hair then stood up, not looking at her. Lucy touched his arm as he turned away.

"I'll have to see what Mark says first." It was a smile laced with mischief.

Lucy sat George at one end of the table then went over to Nora as the other kids got settled. Everything was in place now and Ian counted down as he tried to look at the kids, Nora, and Lucy at the same time. "All right, go!" Little hands started grabbing, stuffing mouths and filling plates. Rose was standing near him.

"God, they're savages." She gave him a quick hug.

"Are you OK? Nora said you were in a bit of a state."

"What?"

"She didn't go into it. Just said that you were having problems with the book and that money would be a bit tight until you'd finished it."

He glanced over at Nora and Lucy. Nora was looking fierce and had taken a step back. What had Lucy said to her? Oh shit, this was a nightmare. He couldn't wait. He had to find out. "Sorry, Rose, I have to have a word with Nora."

"Not about what I said?" She looked concerned.

"No, something I've just remembered and, honestly, I'm fine. I was a bit down but good now." He gave her a quick kiss on the cheek. "Thanks for asking though."

She smiled and turned away as she caught one of the boys stealing a fish finger from a girl sitting two seats away from him.

"No, Carl, that's not on, give it back."

Ian walked towards the two women who seemed friendlier now. "Everything all right? Nora looked like she was going to punch you."

"I had to confess…" Lucy looked at him for a long moment, "that I hadn't read your text properly about not getting George the roller skates and I'd already bought them."

She glanced at Nora who was watching the scramble at the table. Nora looked back at Lucy.

"I overreacted. It's not Lucy's fault and George will love them. I was being a bit too careful about it but she's right, he'll be fine, like he was with the ice skating." She saw George throwing a sandwich down the table and gave Ian a look. "Thought you were in charge. Have a word with George but don't get heavy, it's his birthday and he's excited."

He nodded and headed for the table.

"Well trained," said Lucy as she watched him go.

"You think?"

"No."

The two looked at each other then laughed.

They watched as Ian sorted George out and then, looked round and mouthed. "Just going to the loo."

In the toilets, Ian sat in a cubicle, trying to calm himself down. It would be fine. He would get through today. He looked up as the light above him and the ice rink sounds slowly faded and a howl of wind and the crash of breaking waves edged in.

CHAPTER FOURTEEN

Walter and Cate were on the beach at Robin Hood's Bay. It was cold and there was a strong wind coming off the sea but walking close to the high cliffs forming the valley in which the beach sat, it was bracing, blew the cobwebs away, yet was bearable. They had wrapped up well and, after two days here, were beginning to relax. This was the first time they'd left the town and they'd walked over the cliffs to get here. Walter was pleased that he'd hardly noticed it at all and felt he could have walked miles without his leg playing up. That had to be a good sign. And Cate was beginning to open up, which was an even better one.

"Thank you for bringing me here," she said putting her arm through his. "It's a different world."

Walter laughed. "Wouldn't have been the same without you."

Cate smiled. "I mean it." She looked out to sea. "I know I've been difficult…"

"Cate…" He wasn't sure he wanted to talk about this now. He didn't want her to get upset.

"No, let me finish, love. You've had to put up with a lot from me." She stopped and took a deep breath then seemed to relax. "Both of us know why I was like that and that it was nobody's fault but there was part of me that had to find someone to blame. You were it and I'm sorry that I made it difficult for you. I know you were hurt. But I had shut everything down not to feel anything. I couldn't even come to you that night I heard you crying in the bathroom." Walter frowned, in surprise and embarrassment. "These last weeks I knew that something had to change, one way or another. I had to do something. I didn't want to lose you and the way things were going you'd have eventually gone."

"I wouldn't… "

She put her hand over his mouth.

"That's why I agreed to come away. It was either going to sort things out or break us apart." She took her hand away. "Being here with you now makes me see how much I love you and that I want to try and make it up to you." She looked at him for a long moment. "Is that all right with you, or have I gone too far for you to forgive me?"

They'd stopped and were standing behind an outcrop of rock that took the wind away from them. "Cate, there's nothing to forgive." He stood back and looked at her then laughed. "I think that's the most you've said in one go for months."

She smiled and gently kissed him, then took his hand. "Come on, let's walk out to the sea then go back and find somewhere to eat."

They started walking towards the edge of the water. The wind was getting up and the breakers, starting from as far out as they could see, were crashing before dipping away to a trickle of foam by the time they reached their limit on the sand.

"The mussels place might be open. Would that do you?" he said.

"It would."

Walter stopped and moved in front of her, took her face in his hands, kissed her softly on both cheeks then briefly on the lips. She wasn't ready yet and gently moved his hands. He understood and smiled. "We'll take it easy, got plenty of time before we go back home." Cate nodded, moved into his arms and they held on to each other. Walter felt happier than he had for a long time. Perhaps they'd have a chance after all. It had been good to come here. Not only because it reminded them of their wedding but also, out here, away from everybody, they might find a way back, and if that happened then who knew what else might be possible. It wasn't a time to talk about babies or adoption. They needed to just enjoy the here and now, with the person they loved most. To know that what really mattered was their relationship and to trust that, in time, everything would be all right.

It was too windy to walk back over the cliffs, so they followed the road and as the clouds grew dark, there was a distant clap of thunder. Just as it started to rain they were picked up by an army lorry and dropped off outside the mussels place. They went in to the warm and cosy café, where the young woman who ran it, Gladys, said she was thinking of shutting up for the night soon because of the weather.

"But seeing as you're visitors I'm happy to feed you first! "

The food was as good as they'd remembered it and she joined them for a drink after their meal. Walter and Cate told her that when they were there eight years ago it was run by a large round friendly man with a red face and a booming voice. She laughed.

"That was my grandfather. He retired a year ago after he had a heart attack."

"Sorry to hear that." Walter felt a bit embarrassed that he'd painted such a cartoon-like picture of the man. Gladys smiled.

"He's OK now but has to take it easy. He didn't want to sell, Mum and Dad weren't interested, so he persuaded me to take it over. I'd been helping him out for years and knew how to run it. I don't have kids and my husband is in the Navy so I've time on my hands. It's only a couple of days a week. I'm a civilian clerk at the Army camp just outside town."

Walter was just about to chip in but she ploughed on, saying that the café wasn't really paying its way, but she felt people needed a bit of cheering up in these dark times and home-cooked food always did that.

The rain had stopped by the time they got away. "Thought we were there for the night," said Cate, "I was about to give her a thump to shut her up."

Walter looked shocked then laughed. "I'd better watch my step from now on."

"It's the sea air." Cate giggled and gave him a kiss. "Come on." She grabbed his hand and pulled him after her. They managed to walk around the harbour and get back to the hotel before the rain started again.

By the time they got into bed the storm had risen. The rain pounded against the windows and the old building groaned and rattled. They snuggled down under the pile of blankets, their feet touching, warmed by the stone hot water bottle that had been put in the bed. In the darkness with the ringing chorus of nature outside, safe and covered up from the world, they made love and then slipped into sleep, their arms wrapped tightly around each other.

CHAPTER FIFTEEN

Ian was still in the cubicle and but now everything was normal again. He tried to remember what had happened. But it was too distant now. It had never been this short a time between slips into Walter's world and that brought a burst of panic that he knew he didn't have space for now. There were other things more pressing.

He heard a door open and the noise from the rink increased then faded again as it closed.

"Ian, are you all right in there?" It was one of the dads, but not one whose voice he recognised. "Your friend Lucy asked me to check on you."

Ian took a deep breath. "I'm fine, just having a moment before I go back to the madness."

The guy laughed. "Tell me about it!"

"You have no idea."

"What?"

"Nothing!" Ian stood up and unlocked the door.

The rest of the party had passed in a blur. The noise level was at the edge of bearable and the parents of the other kids seemed happy to let Lucy, Nora, Ian, and Rose do it all while they picked at bits of food and drank more mulled wine that they'd ordered without asking or offering to pay for it. But the cake was a huge success. George's reaction when it was carried over by Sean after the lights over the table had been switched off, was almost worth all the pain and the stress. It was dim rather than dark because of the other lighting around them but it was enough to make the cake and the candles in the shapes of Pooh and the others magnificent and magical. George's face was a delight. It went from surprise to realisation, to laughter and finally sublime joy and disbelief at the wonder of his Winnie the Pooh cake. For a moment it looked like he didn't want to cut it and spoil anything, but once he'd blown out the candles and the singing of 'Happy Birthday' had finished, he was ready to share it.

An hour and a half later all of George's friends and their parents had gone except for Daniel who was just leaving with Rose. George was really cross with Ian because he hadn't let Daniel go in the car with them. But Lucy had taken his hand and headed off as Nora and Ian paid the extra for Sean and the rest of the Rink staff to finish the clean-up.

It was dark and wet. The lights of the traffic, like fuzzy starbursts between the pathetic swipes of the worn-out wipers, made driving less than relaxed. As they finally turned into the station, Lucy and George in the back were playing a game that seemed to be all about shouting the names of animals as loudly as possible until they both said the same one and then whoever shouted 'snap' first won. Nora, sitting next to Ian, looked exhausted. Animal Snap would easily replace water boarding as a guaranteed method of forcing a confession of guilt... or betrayal. That little rapier thought didn't help Ian's paranoia or throbbing head. Nora hadn't spoken since she'd got into the car. It had taken them an hour to get to the station and now they were stuck behind a sizeable old people carrier that was disgorging a large Asian family group with bags, babies, kids, and cases. They all took their time in saying their goodbyes to the driver, probably a relative who had drawn the short straw and who looked as close to a wipe-out as Ian felt. As the last mum rounded up her escaping child and headed towards the entrance, a huge weight seemed to lift from him and he turned, smiled, and mouthed 'sorry' at Ian, then, almost skipping, got in the car and drove off. Lucky bastard, his nightmare was over.

As they pulled into a 'drop off' bay, Mark, sheltering under the canopy, stepped out and waved as he saw Lucy through the misty window, and shouted her name. She was distracted by George and didn't notice until the little boy pointed at Mark. He'd seen him as he wriggled around to grab a balloon that had floated up from the floor.

"That man is waving at us."

Lucy looked around.

"That's my boyfriend. Mark."

Mark managed, despite the rain and the coat, to look stylish in a sort of rough-edged way. Nora had perked up as she looked around. "Bloody hell, he's gorgeous."

Lucy laughed. "He is!"

"What's gorgeous, Mummy?"

"It means really nice."

George looked at Mark, considering, and then said seriously, "He's not as old as Daddy."

Nora laughed. "No, he's not."

"Thank you, George." Ian tried to make it sound funny, but it came out whiny instead.

"He looks like Ryan Gosling." Nora glanced back at Lucy.

Lucy gave George a big hug and a kiss. "I'll come and see you on the way back. Mark and Daddy can play football with you."

George hung on, not letting her go. "Promise?"

"Yes, I promise."

She opened the door, leaned in close to Nora. "Not intellectually stimulating, but then we don't talk much." She caught Ian's eye. "Enjoy the rest of Georgie's birthday. I'll let you know when we're on the way back."

"Yes, I'm sure you will." He leaned towards Lucy and gave her a quick kiss on the cheek.

Lucy backed out and shut the door and was grabbed by Mark, who turned her around, looked at her for a moment. "Hello, babe." He moved in for a kiss.

In the car George and Nora were gazing at the couple as they kissed passionately. "Aunty Lucy likes her friend, doesn't she, Mummy?"

"She does." Ian looked at them for a moment then opened the door and went to the back of the Volvo, took out Lucy's case and backpack, put them under the station canopy and ignored the couple who were just coming up for a breather. Mark gave him a big smile.

"Thanks, mate. Good to meet you."

"You too," Ian mumbled and moved away. He glanced at Lucy. "Need to get George home," he said sharply and hurried round the car, got in, and started to drive off.

"What's up with him?"

Lucy smiled and waved at Nora and blew kisses back to George. "He's had a tough day." She pulled out of his arms. "Come on, let's get the car."

Ian was waiting impatiently for a space in the traffic, or for someone to let him out. That wasn't going to happen though, was it!

"That was a bit quick." Nora said, glancing at George who was looking back towards the station where he could just see Lucy and Mark walking away.

"I want Aunty Lucy to stay. It's not fair." He thought for a moment then remembered. "Mark could have played football with me too."

"I know, sweetie, but she'll see you before she goes home."

"No point waiting for them to finish." Ian said, glancing at Nora.

"Finish what?" Nora said sweetly.

Ian ignored her and pulled quickly out into the traffic, causing a black cab to slam its brakes on. The driver tooted long and loud.

Ian couldn't hold it back. "Piss off." It was louder and more aggressive than he'd meant it to be.

George snapped back into his seat in surprise.

"That's a bad word." A slight pause. "Isn't it, Mummy?"

"It is, sweetheart, I think Daddy's a bit cross."

"Why?"

"I'm not," said Ian crossly.

George and Nora looked at each other and started giggling.

Ian glanced round at them and forced a smile. Better try to ease things now. "I'm sorry, I'm just a bit tired. I wanted Aunty Lucy to stay too."

"What about Mark?" George said through his giggles.

"Yes, of course, him too." He hoped it came out in the right way, light and easy, but from the quick look Nora gave him, it obviously hadn't. "A glass of red and I'll be fine."

* * *

By the time they got home George was fading, his eyes closing. Nora had fallen asleep as they left York and Ian had trouble keeping his eyes focused as the drive had gone on. It had taken them ages to get out of the city and then there were the usual post rush hour in the rain queues and roadworks lights.

At last Ian drove through the gate and stopped. He sat there for a moment as George bounced sleepily awake and Nora snored gently. Should he leave them there for a while and gulp down a large glass to prepare himself for the evening? Perhaps Nora would fall asleep with George and he'd have it to himself.

"Get George straight into bed and I'll come up after I have a pee. You can wait for your wine until then." She was reading his mind again.

"Ian?"

"Sorry, still locked in horror drive."

"Well, you're not doing it now and I want George in bed before he really wakes up."

He nodded and got out. The ground was slushy and saturated although it had stopped raining so heavily. He opened George's door, undid his seat belt, and lifted him out. George wriggled and reached out his arms towards Nora. "I want Mummy to take me."

"I'll come up when you're in bed."

George grumbled a bit more, then his head bounced a couple of times and finally flopped onto Ian's chest, and he was asleep, his thumb shooting into his mouth like a magnetic stopper. Ian felt a surge of love and then, in the same moment, a suffocating cloud of guilt engulfed him. Jesus, if he managed to get through this nightmare without losing them, he would never risk his family again. Never!

He took George upstairs, undressed him, put him into his Lenny the Lobster pyjamas, got him into bed, kissed him, waited as he curled up and his eyes closed. He was just creeping out of the door when there was a cry. "Where's Mummy?"

He turned around. George was sitting up in bed.

"Downstairs."

'She promised to read me a story.' Ian could see his glass of wine disappearing into the distance but that was fine. It was George's day and this was his new and caring dad.

"I'll read to you."

"No, I want Mummy."

"She's having a rest." He went back to the bed and sat down. "Shall I do a made-up one?"

"No, I don't want you to do it, I want Mummy."

Ian could feel himself getting tetchy and forced it down. "All right, sweetheart." He went to the door. "Nora."

George joined in, "Mummy, Mummy, Mummy!"

"I'll go and get her." As he went out of the door, George suddenly exploded into full tantrum.

"Mummy. Mummy. Mummy. Mummy!"

Ian was halfway down the stairs when Nora came to the bottom. She was not happy. "What's the matter with him."

"Over tired, grumpy, cross with me."

"I know how he feels." She pushed past him.

"Thanks."

She didn't respond.

Ian stood in the kitchen trying to decide whether to have red or white. He looked out into the dark night and listened to the wind whoosh and whistle through the cracks in the window frames.

Suddenly someone was looking in at him. For a moment he froze, then glanced towards the door. Had he locked it? He looked back and the head mirrored his movement. He tried again, turning quickly, and it did the same. Shit! It was his reflection, or at least it should have been, but with a different face. One, with a sudden shock and a physical lurch in his stomach, he was sure he'd seen before. But where? Then he knew! It was in the bathroom mirror the morning after the attack in the Lookout on the beach. Jesus, what was going on in his head?

His phone buzzed and vibrated. He'd put it on silent at the rink. He glanced towards the sound. It was on the table. He turned back to the window. The face had gone. He went to where it had been and cupping his eyes and pressing his nose against the glass, looked out into the garden. Nothing there that he could see. He rushed to the door, unlocked it and looked out. There was nobody near the cottage or in the garden. No body… or head, come to that! But his phone was still going. He shut the door, locked it again, and checked who was calling.

It was Janey. He'd switched off automatic voice messaging to stop Lucy leaving anything incriminating. He looked at his phone for a long minute. She wasn't going to give up. What time was it? Half past nine. That wasn't good. It stopped suddenly then almost immediately started again. This time the buzzing sounded impatient and angry. He took a deep breath, grabbed the mobile and answered.

"Janey…"

"How did the party go? I sent him a little present, but he probably won't get it until tomorrow because the stupid girl on the desk left it in a drawer and not in the post pile… then she walked out because she said I'd belittled her in front of everyone."

"Doesn't sound like you." Probably the wrong time to try sarcasm, but when had he ever given the time to think an answer through? There was a loud gasp of silence that he had to fill. "What did you do?"

"Does it matter?" Ice cold and sharp. "Anyway, hope George had a nice time. But you, my sweet, are taking the piss." She made the endearment sound like a stain.

"I've got another two weeks." He'd hoped he would sound in control but the Janey effect always diluted will to weakness.

"Not any more darling. You have a week and then if it's not in my inbox first thing, you'd better start looking around. Is that clear?"

"Crystal." There was a long empty pause. He'd had enough today. He summoned up a confrontational "Is that all… darling?"

Being like that though never worked with Janey. It wouldn't this time, but he'd had a shit day and needed to bite back, and she wasn't close enough to hit him.

"Don't be scratchy or I'll lop another day off." Then she almost sounded warm. "I've tried to talk him round but he's determined to trim some dead wood to make way for his new shoots. You've only got yourself to blame. Give Nora and George my love." She disconnected.

"Fuck!" He leaned against the table then took a bottle from the fridge, poured himself a full glass, took a deep swig and almost choked on it.

Nora came in looking frazzled. "He wants you to do a story now."

"No. I need to sit down for a bit."

"You tell him then." She looked at him for a long moment. "I'm going out."

"What? Where? Why?"

"Somewhere I can be on my own." She grabbed her coat and put it on. "Where are the car keys?"

"Why?"

"Because I want to make a bloody risotto."

"Wouldn't rice be better?"

"Don't piss about. I'm not in the mood."

He looked around, saw the keys on the table, and handed them to her. "How long will you be?"

She didn't even look at him but went out. Ian followed, watched her get into the car and slam the door. She tried to start it. The engine turned over a couple of times then stopped. Nora waited a moment then tried it again. Finally, it began to grumble and spurt then caught and after a couple of pumps on the accelerator, she crashed it into gear and drove off.

"Daddy!" George screamed at full power.

"All right, I'm coming." Ian shut the door, went back into the kitchen and grabbed his wine but the glass slipped and, in the struggle to catch it, his sleeve caught on the rim and it slopped over his shirt.

"Daddy!"

Ian grabbed a tea cloth, dabbed his sleeve quickly, then wiped up the wine on the table.

"Daddy, Daddy, Daddy!"

Ian stood still for a moment trying to find calm, failed, sighed, and went wearily up the stairs.

It was a good story, about a little dragon that lived in a cave on a Welsh mountain and his best friend who was a *very* small pony. They got into trouble with a farmer for taking one of his sheep on an adventure to find its lost lamb. George had taken a while to quieten down, stop grumbling about Mummy leaving him and Aunty Lucy going, and start to get involved in the story. But he did, eventually, and it was just about to reach the point where they had to fight a huge wild boar when Ian realised he was on his own. George was fast asleep. He was almost disappointed and if it hadn't been for a huge clap of thunder, he would have carried on, looking forward to seeing how he'd end it. He waited for the flash of lightning, but it didn't come. He looked at George, thumb in mouth, gently snoring, then lay down next to him, lifted his head and put his arm under him.

His face was close enough to smell the cake that George had somehow got into his hair.

Nora opened George's bedroom door and saw the two of them asleep, the light still on. She stood there for a long moment just looking at them, then went out, pulling the door hard because it always stuck. This time it didn't, and she couldn't stop it quickly enough before it banged loudly. Ian must have fixed it. Why the hell didn't he tell her? It had taken him long enough to do it.

She stopped, holding her breath, but heard nothing from inside and went downstairs.

The noise of the door had woken Ian. He was confused and, for a moment, couldn't make out where he was and why his arm wouldn't move. Then he looked at what was happening and saw that George was lying on it. He gently lifted his head, took his arm away, and then placed it back on the pillow. George moaned, opened his eyes, then turned over, still fast asleep. Ian got off the bed, leaned down, kissed him, turned the light off, and went out.

Nora, with a mug of tea and reading something on the worktop, looked up as Ian came into the kitchen. "I was asleep."

"I know, I saw you. Why didn't you tell me you'd fixed the door?"

"Oh, that's what woke me! I forgot. I did it yesterday. Shaved a bit off."

"Clever boy."

"Yes, I am."

"The car kept cutting out."

"Where did you go."

"Sat by the river."

"Catch anything?"

Nora shook her head sadly.

"Sorry. I'll get the garage to look at it tomorrow."

"Will you?"

Ian was confused. "Yes." Said with a little spike.

Nora knew the signs. "What's wrong?"

A long pause as he looked at her. Then he sighed and sat down.

"Janey rang. They've cut my deadline down to a week from today."

"Is it doable?" Always the pragmatist!

"Yes, if I don't eat or sleep."

"Why?"

"If I can't do it, I'm fucked." It was obvious so why was she asking?

Nora laughed. Ian couldn't stop the glare in time.

"I know that. But why did she do it?"

"I have no idea." He looked up at the clock. It was nearly eleven. "Too late to start on it now."

"Is it?"

"Yes." Ian stood up and kissed her head. "I'm sorry."

There was a long moment as Ian waited and he was just about to give up when she put her arms around his waist.

"So am I."

She kissed him gently on the lips. He kissed her, warily at first, then more deeply. She responded then pulled away. "Let's go to bed." She took his hand. Ian didn't move.

"I need to talk to you first."

She was surprised. "I was going to forgive you and get mucky."

"You still can after you've heard me out."

"I might have gone off the boil by then and you'll have to wait until I'm ready again. Could be weeks."

It was a tough one and Ian almost gave in, but he had to get this out of the way. He needed her to find a focus for him. "It's important."

"You've done something that will piss me off?"

"No." Too quick a response. She picked up on it immediately. "I just need your help." She held his look for a long moment. "Please."

"All right, but I need a glass of wine."

"Is that wise for the bump?"

Nora looked at him for a moment. "One won't hurt, and I've earned it."

Ian half-filled a glass for her then poured his and picked up the bottle. "Let's go in the living room."

"It's warm in here."

"I lit the fire."

"Why?"

"It was cold. I laid it this morning so we could relax tonight. Lit it when you went up to George."

After he stuck another couple of logs on the fire he sat at one end of the sofa. Nora was at the other with her legs stretched across the cushions. He wasn't sure how to start. He saw it all flickering in his mind like the flames as the logs crackled, caught and flared. It didn't make any sense. He glanced across at Nora. She was beginning to move from interest to impatience. He couldn't wait any longer.

"You remember the night I went out for a walk?"

"Yes, you woke me up to tell me."

"I didn't… you were awake."

"Just get on with it."

"When I got to the beach at Brid… "

She looked at him in amazement. "You went to Bridlington in the middle of that storm? You're more deranged than I thought."

"Just listen, please."

"All right, go on."

"I was trying to clear my head and walking towards the cliffs under the zoo when I saw a light coming from that old Lookout…"

"What Lookout?"

"The one on the beach… do you want to hear this or not?"

She smiled, nodded her head.

He'd just talked through the attack and the pain that shot up through his stomach into his chest and how everything went black until he came around and found himself on the floor, when he saw her eyes flatten and fade. It was a sign that she'd switched off. Her normal reaction when he launched into what she considered was the start of a long and rambling flight of fantasy. He paused, looked at her and waited.

It was a while before she noticed he'd stopped talking. "What?"

"Look, if you're not going to listen…"

"I was." She knew it was too quick. She had drifted off, wondering if George was asleep and whether he'd be so exhausted he'd get all the way through tonight without waking up. She didn't know how much she'd missed and tried to remember the last thing that had registered.

"You weren't."

Was this worth a fight? Not when she was in the wrong. "Go on, please." Soft, with a smile.

"Sure?"

"Yes."

He moved across the sofa, lifted her legs, and put them over his.

She leaned over and kissed him. "I'm sorry, you're right, I didn't hear the last bit." She suddenly remembered. "You were on the floor of the Lookout…"

She sounded like she meant it so he decided to give her the benefit of the doubt.

He told her the rest of it then hesitated. "This is really messing with my head. It's not just something I dreamed up. It felt real. It was real. I need to talk to you about it because you're the most clear-minded and pragmatic person I know and… you'll be honest with me."

"I will."

He told her about the sharp pain in his stomach when he woke up the next morning and how the marks on it disappeared and then seeing the face in the mirror in the bathroom.

"I know it sounds unbelievable but I'm not imagining it. I thought that I was going to die in the Lookout."

He then explained what happened when he went back the next day. He wanted it to be real, so it wasn't his usual wordy and witty mix of fact and exaggeration. He could see that she wasn't sure how to take it. Nora wasn't used to this objective uncovering of the facts of a story.

She was also confused at the way it touched her. She didn't drift off again.

After Ian had told her about the arrest and the shooting of the van driver and the trip to Robin Hood's Bay and ended up with the face at the window earlier tonight, he stopped and tried to read on her face the effect of what he'd told her. He couldn't. She was too good at that game.

"That's all of it!" When she didn't say anything, he looked into the fire. For a moment he wondered if it would burn if he put his hand in quickly through the flames. He had a habit of doing that. If something was hot, he was drawn to touch it to see if it would hurt. Usually, for most people, it was only a childhood thing and didn't last, but it had stayed with him. He glanced at Nora. Was she waiting for him to say something else? Of course, she was! He thought for a moment.

"Is it possible to experience something that happened in the past?" He snorted, a mix of laugh and sigh. "Jesus! If you put that into Google there would be millions of hits but if even a small percentage of them had any sort of academic, psychological, or spiritual credibility, then you'd have to keep an open mind... wouldn't you? I've tried to be objective and dismiss it as some sort of extreme reaction to the stress of getting the book finished in time, the storm, even my deranged imagination taking something that I heard about or read or was told had happened to someone else and running with it. Or did I see it in a shit film I've forgotten all about until now? I've been through every possible scenario, and nothing explains it away. 'I was in another time." Then he remembered something else. "My name was Walter."

"Walter?" For once Nora didn't instantly see all the holes and start to explore them with logic. She hadn't seen him quite this convinced about something that seemed without reason. He really believed it had happened and, on reflection, over the last few days, he'd been acting more strangely than usual. Whatever it was that he experienced, or thought he had, had really affected him.

Ian went on quickly. "The second time, when I was lying on the floor of the Lookout, one of the men spoke. He said 'Christ, it's Walter!'" Suddenly he was back there and saw a hand wave over his eyes then felt fingers touch his neck and heard the same voice say, "Taff, call the Station. He's dead." Then he was back to the present, sitting next to Nora.

"Are you all right?" Nora was shocked at the way he looked.

"Yes…" he paused, "What do you think? Am I going mad here?"

Nora wanted to help. He was clearly distressed but it was way above her skills level. She waited for a moment, trying to find words that might work even if they weren't the right ones. "Anything else about that night you can remember?"

He took his time as it came back to him.

"It was during the Second World War. The guy who said it was Walter had mentioned boys in blue and Adolf before he saw me… him… whoever, on the floor." He tried to push down the panic. "Shit Nora, this is barking.

What the fuck's going on in my head?"

She reached over and took his hand. A brief hesitation to line up the words. "I can't begin to find a reason for this… but I think the way to approach it is to do what you know how to do. Research it like a book." She thought for a moment. "There must be someone who's an expert in things like this. People do PhDs and then specialise in the most bizarre and weird theories. Academia is full of them. Find one of those, don't just throw it out to the online world. That will drive you over the edge with all the conspiracy theories and crap that would spew out. There is one thing you can possibly check out. Was there a policeman called Walter killed during the war in a Lookout place on the beach? You've got a short time frame and a definite location. Most of the local paper archives will be digital, microfilm, or archived. Even ours is over a hundred years old.'

"How do you know that?"

"Just do!" She suddenly felt her energy drain away. "That would be a good place to start."

"It would." He suddenly remembered the Starlight Club. "That other time, when Walter was waiting for the exchange of stolen goods to happen, he was near to a place called the Starlight Club…" He paused." I checked that out. It was a real place. Burned down in 1948. And there's the Bay Hotel."

"That enough for now?"

"It is." There was an edge of hope there and he felt that at least he would be proactive, not just swirling it all around his dishevelled mind. And it would also keep Lucy out. Her sudden interruption shocked him. It was a jolt that felt physical, and he checked that Nora hadn't noticed but her eyes were closed.

Nora was done for the night and had stopped noticing much at all. But as she forced her eyes open to hold off slipping into a deep sleep, she saw that Ian had to find a way to de-stress. What could she do? Then she had a thought about a possible solution. If she tried hard she might still be able to muster up a bit of passion. It would help him relax. She couldn't believe she was thinking that but seeing him this troubled made her want find a way to help him. What he'd told her explained a lot about his oddness since he came back from London too. Then something else edged into her thoughts about the way he'd been with Lucy. She'd noticed and it felt odd, different, to the way they were normally with each other. But then it slipped away as Ian shunted out her musings.

"I was going to see what I could find online but the party took over. Are you home tomorrow? It's an inset day for George, isn't it? Would you do it with me?

"I can't. Rose has got some people coming over to look at replacing the doors into the garden and I promised that I'd take George over to play with Daniel. She wants to talk about something else too and she was such a help with George's do that I can't let her down. You just need to concentrate and not wander off if it takes time to find anything. And it will. Use it as a motivation to show me you're not dropping off the edge."

He was a bit put out that she wasn't going to be here, but he felt energised with something positive to do so he didn't try and persuade her to stay and help him. Not that he'd have succeeded in that little quest.

He leaned over and kissed her. "Thanks, I love you."

Nora wondered whether they could do it here but just as she made the decision that bed would be best, there was a scream.

"Daddy, the spider bit me!"

For a moment they just looked at each other. Perfect timing as always.

"Daddy, Daddy! Mummy, Mummy! It hurts."

Ian looked at her and smiled. "I'll go. Don't forget to put the guard in front of the fire."

Nora tried to sit up but her body wouldn't move. "I won't." As Ian went up the stairs, she stretched out on the sofa and fell asleep.

Ian had chased the monster spider away. Luckily the real one that had attacked him before hadn't made an appearance, so he didn't have to fight his own fear. George must have been only half awake when he shouted because it was just a couple of minutes before he dropped off again. Ian was lying by the side of him and listening to his breathing when he thought he'd better move and get into bed before he fell asleep too.

* * *

It was just after seven. George had opened the curtains and it was getting light. Ian was asleep on his bed in his clothes. He hadn't even woken up when George had struggled to get out of the duvet that was all twisted around him. He was confused. If Daddy was here, where was Mummy? He went to find her. She wasn't in her bed, so he went downstairs and saw her fast asleep on the sofa, a couple of rugs covering her, the fire still glowing. It was cold so he picked up two logs, stretched, and dropped them on the fire, pulling his arms back quickly so the flames wouldn't reach out and drag him in. He climbed onto the sofa and snuggled into Nora, kissing her awake. It took him a good twenty kisses before she slowly opened her eyes.

For a moment Nora didn't know where she was or what it was that was wetly and rhythmically tapping her face. Her eyes slowly focused and she saw George. It was a shock. Then she realised she was still on the sofa and there were two new logs just starting to flame on the fire. "Good morning, sweetheart, where's Daddy?"

"Sleeping on my bed. He was there all night."

"Was he? And I was down here. What an odd Mummy and Daddy you have." Then she had a sudden and scary thought. "Did you put the logs on the fire?"

"Yes, I didn't want you to be cold."

"Thank you, Georgie, but you mustn't ever do that again without me or Daddy being here."

"You were here."

"I know, but…" then the words ran out and she couldn't think of what to say next that might make sense to a just-six-year-old. She felt terrible; scratchy, tired, and dirty. She needed a shower and to clean her teeth, drink a gallon of tea, eat something tasty, and then with a bit of luck, she might feel like a proper mummy again and be able to talk to George about fire safety.

"Did you and Daddy fight?"

"No. Why do you think that?" She wondered if he'd

heard them talking although she couldn't think of anything that sounded like fighting unless she'd forgotten it. Might have happened, it often did, not always cross words but usually a lot of loud ones.

"You didn't go to bed together."

"Sweetheart, you were having a bad dream, so Daddy went up to see you and I was so tired after your party that I didn't manage to get to bed and fell asleep down here." God, she was turning into Ian, rambling on without thought or sense.

"Can we go to Daniel's now?"

She'd forgotten she'd arranged that, but of course George hadn't and now she remembered too. "It's too early yet and I have to get ready."

"Daniel will be awake."

"He probably will, but his mummy won't be ready to pick us up, and his daddy hasn't gone to work yet." She moved George, who was still inches from her face, and slid off the sofa onto the floor then stood up. He followed her as she went to the kitchen. "Go and wake Daddy. Do it gently."

George gave her a long look then ran up the stairs and Nora went to the sink, ran the tap until it was ice cold, then rinsed out a mug, drank two fills of it and almost felt better.

Ian was still deeply unconscious when George knelt on the side of the bed, leaned over and gently kissed him on both cheeks, then his nose. It had no effect at all. So he lifted up Ian's arm and dropped it onto the bed. Still nothing. He sat back on his heels, thought for a moment then leaned over and blew in his ear. That didn't work so he turned it into a whisper. "Daddy, wake up, please." Ian gave a loud snore which made George jump and then giggle. He tried again but louder. "Daddy. Daddy." Perhaps he needed to be really loud to get past the sleepy bit so he'd hear him. He leaned over him again, got really close to his ear and shouted as loudly as he could.

"Daddeeeee!"

Ian's eyes shot open and he saw a face almost touching his. He roared. George screamed, shot off the bed backwards and onto the floor and carried on screaming.

Ian's heart was pumping hard and he frantically searched around to see what it was that attacked him. There was nothing, only an inhuman screeching that sounded like an angry eagle. It was coming from the floor.

Suddenly Nora flew in through the door. "What's going on?"

She saw George half under the bed and Ian pale and shaking on top of it. George saw Nora and scuttled over to her. She scooped him up and held him as he slowly calmed down.

"Daddy shouted and frightened me."

Ian, slowly coming to his senses and trying to understand what was happening to him, saw Nora and a clutching, trembling George both look at him in a way that wasn't concern or love but shock and disbelief.

"What? I didn't do anything. Georgie, I didn't mean to frighten you. I'm really sorry." He held his arms out. "Come here."

"No." George slid down out of Nora's arms and hid behind her.

"Who did what? George, you first."

"I tried to wake up Daddy gently like you told me to but I couldn't make him open his eyes, so I thought if I shouted loudly enough he'd hear me."

She tried not to laugh but failed. "It worked." She pulled George in front of her and walked him to the bed and sat him next to Ian. "Say sorry to each other. You both shouted."

George wasn't convinced.

"I'm sorry." Ian was first. It took George longer and he waited for a moment, looking grumpy, then smiled warily.

"I'm sorry too."

Ian opened his arms and George went and hugged him as Ian squeezed him tight.

Crisis over, although she wasn't sure Ian would fully recover. "You're like a couple of six-year-olds."

"I *am* six," George said proudly. He thought for a moment almost back to normal again. "But Daddy's not, he's really old."

"Only in his body." She smiled sweetly and walked out. "Get George dressed and ready. We've got an hour before we have to go to Daniel's."

CHAPTER SIXTEEN

In the Lake District, the mist swirling over the water added a magical reality to the filtered landscape. Lucy was looking through the large wall-length window of the breakfast area in the Lakeside Hotel.

Mark was still in the room doing a quick workout before he showered, shaved, completed his daily skincare therapy and then carefully chose what to wear. She had yet to start any sort of sleep to stun transformation although she'd managed a face swill and a finger comb. She'd then thrown on yesterday's discarded clothes and headed down to eat. It was always food first then facials. That was her ritual wherever she was, home or away.

Last night she'd slept on the journey from York and then once they got to their room and the large super king-size bed, she had turned animal and driven any thoughts of Ian out of her mind with an hour of wild and wanton sex. Once Mark was satiated and asleep, she'd realised that she was starving but by then it was too late for room service and she had to make do with the two packets of Highland shortcake biscuits. So, this morning, before Mark was awake, she was ready to go down for a cup of tea, some toast, and a moment to herself.

As gently as she moved, he'd woken with "Where are you going, babe?" as she got out of bed.

"I'm hungry," she'd mumbled.

"OK, lemme do my daily prep and I'll come with you."

She'd waited until he went for a pee then shouted that she'd see him down there and left before he could answer. She knew she had at least forty minutes before he felt buffed enough to show his face.

She was trying to understand how she felt. It was certainly not like she'd hoped she would. She thought it would be easier after getting through George's party without bloodshed and fleeing with Mark before she gave herself away, or Ian did or said something that Nora picked up on. She should have been relieved. It was over now. She didn't have to see him again. There was only the necessary manufactured fight between them that would end their friendship but still allow her access to George. That might take a bit of working out. Tricky balance between estrangement and the occasional visit.

It wasn't just that though, distance was only a small part of it. She felt sick at the way that she had treated Nora, knowing she had no idea of what had gone on between her and her shit of a husband. She had almost, after Mark arrived and Ian had dumped her cases, gone back to Nora and told her everything. She wasn't convinced she would really have done it though. If it had only been once, a drunken slip from friendship to fucking, it wouldn't have mattered so much. They could have moved on without it changing anything, and probably only leaving a faint whiff of betrayal and guilt, not the foul stench it had become.

One of the young women serving came over to her table. She was gorgeous, probably seventeen or eighteen with a dazzling smile. She made Lucy feel jaded, weary, and very old.

"Are you ready to order more?" She had a husky catch in her voice that only enhanced her perfection. Obviously, she thought toast wasn't going to be enough for this ageing woman in black leggings and a thick purple jumper, with a hungry look and tired eyes.

"Just waiting for someone. He shouldn't be long."

"No problem." She smiled again for a long moment, bemused by the vision of what she might become, then walked away. Jesus, she had style and grace too… the little cow. Lucy wanted to stuff her face into the large pot of ferns at the entrance.

But she didn't. Just then Mark came in, skinny black trousers and a tight white T. He didn't feel the cold. The girl clocked him immediately and moved towards him. He smiled at her but was headed for Lucy. He gave her a hug and long kiss and Lucy saw the girl's delight turn to disgust.

Mark sat down. "I'm going to die if I don't eat. Have you ordered anything?"

"Just had some toast. Was waiting for you." She looked over at the girl, who was trying to look busy, and smiled. The girl looked for someone else to serve but Lucy and Mark were the only ones there. She approached the table.

Mark smiled at her. Lucy touched his face. "My son and I are ready to order now."

The girl looked horrified. "Your what?"

Mark had just realised what she'd said and thought it was funny but wasn't quite sure why. So he smiled to cover both.

The girl was rooted. Incest sometimes had that effect. "Sorry, that was misleading. I'm not his mother, just old enough to be." The girl was confused now too. "I'll have kedgeree please, with mushrooms."

That Mark understood. "Full English for me."

The girl looked at him like she was horrified at what he could possibly see in this pile of wrinkled flesh and coloured wool. Mark, bless him, was oblivious. "Thank you, doll."

* * *

Nora and George had just left, picked up by Rose and Daniel. Ian, exhausted but enjoying the calm as the house settled, was sitting at the kitchen table on his third black coffee of the morning and thinking about the best way to attack the research. As an occasional guest lecturer on the creative writing course at Hull University, he had access to both the online library and the campus one. What was best? If he stayed here and got on the laptop, he could easily get distracted, by spinning off at tangents as he threw out his nets of queries or getting lost in something that was easier to focus and narrow in on as a search. One of his regular masochistic trawls was through the ranks of more successful writers whose books were being made into TV dramas or films or becoming bestsellers or getting nominated for awards. It was torture but, like the hand in the flame to see if it was hot, he had to see what was not happening to him but to the bastards who didn't have his talent, or were, at best, his equals. That would depress him and he'd probably go to the pub, have a couple of pints, a pie, and a moan to Josh. After he came back his powers of concentration would be slipping and, by the time Nora and George were home, he wouldn't have done anything. She would want to know how he'd got on and he wouldn't be able to fool her nor want to, really. He needed her help on this to keep him sane and on track.

Then another choice elbowed its way into his consciousness. Should he go to the beach again and see what fate awaited him there? Part of him wanted to face his fears but he was afraid that they would overcome him as he entered that world that wasn't his own. Jesus, it made no sense at all. He looked at the clock. It was ten already. He got up quickly. He had to focus. He'd go to the university. He phoned Alex Price, a friend and assistant professor in the Psychology department, to see if he was free for lunch. He was and they arranged to meet at one in the Library Café. It was sunny now. He wasn't convinced but expelled that negativity by cleaning up in the kitchen, making sure everything was off and getting sorted with what he needed to take with him.

Alex couldn't stop the laugh that had threatened and then bubbled up after Ian had gone through all that had happened from his first visit to the Lookout to the face at the window and Nora's advice. He tried to force a serious face and almost managed it. "Sorry, mate, but it's a bit of a stretch even in the weird and wispy world in which I exist and not something I know much about. If you really thought you'd slipped over the edge and needed to get a bit more balance, I might be able to help, but not sure I can add anything to the possibility that it really happened without having seen it for myself."

"I know that, and I certainly don't want you to start looking for reason inside my head. We both know the fun you'd get doing it and I'm not ready for that disturbing little scenario yet. I just want to know if you can point me towards someone who might be willing to discuss the theoretical supposition that there are parallels of time that exist alongside ours and that if they do, then is it possible that they can somehow crash into each other… and what would happen if they did?"

Alex glanced over at a couple of students coming into the cafe and got up. "Just got to make sure these two come to their tutorials in the morning."

Ian, frustrated at the interruption, watched as Alex spoke to them. They took out their phones and tapped something in then went to the counter. As he made his way back to the table Alex took out his phone and checked it. "Sorry, I have to go. It's my day for pastoral guidance and I'm late for the first one. She'll be fine for another five minutes. I'll take her a cappuccino and a ginger muffin, wonderful for wellbeing." He paused. "So, I did have a think and a google about it after you rang and came up with a few people studying the possibilities of time layers and parameters. It's a subject at the very strange and misty end of the metaphysics spectrum. In fact, I realised that, sadly, I had read a paper by one of these weirdoes when I was asked to be part of a panel discussing "Psychology and the Presence of the Poltergeist". Cutting edge stuff!" He laughed. "Listening to a lot of slightly deranged academics trying to justify the money they screwed out of the Department for Pointless Research was time I will never get again. I think the real title is Psychic Research, but my version is closer to the truth."

Ian's body language was 'loudly impatient'. Alex smiled. "Sorry. Give me a minute." He thought for a moment. "Ron Baylis, no, Roly Baylis. He's an expert on the effect of trauma in understanding criminal psychology but, in his non-academic and odd habits life, he has a wild and diverse theory about the logic and perception of the reality of time. He's a prof at Leeds, I think. He wrote a book that was recommended by one of the other panellists." It took him a long moment to find it. *"Parameters of the Paranormal.* I did try to read it. Not many jokes. It began with an incomprehensible supposition, ended with a nonsense summary, and was a pile of shit in between..." he stopped for a moment, "no, I'm wrong, not about the shit, but the writer, and I use that word loosely, it wasn't Baylis, it was Seamus Flint." He took out his phone and googled Roly Baylis. "Now, this is more like it, Baylis published a book five years ago called *Space Between Time*, a study of the parallel connections and mysteries of time." His phone pinged. He glanced at it. "Got to go. She's getting twitchy, thinks I've given up on her. Just as well the fifth-floor windows don't open wide enough for her to jump." He sent a quick text. "It's probably in the Philosophy section of the library, in the Barking but Brilliant dark corner of Absurd Metaphysical Sciences. Let's catch up after you've had a hunt around. Love to Nora. Georgie all right?" He started to move away then stopped.

"When's your mate Lucy up again? Thought I might have a chance with her now I'm single again."

"Fuck off."

Alex laughed. He didn't know the reason behind Ian's tight smile.

* * *

Lucy and Mark were walking along the edge of the lake. Its surface glistened in the early afternoon sunshine. It was a beautiful place. There was no one else where they were and no sounds apart from the gentle creaking of a couple of boats, the wildlife, and the lapping of water. They were holding hands, taking their time and enjoying the peace and space around them. Neither had said anything for the last ten minutes. Lucy was surprised that she was feeling so relaxed and easy with him,

They had come out of the hotel after a morning of sex and sleep followed by a long and lazy lunch. Sometime between yesterday and today, something had changed in the way they were with each other. They fitted together more comfortably and their conversation walking by the lake was easy and chatty, and different. For the first time since they'd got together, they talked about things that didn't consist of the carnal, culinary, sporting, or social. She told him about her family who had a farm in the Cotswolds and her sister, Allie, who lived in Australia and had four kids, the latest, two-year-old twins, who she hadn't met yet but was desperate to see in person, not just on Zoom.

"I thought I'd be able to talk my boss round into me doing some research on indigenous literature at the university where Allie's husband heads up the Aboriginal Studies department. I'd perhaps take four months out to write a novel too." She laughed. "She was positive about it, but then life got complicated and other things took over and I didn't follow it up." She looked out at the lake. "But it might be the right time now. I could do with a complete change and a new start with a year in the sun would be just right."

She didn't say why and he didn't ask. Then he surprised her.

"I'll go with you if you want, babe."

For a moment, it sounded possible and almost plausible… but then she knew it wasn't at all and so did he. That reality hung over them like the mist this morning but quickly cleared when Mark, never one to hold on to moods, told her about his parents who'd run a pub in Pinner until his dad had a heart attack and had to give up the excessive lifestyle of a landlord. His mum retrained as a special needs teaching assistant and in the last couple of years his dad had invested in a small taxi firm with his brother, Mikey, and drove the cars three days a week.

"Uncle Mikey was a professional footballer who never made it to the Premier League but played for a couple of teams that almost did. He retired when he was thirty-three and his knee finally packed in and he had to get the joint replaced." Mark laughed. "Mikey thought I had a talent for footie too and, if I really worked at it, might even make it to the Championship. I knew I wouldn't put in what was needed to make it as a pro. It was too tough a world, and you had to want it so badly you'd be happy to give up everything else. I knew I couldn't do that."

He stopped talking and Lucy gave him space to carry on. They walked on for a bit and then he told her that his dad now wanted him to come into the taxi business, but he wasn't ready for that sort of responsibility either. He liked being on the edge of minor villain celebrity and that would do him for now. Lucy had studied him as he talked. He was incredibly handsome, open, friendly, and warm and, best of all, what you saw was what you got. A great mix in a man and not often found, but he was too young for her and, if she were honest, too normal. She needed an edge in her relationships, intellectual stimulation and shared interests. It wasn't only a matter of sex and comfort. She also knew he'd get hurt if it carried on much longer, particularly now that they were relaxing and opening up. She felt a wave of affection for him and was just about to lean over and kiss him when he suddenly stopped and turned to face her.

"Did you ever sleep with your mate Ian?"

It was like somebody had hit her with a cattle prod on full power. It took her breath away and she had to fight to try and sound normal. The pause before she spoke seemed huge but was only a beat. "No, of course not. Why did you ask that?"

"Just wondered, that's all. There seemed to be something going on when he dumped your things from the car on the pavement. I was going to ask you on the drive up, but you fell asleep and when we got here other things took over and I forgot about it."

She held his eyes for a moment, forcing disbelief and surprise into hers to cover the shock and horror that must have been there. He looked away. She knew it wasn't because of what he'd seen in her eyes but because he wasn't sure he wanted to hear the honest answer if it was going to be a yes.

"It was just the way you looked at him. Hurt, like something bad had happened between you. And it didn't just look like a falling out with a best mate."

Jesus! Don't say she'd misjudged Mark all this time and that he was much brighter than she thought... or wanted. That would be a nightmare. And if he'd noticed it, what about Nora? There was nothing slow about her. She'd been watching too. She had a sudden image of Nora's face through the rainy window and the smile she'd given her. It was just a smile, not a knowing one, or an 'I know you're shagging my husband, you fuckhead' one. It was more of an envious 'Lucky cow' one at Mark's hotness and youth, wasn't it? Fuck, fuck! She hoped nothing showed on her face. She was good at hiding things. Had a lot of practice since she and Ian had entered their betrayal stage. The eyes were the tricky bit. Luckily Mark was looking out over the water. It gave her time to centre and calm. There was no way he could have guessed anything was going on. She had to control her voice too. Try and make it sound normal and give him enough to take the edge off his reasoning. A simple explanation that he would accept.

"It had just been a long and difficult day for everyone with the party, they were all exhausted and I'd hardly had any sleep, getting the early train. And Ian was having problems too with finishing his book and we'd had a bit of a fight about him not helping Nora with the arrangements and generally being a bit of a selfish dick. Sometimes he will listen 'cos I'm his oldest friend, then others he just gets really pissed off with me and says something that hurts. This time it was about having kids and me not understanding because I would never be in that position."

She stopped, realising that she was starting to get into too much detail and that was when things fell apart and you were caught out. They both stood there as if her last words had frozen time. Just when the stillness and quiet started to crackle and she felt the need to break it, Mark turned back to her, put his hands either side of her face, and gently kissed her lips.

"I love you," he said softly and put his arms around her and held her tightly. Without warning tears welled up. She didn't need this. Why? Was it because of the truths they'd both just let out? Or his gentleness and desire to comfort her? Or that she was a cruel and selfish bitch? Or because he had broken the spell and said he loved her and that wasn't part of the deal at all.

* * *

After leaving the café, Ian made his way to the Brynmore Jones Library science section help desk and waited for someone to appear. There didn't seem to be anyone manning it and he had just decided to head off and explore the shelves looking for philosophy, inspiration, metaphysics, and Roly Baylis, when a young woman popped out from behind a large display advertising a series of talks on the science and truth of magic reality.

"Sorry, just needed to make sure this stayed up." There was something familiar about her. She was in her late twenties, with multi-coloured hair and an impressive selection of piercings and tattoos. Not someone you'd forget. She suddenly smiled at him. "Oh, Ian Chambers."

There didn't seem a lot of point in denying it as he was the only one there. "Yes, that's me." Hopefully she was a fan and had read one of his books. He needed a boost to his flagging ego.

"Sally Ryan. I came to your masterclass on character, four years ago. You read my novel *Shadow* and gave me some brilliant notes on Naomi, the main character."

He tried to place her. He did one masterclass a term, except for this year when he was only booked to do an online one in the summer term. Saving money, so they could just pay him once and then reuse it. He must have had about forty students a year before, though…

He realised that she was waiting for a response. He didn't usually offer to read manuscripts so it must have been something special. Suddenly it came to him. It was about a woman caring for her mother, and a road trip they took across Canada to solve the mystery of her father's death. It was based on personal experience. The story had its problems, but the characters were beautifully drawn and their relationship funny, moving, and intense. The ending was shocking and left you emotionally drained. It was excellent for a first-time writer and, of course, he wished he'd written it. It was hard to think it was her first book.

"It was a wonderful story. Didn't you have a

publisher interested, and an agent?"

"I did, and you offered to talk to your agent if it didn't work out."

Oh, shit, did he, and if he did, please don't let Janey have taken her on, particularly as she was young and had a full creative stretch of life ahead.

"It was amazing, they both worked out and it was published last year."

Great, just great! "That's fantastic. How's it doing?" He held his breath and swallowed hard to expel the bile of envy that was already forming in his throat before he spat out a vitriolic response.

"Really well and they've just sold the film rights. Hopefully they'll let me do the first draft screenplay. I've met the producers and they seem keen to give me a chance."

Brilliant, not only taking his legs away but slitting his throat on the way down. He dragged a smile from somewhere deep and tried to sound sincere.

"It will make a great film."

"Thank you. How are your books going?"

Well, that's good of you to ask, colander face. "Yes, great. What are you doing working here?" He laughed. At least he hoped it was a laugh and not about to turn into an uncontrollable sob. "Haven't you got another one on the go?"

"One coming out next month and the next almost finished. I needed to do some research and they had to find someone here to cover for a month. I'd spent so much time on it and was getting my partner down by moaning about finishing it in time, that she thought a break would be good for both of us. So, I came back up here and one month turned into three. I'm finishing next week though."

The trouble was that she was nice, open, and honestly amazed at her success, and the generous and giving side of him was pleased for her. She'd had a tough time caring for her mum. He'd met her to do the notes face to face and she'd told him how hard it had been, particularly when her dad had died in strange circumstances. Writing the book had been cathartic and helped her through the grief, loss, loneliness, and that emptiness when you, as a carer, no longer have to care. A friend of his, Audrey Jenkinson, had written a wonderful book, *Past Caring*, about who cares for the carers when their role is over. She'd looked after both her parents. He hadn't spoken to her for ages. What sort of a friend was he?

"I passed on that book you sent me written by your friend. It was very helpful." God, she's telepathic too! He hoped she'd only read this latest thought.

"I'm glad. Look it's great seeing you again but I need to get move on."

"Sure, what did you want?"

"I'm looking for a book by a psychologist, Roly Baylis. *Space Between Time*. It should be in philosophy."

She smiled at him and went to the computer and tapped around for a couple of minutes. "There's one copy." She scribbled the reference on a bit of paper and gave it to him. "Do you want me to show you where it is."

"No, just point me in the right direction."

She did. "Lovely to see you again. Sorry if I've banged on about myself but I thought, as you'd helped me so much, that you'd be interested."

"I was. I am! Good to meet you again and best of luck with the film."

"Thanks…"

Luckily someone came up to the desk and distracted her and he was able to make his escape before she saw the taint of jealousy in his eyes.

* * *

Rose and Nora were sitting at the huge table in the large sprawling kitchen, a glass of wine in front of Rose and a half pint of Guinness for Nora. They'd fed the boys, stuck them in the playroom to watch a video, and cleaned up the lunch things. "How long has he known Lucy?"

"Years, since before we met, she's always been a part of our lives. Georgie's in love with her and she adores him. You must have met her on one of the times she's been up here with us."

"Yes, I think I did, but I hadn't really talked to her before yesterday. She seems fun and was a real help at the party."

"She was. I was hoping she'd stay over for a couple of days, but she went off to the Lake District with Mark, her very young and sexy lover. Ian was a bit put out with her though. I think he was hoping they'd stay with us. I have a feeling they had words about it." Nora took a sip of Guinness and, just for a second, she wondered again about Lucy. "And talking about my deranged husband, he's being weird."

"That's normal, isn't it?"

"Yes, but this is really weird."

"He wants to tie you up, dress in your knickers and sing the Hi Ho song from *Snow White*?"

Nora laughed. "Oh, yes, that of course, but something else too."

"Tell me."

"Don't know where to start really, it all sounds totally insane. He only told me last night. He'd been having problems with the book and his agent was getting snappy with him plus things, as you know, are a bit tight, the car's playing up, George was being difficult, so I thought the way he was behaving was probably a mash-up of all that, but it wasn't." She paused, then took a deep breath and when she couldn't remember word for word, paraphrased what Ian had told her.

When she'd finished, Rose just sat there looking at her. "That's way beyond weird. Does he really believe it?"

"He does. Or thinks he does. I should..." She stopped and struggled to find the words.

"Have him sectioned." She screwed up her face as Nora gave her a sharp look. "Sorry." The two women held the look for a moment longer, then Rose started to giggle and, after a minute, Nora cracked and joined in. It took them both over then slowly eased off. "OK, mad as it might seem, are you just a little bit..." she searched around for the right word, "concerned that something might actually have happened to him in that Lookout place?"

"I don't know what I think." She hesitated. "It's that it didn't just happen once but a number of times. I know they weren't always on the beach with him being attacked. The face in the bathroom mirror and at the window could just have been his vivid imagination, playing tricks with his reflection; and the other things could be a jumble of stuff he'd read or heard about that his brain just ran with when it was emotionally open to it. Like at the party when the stress of it all had left a raw space to be filled. But the two times on the beach are worrying unless there's such a thing as repetitive barking-writer nightmare syndrome!"

"If there's not, there should be. What are you going to do?"

"See what happens today, perhaps write down what he's already said and keep a record of everything else he tells me. If nothing else, it will give me proof of what he told me when he gets confused and changes it. He's looking into it today and checking out the possibilities of someone sensible having written something definitive on the subject."

Rose suddenly looked thoughtful.

"What?"

"I just remembered something I heard on Radio Four when I was painting the hall. About what is meant by something being light years away. It's the speed at which light travels from one point to another. So, if a star is six light years away then that's the time it takes to reach us on Earth. But then someone said that if your twin lived there, they would be six years older than you and always would be even if they came to visit you."

"And you remembered all that."

"Some of it. I might have made up the rest."

"So why are you telling me this?"

"I don't know… oh, yes, if it is possible to travel forward in time at a hundred times the speed of light then it might be possible to travel backwards too."

Nora slowly finished off her Guinness. "And that means what as far as Ian and his trips to past times go?"

Rose looked at the table for a good minute then back at Nora. "I don't know. Just trying to help."

"You don't understand any of what you said, do you?"

Rose smiled and sighed. "Not at all, just thought it sounded…"

"Like shit." Nora finished for her.

"Yes!" She picked up Nora's glass. "Another?"

"I'd love to have another, but no."

There was a moment when something passed between them, a silent agreement to move on. Rose got there first. "Let's see what the boys are doing?"

"Good idea!" Nora got up quickly as if moving would ease the onset of more mutterings on madness.

* * *

Ian, with a small pile of books in front of him on the table he was sharing with a student of Anthropological Behaviourism, was no nearer to having uncovered anything that might help him in his search for parallels of time and space.

Although he'd spent time looking, he hadn't found Baylis's book in his first trawl of the shelves, but the selection he'd chosen explored different philosophical views, none of which made any sense to him at all. He didn't even understand the way the words were put together, let alone what they meant. What he thought he did get, up to a point, about their 'takes' on time and space, was that there seemed to be two main theories. Absolutist and relationist. Were they autonomous entities? Do times other than the present exist? If they do, are the past and the future accessible too? Is it possible that time flows both ways? Neither the absolutist or relationist conclusion was definite, and that seemed to suggest that they hadn't got a clue what might be real or not. He'd struggled through parts of the first books he'd picked out, *The Order of Time*, *Time, Space and Philosophy*, and *Time, Space and Metaphysics*, and none of them would slip on to his reading list alongside Fred Vargas and James Lee Burke. However, the one thing that seemed to shout out at him, perhaps because he wanted it to be there, was that there was no definitive and provable answer to the question of whether what happened to him was possible or not. Although none of them had mentioned parallels, they had all signalled that there was still a long way to go to know, beyond reasonable doubt, whether anything like that was feasible. No one seemed to have won the argument yet. Still, a couple of hours of research couldn't really be seen as deep study. He'd scribbled down a couple of things.

'The only way we can tell past, present, and future apart is by observing change. If everything stays the same, those time frames become impossible to disentangle.'

'Nothing can travel faster than the speed of light. But if it could, the conventional wisdom goes, it would travel back in time.'

'The investigation brings to the fore questions of the nature and reality of time and space, and leads on to more recent debates, as those relating to their possible infinitude, to anti-realism, time travel, temporal parts, geometry, convention, and the direction of time.'

He read through them again. Perhaps if he was able to separate and scatter the letters then reassemble them, anagram-like, into a couple of bullet points that made past and present parallels of time and space seem possible, he could show it around as the result of his clever and focused research. He might then, at a push, be able to fool someone into taking him seriously. But then what would that do or prove? Fuck all! It would still be made up proof of nothing! Although saying that he'd quoted credible sources wouldn't be a total lie, as all the letters that formed his restructured words and sentences would have come from those written in books by respected experts in the fields of Philosophy and Metaphysics.

Bored with his inane theoretical pondering, Ian started to drift off into an imagined animated movie of a dancing alphabet as the letters touched, twirled, and formed into whirling groups of words that now said all was possible in time and space. He could feel his bum getting achy and numb from sitting on the hard seat and he had to move. He put his iPad to sleep, asked his unfriendly tablemate to keep an eye on it for him and, without waiting for a reply, gathered the books and took them to the 'read' shelves, then wandered down the aisles again to the reference number he'd been given by Sally for the Roly Baylis book. This time when he couldn't find it, he started to look around where it should have been in case it had slipped over the back and was behind another one or had been put back in the wrong place. Finding nothing on that shelf he slowly worked his way down to the bottom one. He found it, at last, laid flat on other books, its spine facing away from him. He looked at the front, a mishmash of swirling colours and clocks, then at the author snapshot on the inside of the back cover. It showed a man, probably in his sixties, with a mass of white curly hair down to his shoulders, a shaggy beard, and bright blue eyes that were intelligent, mischievous and seemed to follow you around. He moved the book, rotated it and the eyes still seemed locked on to him. That was a good sign, unless he'd finally gone mad. Anyway, the guy looked weird and that was good. He should be! He hoped the book would be easier to read. He opened it and checked out the first paragraph.

For any of you to make sense of what I am going to discuss over the next 150 pages, the analysis has to be clear and not jumbled in scientific language or theory. So, it will be a simple assessment of the possibilities of time and space not only existing on one level – the present - but on multiple ones – the past and the future as well.

"Fuck me, that's a good start, Roly, old mate. If you carry on like that, I might even be able to make sense of this load of old bollocks."

He suddenly realised he'd said it out loud as the people-watcher, a backpack on one shoulder and carrying Ian's iPad, hesitated in approaching him and looked ready to run if a threat was imminent. "I've got to go, and I didn't want to leave your iPad there. Someone would take it."

Ian was touched and sorry he had misjudged him. It was thoughtful. He took the iPad. "Thanks, that's really good of you." He held up Baylis's book. "I've found the book I wanted." He smiled, hoping it would show that he was nice and normal. It didn't work and the student scurried away, his behaviour suggesting that Ian, although with his ageing body and weakening mind the antithesis of a young Byron, might still be 'mad, bad and dangerous to know.'

The pleasure that literary moment gave him was shortened when Ian remembered that he'd promised to be home in time to take George out on his skates before bedtime.

He checked his phone. He should go. He'd take the book out. He was an honorary associate in Humanities so his pass would do it. He'd lost the library card but was sure Sally, the future BAFTA winner for best screenplay, would let him. Perhaps she'd mention him as a big influence, in her acceptance speech. He could bask in that little bit of reflected glory.

He was heading for the desk and, seeing the small, bearded man behind it, was pleased that it looked like Sally had gone and he wouldn't have to smile and survive her success again, when he remembered that he'd had a bag with him that he'd tucked under the table with his coat. Why hadn't the guy brought that to him too? He was probably punishing him for being such a twat. Then he realised he probably wouldn't have seen it and apologised loudly to the invisible student. Several people glanced at him and put a little more distance between them. He ran back and found everything where he'd left it.

As he reached the desk again, he wondered how he'd get the book out without Sally, but she had printed out a new library card for him with a note attached.

Knew these only lasted a year so checked and printed you out an up to date one. Remembered I had a copy of Shadow, *so I thought I'd save you buying one, hope you don't mind, I've signed it Sxx.*

He looked at the inscription. *Thank you for all your help and advice. Love, Sally.*

"Brilliant book," said the hobbit as he signed out the Baylis one. "You'll love it. It's going to be made into a film next year, hopefully with Kate Winslet as the mum, can't wait to see it."

Ian smiled and nodded, took the book, then thanked him and hurried out, saying, "Fuck off" almost under his breath. Nobody heard this time.

The rain started as he got into the car and within minutes it was torrential, so he just sat there, waiting for it to ease and noticed a leak running down from the roof on the passenger side. Great. Another little thing to add to the garage list. He called Nora, who said that George was staying over at Daniel's, so she wanted him to pick her up. Just as he decided it wasn't going to stop and he'd be there all night if he waited, his phone rang. It was Alex.

"How did you get on?"

"Got his book. Tried a few others but they made no sense even when I got past the long words. Haven't looked properly at the Baylis yet, but at least I understood the first paragraph."

"Sorry, in a bit of a rush. Going out with one of the wellbeing lot for a meal and a bit of therapy. Just wanted to say that I've spoken to a mate at Leeds teaching Maths and he and Baylis try to outdo each other with Japanese number games. Anyway, he said he'd give him a call, if he was in the country, and ask if you can contact him. I told him in brief what it was about. He thinks you're barking and knows that Baylis is, so reckons you should get on. He's going to text it to you if he agrees. That work for you?"

"Great, Alex, thanks."

"You owe me, buddy."

Ian sat for a moment watching the downpour on the windscreen, then closed his eyes, prayed to the Volvo god to be good to him. and turned on the ignition. The engine started. As he left the car park, there was a huge crack of thunder and seconds later a flash of lightning.

The Volvo suddenly and unapologetically ran out of energy and hope as he tried to overtake a lorry and he had to drop back and edge the car to the side of the road. It was a stupid thing to do on the crest of a hill with a bend ahead, but he thought he'd just make it. Surprisingly the moment of panic had turned to calm as the practicality of what he had to do to get out of the way of the car suddenly appearing and heading straight towards him took over. He felt a moment of regret that Nora wasn't here to see his 'good in a crisis' moment as he steered onto a narrow muddy apron between the hedge and the road. Unfortunately, it left him sticking out and upsetting the constant flow of traffic that had to swerve as they just caught the shadow of the shape in the dark and the rain. A top of the range BMW 4x4 passed just a few of its many layers of paint away, and the raised middle finger and exaggerated mouthed 'Twat!' of the female driver left no doubt to her assessment of him and his crap car. And that, as if he needed any more negative stimulus, really pissed him off too.

"Fuck off!" Ian roared, and then as he realised how pointless that waste of breath and emotion was, he sank into a slumping and pathetic, "It's not my fault." This was a nightmare. What was happening to him? Lucy, the Lookout, the book, Sally fucking Ryan, and now this! What had he done to deserve it? He managed to stop that thought before the long list of screw ups could tumble out and overwhelm him.

A sudden cacophony of blasting horns shot him out of his misery. He had to do something. Phone the RAC. He had the number in his phone. A momentary panic that his phone, low on battery when he left Hull, would be dead, but then he saw it plugged in and checked it. Just over a quarter, that would do. He eventually found the number, unhelpfully under V and not breakdown, and rang it. After a few minutes it was answered. He gave his details and the problem with the car to the friendly and sympathetic woman.

"I'll just check availability. The line will go quiet but you're not cut off."

"Thanks." It took a couple of minutes by which time he was convinced that she'd lied and was having a laugh at his expense and had gone for a pee or a coffee… or on to someone more worthy of her time.

"Sorry to keep you waiting. Someone should be there within an hour. It might be sooner but it's a busy one tonight so try and be patient."

"Thank you.'

"If they're not there in an hour, call us back."

"I will."

She ended the call. What fucking good is that? I could have been crushed before then by a sixty-foot wagon with a moron at the wheel.

He checked the hazard lights were on. The traffic seemed to be ignoring him now and the stream had slowed. He tried the engine and was shocked when it started, although it was stuttering and not happy. Thinking it through, he decided not to pull out straight away but to move further onto the verge, hope there wasn't a ditch, and keep the engine running for a couple of minutes, before getting back into the flow of traffic. Luckily there wasn't a ditch but as soon as the four wheels were off the road, the engine gave a groan and died. He tried to start it again. Not even a weak attempt at turning over just a horrible clunk.

"Shit."

That didn't sound good. It was getting colder, and the leak was now pouring in as the rain seemed, impossibly, to get heavier. He pulled his coat from the back seat and managed with a lot of struggling to get it on. At least he would be warm. Then a sort of acceptance came over him and he caught a flashing positive thought and held on to it. If you were in a situation where your life depended on it, you'd come through it because you had to or die. Perhaps that was going to be his way out of everything that was going on. He'd survive on all levels because there was no choice. This philosophical moment faded into the here and now when he realised that he hadn't told Nora he'd broken down and would be there late... Or never. He texted her explaining and waited for her reply. Then he caught the reflection of blue flashing lights as a police car weaved its way through the traffic its hazard lights flashing. As he waited for it to reach him, the lights and noise began to fade and he saw dark shapes like mounds around his car. Only the sound of the storm stayed the same.

CHAPTER SEVENTEEN

The raid on Jimmy Douglas' new warehouse was going to happen at midnight but the police had been in place since ten. They were in a mix of old vans and a couple of cars with tuned-up engines in case they had to give chase. The warehouse was next to a car breakers and scrapyard, so their vehicles, sitting amongst the other wrecks, wouldn't look out of place or suspicious. They'd nicked the owner a couple of weeks before for stealing lead from church roofs and, for a free pass, he'd agreed to them using it, but they had to make it look like they'd broken in without his say-so. He knew whose warehouse it was. Jimmy didn't give narks a second chance and made their end a beacon to others not to stitch him up. Sadly, Don Keyes was witness to this fact, and had not long been out of the prison infirmary with a couple of broken arms, blinded in one eye, and a slash on each side of his face that would be a constant reminder, and an example to others. Don was lucky, his sister had persuaded Jimmy that it would be better to have him alive and showing the results of being a grass than dead and forgotten.

The police knew Jimmy was already in the warehouse with a bunch of his thugs and Ray Bolton, a butcher, who ran the meat-hacking team for him. They were going to distribute stolen meat and the three lorries moving it on were already there.

The day before, Walter's boss had received a call from headquarters, saying the job was on and his nick was in because they had a history with Jimmy. There were two other local stations involved in the raid as well as the heavy mob. The information about the distribution had come from an informer who worked at a large illegal abattoir in the Dales, where Jimmy slaughtered cattle that had been stolen from all over Yorkshire. The carcasses were then taken to one of his warehouses where they were dispatched to Leeds, Manchester, and Newcastle. It had to happen the same day, so the meat didn't go off before reaching its destination. Once Jimmy had been paid for it and it was en route, he didn't care what happened to it, but if it arrived fresh and still edible then he'd get repeat orders. So, before each truckload was allowed to leave, cash had to change hands once the meat had been checked. Ray's team would cut up three or four of the carcasses into smaller portions for local butchers who went for money over morals, and then a couple of Jimmy's drivers would do the drop-offs, usually before five a.m.

It was a good earner and the police had been trying to catch Jimmy at it for the last year. Up until now he'd always managed to elude them, rearranging locations, times, and sometimes days. How Jimmy got wind of it, they couldn't fathom, unless one of the copper's was on his payroll. So far nobody had surfaced. This time, though, nothing seemed to have got out and it looked like they might catch him on the hop. So, tonight, could be a game changer and, if luck was on their side, they'd crack it and put Jimmy away for a long time.

Walter, Arthur, and Taff were in a small, rusted van with a faded sign on its side: *Bert Timms. Painter and Decorator*. There was a real Bert Timms but he was in the thick of it somewhere overseas, doing his bit for King and Country. Walter, in the front, was asleep and Arthur and Taff were talking quietly when the back doors opened and Billy came in, dripping rain off his helmet.

"That better?" said Arthur.

Billy smiled and then jumped as there was a scratch on the door he'd just closed, and a head popped round. "We're on, they've just passed the crossroads, Boss said to go on the whistle. About fifteen minutes."

He looked at Billy. "Next time piss in a bottle, you could have been seen, blown the whole thing, and then you, me and the rest of us would have been well and truly fucked." He turned to Walter. "Gates are open. You're in front so give them a shunt and put your foot down. We'll come in from the other side. The guv'nor managed to get a few more bodies from York so we shouldn't have too much of a problem"

He disappeared and the door shut. Walter leaned across the seat and gave Billy a slap across the head. "I told you to do that."

"Couldn't with all of you here."

"All got the same bits, boy, just a matter of size is all that's different," said Taff. "Some of us got to go for something a bit bigger to piss in." He stopped and thought for a moment. "Bugger, now we're talking about it, I want to go too. Pass me that bottle, Arthur, should be a jam jar but hopefully my aim's good. Don't want to wet myself on the gallop. Mind, in this bloody weather, nobody'd notice."

Taff wasn't usually this chatty. He must be getting the jitters. Still, even Walter felt a bit apprehensive at times like this, but once it was on, the old adrenalin took over and you did what you had to do. He'd have to keep an eye on young Billy though, give him a push if necessary.

Walter laughed. "Hurry up then, Taff." He glanced at Billy and Arthur. "Make sure you can get at your weapons."

"Way ahead of you there, Walt," said Taff, laughing.

"Sod off, you daft bugger." Billy was shuffling around. "You all right, Billy?"

"Yes, think so."

"No point thinking, you've got to be bloody sure. Can't afford to slip or be careless on a jump like this. Stick close to me and don't get your head in the way of anything, iron bar or bullet. If you need to shoot, just point and fire, don't hesitate. They won't!"

Walter remembered what it was like his first time. He was terrified. He'd almost run but his sergeant had grabbed him and thrown him into the mess of the brawl. That time there weren't guns just a mix of clubs, bars, fists and knives. He got through it but as they rounded them up, realised he'd wet himself. That was worse than being scared. He squeezed Billy's shoulder. "You'll be all right."

Walter turned and glanced out through the windscreen at the sound of engines. He saw two big trucks, lights off, roll up to the warehouse and stop in front of the big double doors. Walter and the others started up before they were switched off. It would muffle the sound of their engines. It wouldn't have mattered tonight though with the pounding rain and the wind threatening to rip off the corrugated roof of the warehouse as it found and rattled every loose edge. The two truck drivers, caps tight on their heads, collars of their coats up, got out and ran across without looking around, knocked three times, then twice, then once more, and as a door opened at the side of the main ones, went in, slamming it hard against the frame. Then the whistle blew, and all hell broke loose. There was a loud boom of thunder then three sharp cracks and streaks of lightning.

"Right, lads, looks like the good Lord's on our side, hold on." Walter slammed into gear and hammered towards the gates, hitting dead centre, snapping them open. The others followed close behind and three vans came from the other side of the warehouse. They'd blocked the trucks in and as Walter jumped out, a large, armoured vehicle roared past and smashed into the double doors, crashing them open.

"Bloody hell…" said Arthur, "that'll do the job," as he, Walter, and the others followed at a run, guns and truncheons out.

Inside the massive warehouse, there was chaos at the shock of the attack. As well as the three trucks there were a couple of cars, including Jimmy's Jag. There must have been twenty of his crew there plus the drivers. Some immediately found their feet and went on the attack. Others were heading towards the doors at the back of the warehouse when a truck crashed through them, followed by another load of coppers.

"Fuck me," said Taff, "the cavalry's arrived."

Walter saw Jimmy run for his car, its front end pointing towards a side door, as his driver started it up, and shouted at Arthur to follow him. Jimmy turned around, a gun in his hand. Walter twisted to one side and Arthur fired and hit Jimmy in the shoulder. Jimmy's bullet missed both of them. Walter dived for Jimmy's legs and dragged him down, smacked his head hard on the concrete floor. Freddy, Jimmy's driver, leapt out of the car. He must have been six foot four and eighteen stones, but Arthur was no lightweight and when he hit Freddy with his shoulder, they both went down. Freddy wasn't a pushover but with a bit of help from Walter after he'd cuffed Jimmy to a pipe, Arthur managed to hit him hard enough with the butt of the gun to make him lose interest.

There was a lot of shouting and shots being fired but it didn't take long for the heavily armed police to get the upper hand. The drivers of the meat trucks managed to make it back to them but had nowhere to go and when they tried to run found that the police were everywhere.

It seemed to Walter that there were a lot more of them than villains. Didn't often happen like that, not with a lot of the boys away. In the calm after the noise, he looked around for Billy and saw him slumped not far from him against one of the trucks. He ran over to him. His eyes were open.

"Billy, are you all right, son?"

Then he saw the blood and bits of brain on the front of the truck. For a moment he was stunned, then the horror hit.

"Oh, Jesus, Billy. I told you to keep your head down." He touched him gently then a rage came over him and he ran back towards Jimmy and kicked him in the head. "You bastard!"

Jimmy just managed, "I aimed for you, but that young copper down is a good result too," before Walter kicked him in the head again, then started to punch him in the face. It took all Arthur and Taff's strength to pull him off.

"Leave it to the rope, Walt." Arthur held him in a bear hug as he calmed down and pulled away from the big man.

"He trusted me and I let him down. What am I going to tell his mum and Doris?"

It was a couple of hours later. Billy had been taken to the mortuary at the hospital and those, both villains and cops, who needed treatment had been ferried there too, in one of the vans. The first load of arrests had gone to the cells in each of the local stations. Billy had been the only fatality, but one of the coppers and two of Jimmy's boys had more serious injuries.

Walter and Detective Chief Inspector Ron Bryan from Leeds were questioning Ray Bolton, who was repeating that he didn't know they had shooters and that his job was to check out the meat and nothing more. Bryan was a big hard man in his fifties and not about to take any shit when one of his own had been killed. As Bolton started to deny that he knew where the three wagons were going and who was getting the meat, Bryan butted him so hard that he dropped like a stone without a sound. It happened so quickly and brutally that Walter had taken a step back in shock.

"Piece of shit," said Bryan and walked off. He stopped and turned back to Walter. "I want to know who and where… and you have my permission to feed his genitals through that mincer…" he pointed towards an industrial meat mincer clamped onto a rubber-covered table "and then force him to eat it if he isn't forthcoming. That should either finish him or get him talking."

"I need to go and see Billy's mother, sir. Wouldn't like it to come from someone else. She thought I'd look after him."

"You're a copper, not a fucking nursemaid."

Walter felt the anger rise and moved towards him.

"Don't do it, sergeant." Behind Bryan a couple of the Leeds squad were ready. But suddenly the inspector softened. "I'm sorry, I know he was one of your lads, Walter, it pains me too." He looked hard at Walter for a moment. Walter held his gaze. "You'd better go. Give her my condolences and tell her we'll make sure the bastard hangs." He looked around and saw Taff standing looking at them stunned. "What the fuck's he doing? Is that miserable streak of piss one of your lads?"

"He is, sir, Taff."

"Welsh, is he?"

"Yes, sir."

"That's all I fucking need. All right, get him to do it. Bolton will think the Grim Reaper's popped in to give him a pull. Might loosen him up."

"You don't think both that and the mincer would be too much?"

"Take care, sergeant, I'm not in the mood." Bryan headed off towards one of the truck drivers, pulled him up and slammed him against the wall. Walter went over and joined Taff.

"He eat babies for breakfast, does he?"

"Wouldn't be surprised." He walked Taff away. "I've got to go and see Billy's mum. Bryan wants you to have a word with Ray Bolton when he comes round." Bolton was starting to moan and move.

"Off you go." Taff took hold of Walter's arm. "Tell her he was one of the best and I thought the world of him even if he pissed me off sometimes." He looked close to tears.

Walter couldn't cope with that. "I will." Taff watched as he went out of the doors, then headed for Bolton as the butcher tried and failed to get himself up.

Outside Maud Wilkinson's small, terraced house, Walter checked his watch. It was six thirty and the darkness was moving towards a shadowy dawn. The rain had stopped although the wind was still sharp. There was a dim light showing through the small window above the front door. Billy said his mum was always up before six no matter when she went to bed, especially after his dad, Ivor, was killed in a bombing raid on the Victoria docks in Hull where he worked as a loading foreman. He wasn't even supposed to be at work. He was doing it so a mate could take his missus on a trip to Scarborough. That had knocked her for six, and this would end her world. Billy was their only child. They'd wanted more but somehow it didn't happen. Walter rubbed his head and tried to remember if Billy had mentioned an aunt or uncle. He knew he was putting it off. Sitting here in the car wasn't going to make it any easier to tell her. She'd know something was up as soon as she saw him. It wasn't like he could put a smile on his face and then say her son was dead.

It was never easy delivering news like this but usually there was a distance, but now it was raw and close.

Slowly he got out of the car. He was exhausted and his leg was aching. His own fault for laying into Jimmy. It was worth it though. He pushed all these thoughts away. He was only delaying it. He knocked on the door with his knuckle not wanting to use the metal knocker. It felt wrong somehow to have the loud and harsh sound it made.

Maud came to the door in her dressing gown. She was a small woman in her fifties, strong, worn down by tragedy but quick and intelligent with a bright laugh that was never far away even after everything she'd been through. Walter hesitated for a moment, and she knew.

"Mrs Wilkinson, I need to come in. We can't do this on the doorstep." The formality was odd. He'd known her for years. She heard it and knew!

"What's happened? It's Billy, isn't it? He's been hurt. Tell me now, Walter Robbins." The colour drained from her face and fear filled her eyes. She bit hard on her hand then took it away and grabbed Walter's coat and pulled him towards her. "I knew something was up, I felt it."

Gently Walter moved her inside and shut the door. "I'm sorry, Maud, there's no easy way to say this. Billy's dead." He waited for the shock to explode, and it did. She started to pound against his chest with her fists.

"No. Why are you saying that? God wouldn't let it happen. Billy's all I've got!"

Walter held her tightly to him and suddenly all the life went out of her, and she dropped in his arms. He picked her up, carried her into the kitchen, and put her into a chair next to the open range that must just have been lit, as it was slowly heating up, the flames small but stretching. She was in shock, her eyes were screwed shut, her mouth open, her breathing in short bursts. Walter pulled up one of the kitchen chairs in front of her and sat on it. Although he knew a bit about basic first aid, that was for physical hurt and not something like this. He'd just have to do what he could, let his instinct take over. He wondered whether he should go to the grocery shop on the corner and get them to ring the doctor. The owners lived in the two floors above it. He didn't want to leave Maud alone though so decided against it.

He held her hands and rubbed them softly. It sometimes comforted Cate when she was distressed. Perhaps it would help Maud. It had no effect though and after five minutes he stopped. Slowly she opened her eyes and the life had gone out of them.

"What happened?"

He could barely hear the words.

"We were on a raid…"

She jumped in before he could say any more. "Billy told me. He was scared but excited too. I didn't want him to go." Tears started to fill her eyes. "I should have stopped him. Locked him in the cellar. I felt something bad would happen if he went but I also knew I couldn't protect him for ever and he had to live his life, danger and all. I didn't want to drive him away. After his dad died, I didn't want to let him out of the house."

Suddenly she punched him hard in the face. It was such a surprise that he almost toppled off the chair. The she was screaming, "Why didn't you look after him? You promised. After I let him join up, you promised no harm would come to him."

Walter wasn't sure that it had been that strong, but she was right, he had said something like that to make her feel better about it. She lashed out at him again but this time he caught her hands and they struggled as she tried to free them. Then she slumped. "Tell me what happened."

He had to be straight with her. "Billy was shot. He didn't suffer. He wouldn't have felt anything. The man who did it will hang. He is in custody and there were too many saw it for him to get off with just a prison sentence."

Maud looked at him for a very long moment then a determination came into her face. "I want to see him. Billy!"

"I don't think that's… "

"I don't give a bugger what you think. I want to see him now." She pushed herself up from the chair, waited for Walter to move, then went to the door.

He'd hoped this wouldn't happen but deep down, he supposed, he knew it would. You couldn't ever plan for something like this, you just had to go with your sense of right and what was the easiest way forward for those who are in pain and grieving. It was against protocol to do this without checking it with the boss, but tonight the rules could get fucked, even if he ended up with his fingers burned. He followed her out of the kitchen.'

It had been awful with Maud at the hospital and he'd eventually left her with Betty Johnson, the only female officer at the station, and one of the nurses, Aggie, who lived in the same street as Maud and was going to take her home and make sure there was someone with her when she had to leave. If Aggie couldn't find a neighbour willing to stay with her then Betty would go over. She was sure someone would though. Even in the constant crisis of wartime, people still pulled together, particularly when something like this happened and, especially, if you lived close by them.

Walter would have stayed longer with Maud but he had to get back to the station and brief Sid Barnes before he could get off home. And he was desperate to see and hold Cate. Things like this had a way of focusing you on what was important in your life.

Barnes, called in on his day off, was, although he tried to cover it behind bluster, in as much of a state as the rest of them. Billy's death was hanging over the station like a dark cloud and there was little of the banter that would loudly and irreverently come after a successful raid. No one seemed to want to say anything, and more than a few had tears in their eyes, some instantly wiped away, others too shocked to hide them. Even Barnes, not normally one for a sympathetic ear, spoke in a whisper, his voice flat and toneless. It had affected them all and would for a long time to come. Any death of one of their own was taken personally but in one with so much life ahead of him, it hit them hard. Billy was too young to be snuffed out like that. He was a bit clueless and naïve but that would have been knocked out of him soon enough. He had the makings of a good and caring copper. Since his dad had died, Walter and Arthur had kept an eye on him, and the small team at the nick had been like his family. Of course, they wouldn't feel it like his mum and any other relatives he had. It would however leave a big hole in all their lives and getting back to the daily grind of the job would be hard. They would do it though because that's what they did. They had no choice but to put it behind them, not forgotten, just out of sight until there was space and time to work through it. There were a lot more villains out there that needed slapping down and they were the front line.

Barnes had been quiet for a good few minutes and Walter was starting to think he might have to give him a nudge to get him going again. "Good thinking to get Bryan to take him, not sure he would have lasted if he'd been here. Still, with a Neanderthal like the DCI, I would be surprised if he got there with all his bits intact." He looked sharply at Walter. "That's not to leave this room."

"Of course not, Sid. I'd have been right behind you making sure that it was a painful and fatal accident if he'd been close enough to touch. So whatever Ron Bryan does to him is good for me."

"It's Detective Chief Inspector Bryan to you, Sergeant. I didn't hear what you just said but don't repeat it even to Arthur and Taff. You're their superior officer and need to show a good hand.
I know hanging is too good for that evil bastard, but it will show the rest of the villains that you can't kill a copper and get away with it, even in the middle of a war."

He paused and Walter realised that he was getting himself under control and shutting down his personal feelings. "Hard choice with Maud but it was the right one." That was his way of saying that, despite breaking regulations, it was all right, this time, and wouldn't go any further. He looked at Walter as though he was considering something, then, decision made, gave a slight smile which went almost as soon as it came. "I think, Walter, that it's time you moved to plain clothes. I'll have to have a word with District. They have to put it to a Board but it shouldn't take too long if you get through the exam. You're a good copper and we need more like you out of uniform."

This was too much praise for Barnes and he moved some papers around on his desk to distract himself. Walter waited but nothing more came. He stood up.

"All right if I get off home? I'm about to drop. I can do the report first thing in the morning. Expect there'll be some brass coming down from headquarters to investigate and then the boys from internal will have a go too so a good night's sleep will give me a heads up. Is that OK with you…" a slight hesitation, "sir?" Even now he couldn't resist trying to prick Sid's bubble. Barnes glanced up at him.

"Yes… and don't push it, Sergeant, I may have known you a long time but I am still your helping hand on the slippery ladder… for now."

Game to Sid Barnes, but now that his move to mufti was in sight it was probably best to concede the match.

"I won't, Inspector!"

Walter and Cate were sitting at the kitchen table. He'd got home at half past eleven and she'd made him a fry up. He didn't think he'd be able to eat but he did, and it helped. Cate hadn't said anything while he was eating and now waited for him to start. She was worried when he told her about Billy. He was too calm and in control. She could see he was stretched tight and had to let it go. Since they'd come back from Robin Hood's Bay, they seemed to have found their balance again and she was happier and less centred on what she couldn't have than what she had. Their sex life had been good too and sometimes it felt the way it had those first times, exciting and a bit naughty, and there was laughter there as well as the passion and easiness with each other's bodies.

She wanted to take him to bed now and hold him. Then there was a sudden flash of guilt that she was thinking these things when Billy Wilkinson was lying dead in the hospital. She'd met him a few times and liked him. He was shy at first but once you got past that he was chatty and funny. She even thought, sometimes, that he felt more comfortable in her company than Walter's. She realised that Walter was looking at her.

"I was just thinking about Billy."

He nodded then smiled. "I know this is the middle of the day but will you come to bed with me?"

"Yes, I'll just clear up, give you time to have a quick bath, then I'll be there."

He glanced at her, surprised.

"You're filthy." She laughed. It was awkward but broke the moment.

Walter was lying in Cate's arms, sobbing uncontrollably.

They had made love. It had started gently but then there was a desperation and roughness that hadn't ever been there before. It was uncontrolled, and exciting, and when they came together, the first time it had ever happened, it was like something had changed and they were a single entity, a whole, not two halves that just fitted together. Then as the world calmed around them, Walter cracked, and the dam had burst. She had never seen him like this. He always kept her away from anything that was dark and violent in his working life. Now she saw him at his rawest, damaged, and despairing that he had been the cause of Billy's death. She knew it was not the time to tell him that if the bullet had gone where it was meant to go, he would be the one dead, and she would be distraught and grieving. Seeing her strong and capable husband like this made her realise how much she loved him. He was a good and caring man, and she would help him through this. Then as Walter's tears slowly stopped and he was spared by sleep, a strange and uneven thought came into her head. It was so unexpected that it had to fight its way through. What if she had conceived tonight? If, in the middle of all this horror, a new life could replace the one that was lost? Then something inside told her that it wasn't now. It wasn't right yet. It would happen soon though, she was sure. Something had changed in her mind and body, and she knew that she was ready for it. The blockage that had prevented it had gone.

She knew that she wouldn't talk about it to Walter, this was only for her until it happened. She couldn't even allow herself to think too much about it. It was her secret, a hidden way of healing both her and Walter. She would only have a month or so to wait and if it wasn't, as she knew in her heart, true, she'd always know now that it would happen. The curse had been lifted. She'd had her time of pain and desolation.

CHAPTER EIGHTEEN

The breakdown truck dropped the Volvo outside the garage and then Ian at home. It was just after ten by the time they got there. Ian had phoned Jed, who owned the garage, and he'd promised to see if he could do it earlier than they'd arranged for the initial repair, perhaps he'd even find time to get to it tomorrow. If he couldn't, then he'd lend him a car, it wouldn't be classy but not a banger either. He was a good man, Jed, and Ian got on well with him. They were on the pub darts team together. He lived in the village too and knew the nightmares of ferrying young kids around with a problem car and hardly any buses. That was one of the good things about being in a small community, people rallied round when there was a crisis, big or small. The downside was that, if like Ian you were a bit on the edgy end of creative and didn't have a proper job, then it created gossip and over-imagination. But at least it got them invited to parties. Some they went to but most they managed to evade. Why they couldn't just say that they didn't want to go always irritated Ian, but Nora was more sensitive. They were living here and shouldn't upset people for the sake of it. There were, however, three couples, with kids around George's age, with whom they were friendly. The pub was good too and Ian had even been asked to join a committee to set up a village Arts Festival.

Earlier and after the police had checked him out because, unknown to him, only one of his hazard lights was flashing, and warned him that in this sort of weather it wasn't the cleverest place to be, Ian had gone for contrition, rather than the instinctive sarcasm, and thanked them. He then had another hour to wait for the RAC. With nothing but the fear of being hit by careless cars to distract him, he kept thinking about his latest slip into Walter's world. An image of the young man shot in the head floated in and out, then he must have dozed off because he was jolted awake when the breakdown truck pulled up. The traffic had died down by then. He was getting very cold, even in his coat, and he sat in the cab of the truck to warm up while the car was checked out. It wasn't a problem that could be fixed so it was loaded up. The guy was chatty and had some horror stories of people stuck in out of the way places, and the stupid and unbelievable reasons they came up with for calling him out. Ian managed to stick some of them in his phone. Always good to have someone else's truth to use as his fiction or even, at a push, someone else's reconstructed fiction. The only thing wrong with plagiarism was getting caught.

He watched the truck drive away. It was freezing and the wind was starting up again, and the rain getting heavier. The house was in darkness and looked cold and unwelcoming, but it was better than being out here. He took his keys out of his bag. He'd almost stuck them all through the garage post box but had just stopped himself in time and taken the house ones off the ring. That would have really finished him off. He wouldn't have been able to get in at all. The spare key wasn't back in its not-so-secret place outside but on the kitchen table. He'd meant to put it back the last time he used it but forgot. The house was chilly so, although it was late, he decided to get the fire going. It didn't take long. He'd taken the ashes out and laid it this morning. He went into the kitchen, put on the light over the worktop, poured himself a glass of wine then, suddenly starving, looked in the freezer for something to eat. He took out a chilli con carne, stuck it in the microwave, then took off his coat, hung it up, checked the fire, took his iPad out of the bag, put on a jumper that was on the sofa and went back to where he'd plugged his phone in. He rang Nora. It took her a while to answer, and he was just about to hang up. He could hear Rose talking in the background, but it didn't make sense

"Hello, sweetheart, just got home. I broke down and had to be towed back. We dropped the car off at Jed's."

"Are you OK?" She sounded a bit distant

"Yes."

This time her voice was warmer. She was obviously trying not to be heard. "Me too. Except Rose is a bit pissed and on her own tonight, so I'm on duty."

"Tell him you're staying here and to fuck off."

"Shut up, Rose!" Nora sounded spiky then her voice softened. "How did it go at the library?"

"Good. I met up with Alex and he knew someone I can talk to about it all."

"Alex? Oh, Alex, is he still there? I thought he was leaving. Got a better offer. Got rid of his wife, what's her name… Masie… and job in one go. Has he found another woman yet? A new start and a new tart! Haven't seen him since he tried it on with Lucy at that pub with the theatre. She told him to piss off. He's a dick. How is he?"

He didn't know that she'd given Alex this much thought and it was unsettling. But throwing in Lucy was the big jolt. He hadn't been ready for her to surface. He'd managed to push her out of his mind for the last few hours but now she came galloping back in like all the horsewomen of the apocalypse rolled into one. He had to take a moment before answering, even distracted by Rose, Nora would pick up on any unusual intonations and hesitancy in what he said. She could cut out guilt and lying like a surgeon. Luckily the microwave pinged. Thank you!

"He's fine. I'll tell you tomorrow. My food's ready. I haven't eaten since lunchtime."

"That's a bit abrupt, even for you. Are you cross with me?"

"No, just hungry. I'll call you back after I've eaten."

"No, I'm going to get Rose into bed, check on the boys and the baby. Can you pick me up tomorrow?"

"Not first thing. Is Georgie asleep?"

"Yes… why not?"

"Why not what?"

"Why can't you pick me up."

"I told you, the car's in the garage and I don't know when it'll be fixed or even if it can be fixed and if it can be, what time it'll be ready."

"Fuck."

"Sorry, but it's not my fault."

"I know, but I don't understand what you're talking about. I'm too tired."

"I'll go then. Give Georgie a kiss from me. Love you."

"Do you?" What the hell was happening now? Paranoia immediately started to edge in between the cracks of his guilt. He knew she'd pick up on something and connect it.

"Yes, but you're confusing me, and my food is getting cold. So, I'm going. I'll ring after I've spoken to Jed."

"In the morning?"

"Yes."

"I love you too and… what?" She paused as Rose mumbled something. "Rose will drop me off after the school run… oh, shit, she's going to be sick!" And she'd gone.

He tried to get Lucy out of his mind and failed. "Will you fuck off!" He had a sudden panic that the phone was still live. "Not you, Nora." It wasn't of course.

He finished off the wine, took the chilli out and put it into a bowl, then filled up his glass again and went into the living room. The fire was starting to flare up and he threw on a couple of logs, sat with his back against the sofa, and tried to eat without thought. Of course, he failed. They swirled from Lucy to the beach, the knife, the storm, and the face at the window, then sprang to Sally Ryan and her book, then back to Lucy and, bizarrely, the hobbit at the library. Did this confusing kaleidoscope count as multi-tasking when he was eating and watching the fire as well? Did he always have to have this inner debate? It was so fucking exhausting.

He finished his food without any memory of the taste

and, determined to occupy his mind with something else, switched the TV on, changed the input to Chromecast and opened the All4 app on his iPad, scrolling through to *The Border*, series two. It was about a border force team chasing refugees and drug runners and was something else he wished he'd written. He and Nora had watched series one and loved it. It was good snuggled up together to binge on it, but tonight he needed distraction. Just as it started his phone rang. It was quarter past eleven and the phone was in the kitchen. It could wait.

It carried on ringing. He paused the show. His phone was almost charged so he unplugged it and, still ringing took it back to the sofa. He didn't recognize the number, then he wouldn't unless it was in his contacts and had a name attached. If it hadn't stopped by the time he sat down, he'd answer it. It hadn't, so he did. "Hello?"

"You took your bloody time!" The voice was deep, full of resonance and sharp.

"Who is this?"

"Roly Baylis. You wanted to talk to me." Ian tried to get his head around it.

"Mr Baylis, yes, I wasn't expecting you to ring so soon."

"No point wasting time. Sorry it's so late but I thought if I caught you tonight, we could meet tomorrow. I've got a free day and from what I've heard, the sooner you tell me all, the better. Where are you?"

"About twenty miles from York."

"Meet me at York station. I'll be there about one."

"I've seen your photo on the book."

"Good." Baylis disconnected.

He hadn't expected such a quick response. That was good, though, wasn't it? Yes, of course it was. He realised that he hadn't had any 'moments' of disappearing into the past since last night. What if they'd stopped? How would he explain that? Bit like going to the dentist. In pain until you made the appointment then it wasn't there when you got to the surgery. Shit! Then the one he had tonight flashed into his mind. Jesus, loss of short-term memory now! That wasn't good. But with what was going on in his life and head, he was lucky there was any recall at all. Still, he had to get himself in some sort of order before tomorrow. Make some notes. Check his timeline and put down everything he remembered from the beginning. Baylis sounded like he believed there was something. What had Alex's friend told him? It was obviously enough to get his interest. Then he remembered he wouldn't have a car. He'd have to ring Jed first thing and then if he couldn't work something out, he'd ask Josh at the pub. Sounded like a seventies folk band, Josh and Jed! Should he tell Nora? No, best to wait until he'd seen him, then he'd hopefully have something more than his imagination and paranoia to go on.

He opened his *What the fuck happened on the beach?* file. Just before he clicked on it, though, he noticed that he had mail. He decided to ignore it, then couldn't and opened it up. There was a pile of junk in his general email, then in his work one there were three. One was from Janey. What the fuck was she going to do to him now? Of the other two, the first was from a production company who had an option on his thriller. He opened that first. They'd had some interest from Amazon and Apple and wanted to set up a Zoom call with him and someone in the US. The second was from a journalist he'd met at an awards show, another one where he came away with nothing except a hangover. He wanted to chat about a story he thought might interest Ian to co-write with him, changing the factual reality into fiction. Bloody hell, that was unexpected. Before he enjoyed the anticipation of hope for a moment, he thought he'd better see what Janey had to say.

It was only four words in red capitals: *NEXT FRIDAY YOU'RE TOAST!* And two kisses followed by a *J*. Great, fucking great! Then he pushed that away. There were two positives to balance that negative. He'd manage somehow to get it off by then even if he had to do an 'and then they all died ending' for now but make it look clever and surprising. Could he manage that? Sure. He quickly replied to all three, sending the two others to Janey too. Would that work? If she saw big bucks, yes. Also, when one big player showed an interest, the others wanted to get on board too: Netflix, BBC, HBO.

Suddenly things didn't seem so bad, then, as always, that 'change of luck' moment of cocky optimism withered, this time with the reality of what was happening to him now. He opened the file and tried to make sense of what he'd already written. It was difficult as his focus immediately, with its own spark of priority, jumped to the end of his book. He knew he'd have to follow that focus first or the two things would battle for space, and he'd end up with nothing. He slipped into novel mode and his mind began to spin out possibilities. They were tumbling out, disordered and ragged, and he had to write them down before he forgot. So, he went into the book folder and started a new document of these ideas. It wouldn't take long and then he'd get back to Walter and the beach…

He was wrong, it had taken him over two hours, but he had a good plan loosely mapped out of the way he would tie it all up. He decided to stop and get some sleep because, by then, he was so exhausted that he wouldn't be able to think about anything else, let alone write something that made sense. The brilliant, positive thing was, though, that what he'd worked out wasn't a 'just for now' but a perfect storm ending. He'd have time in the morning to list all that he wanted to tell Baylis. He'd cracked it and now it would be easy.

Just as he was putting the guard in front of the fire, his phone pinged. A WhatsApp from Janey… a 'thumbs up' emoji. Perhaps everything else would come right now too.

He left his iPad where it was, switched off the TV and lights, and went upstairs.

He was standing alone on a small stage waiting as the applause died down. 'Thank you, it is a great privilege to share this stage with Sally tonight, but it is all her own work and not anything to do with me. I was just pleased I was able to suggest a few things that would…' he paused for a few moments as his face became grotesque and his mouth opened and with a harsh laugh spat out, 'turn her pathetic ramblings into something that took it...'

Suddenly there was a scream and a naked Sally Ryan rushed from the side of the stage, a large knife in her hand, and before he could defend himself thrust the blade deep into his stomach, twisting it and forcing it up into his heart. As she gasped with the effort her face became Lucy's and she leaned towards him, her tongue pushing its way into his screaming mouth.

"I want you to taste me as you die."

Despite her tongue growing and pushing down his throat the words were clear. Then suddenly he felt hands squeezing what he could see was a massive trembling erection and before he could work out what was happening, he cried out "Cate" and exploded, the pain and pleasure intense...

Ian crashed awake with a scream and lay there shaking as slowly he came back to the now and the dream slipped away. He suddenly felt uncomfortable and put his hand to his stomach and felt a stickiness. Jesus, what was happening to him now! Before he could follow this thought, his eyes closed and he slipped back into a deep and, this time, untroubled sleep.

It was as he was buttering toast the next morning and waiting for his tea to brew, that the name flashed into his head. Cate! Cate! Who the fuck was Cate? He didn't think he knew any Cates, and then suddenly the mists cleared, and he remembered the dream. A dream that was, embarrassingly, apart from anything else, the first 'wet' one he'd had in thirty-odd years - and that was, of course, the memory that would stay with him after the other horrors faded. He always tried to analyse those dreams he could recall in entirety and give them intent and purpose. The strangest thing about dreams were those small fractional elements of truth that were taken to the most shocking extremes of their worst or, sometimes, their best, conclusions. This time, the dream theme was easy. It was Sally and his pathetic despondency and irritation at her success, blended with the stabbing from the beach and his guilt about Lucy. Did the weirdest of dreams signal a pathway of confusion to come in later years as the mind deteriorated and lived in a shadowy world of real and unreal? Not that it would be a great step into the unknown for him. He had been living in that little bubble all his adult life and probably most of his childhood too.

He checked the time. It was eight thirty. He'd been up since five and strangely, after he dropped off again, had the best sleep he'd had for ages and felt physically refreshed if not completely clear headed and focused. He decided to see how far he could get with the end of his novel and realised that he'd been so caught up in word count that he'd not seen the simplest of endings that was right and perfect, at least until Janey read it. It was going to come out at eighty thousand words, not the hundred and ten thousand that he thought he could stretch it to. By seven thirty he'd finished it. It was the fastest two thousand words he'd ever written, and they might well be the best. He'd ask Nora to read it before he risked sending it off. She'd do it in a day. She was a speed reader and somehow managed to point out the worst bits with the briefest of sharp and focused notes.

God, he was flying this morning. Perhaps it was a

rush to do all before he fell into the pit of no return.

He'd also managed to jot down some more of his notes for Baylis too before his phone rang. He looked at the screen. It was Jed.

"Jed, morning."

"Hello, mate, I've had a quick look and it's going to take a bit of time to get patched up because I've got to get some parts from Volvo. The bastards make sure you can't get compatible ones especially for the older models, like yours."

He paused. Ian's heart dropped. He'd a feeling that what came next wouldn't be good, though it was probably the least of the problems he had at the moment and, if things worked out, he'd have some money in from the production company and the journalist.

"If you want my advice, I'd dump it and get something else. Billy Thorpe at Driffield Motors has got a newer version of yours that he'll let me have for fifteen hundred. If I keep yours for spares, you can have it for the same price. What do you think? It's your best bet. This one's going to cost about a grand to repair anyway and might be more if the engine's knackered."

"Shit!"

"Think about it. I'll let you have it for five hundred up front and the rest over twelve months if you're a bit strapped. In the meantime, I can let you have Dawn's Clio for a couple of weeks for free. She's gone to help her sister in Newcastle run her café while her old man's off sick. Talk to Nora and give me a ring back. What time do you want the Clio? I'm just doing an MOT on it. Should be an hour at the most."

It ran through Ian's head at super speed. He could put the five hundred on his card and they'd probably be able to manage the eighty-odd a month and then pay it off if he got a chunk in. He should talk to Nora about it, but they needed a reliable and solid car and Jed would make sure it was.

"We'll have it. Nora'll be fine! I'll be over about twelve. Will that give you enough time?"

"Perfect. You made the right choice." A phone rang in the garage. "Got to go. See you then."

"Thanks, Jed, you're a star."

"Aren't I just." Jed disconnected and Ian stood there for a moment wondering whether he should phone Nora. No, he'd wait. She'd be home soon. Just then a WhatsApp pinged in. It was Nora. How did she do that? Sometimes he'd just think about her, and she'd ring or text.

We're going to go swimming then shopping in town. What I mean is that we're both going swimming then Rose is going shopping and I'm going to help and be envious. Nothing will fit me anyway. I'll see you later. George sent you a hug and a kiss. I love you. Sorry I dashed off last night, it was Rose's fault, and this morning I've got a headache and she's fine.'

He felt a surge of love, followed by a barb of guilt, and made a silent promise not to ever do anything again to risk losing her. He replied, having to keep correcting the predictive text, as he hurried to get it off. Why did it replace words with those that made even less sense than the ones he'd written? It had to happen to other people too, didn't it? Although the way his life was, he wouldn't bet on it.

Hope it goes soon, sweetheart. Got a meeting today with a guy from Leeds University, Prof Roly Baylis, he might be able to help. I'll tell you all about it when I get home. Have fun. Love you xx.

Just as it went a text message came in. *One fifteen. RB.*

Short and to the point. He could do that too.

See you then. IC.

He made another cup of tea and more toast, took them into the living room, found the book in his bag and settled down to read as much as he could before he picked up the car. He'd have more than enough time to try and get into it.

It was just after one when he walked into York station and looked for the Leeds train. It wasn't on the board. He asked one of the ticket checkers by the gates, who looked at him as though he'd suggested they get naked by the buffers. After a lot of glaring, muttering, and phone swiping, she told him it was going to be thirty minutes late and would be coming in on a platform that hadn't yet been designated. She said it as though it was his fault, then lost interest and found something else to sneer at. He boiled gently but had enough on his mind to hold back a response. It wasn't long to wait and gave him time for a coffee. So, he went to Costa and treated himself to a ginger muffin and a double shot cappuccino and sat watching the people milling around the concourse. People watching was one of his escape tactics to drift, push the uncomfortable aside, become faceless, and generally pass time. It also counted as work as it gave him a diverse bunch of material to store away and was therefore guilt free too.

He ate his muffin then stopped scanning the crowd and tried to summarise what he'd read in the first fifty pages of Baylis's book. A lot of it went over his head, particularly the graphs and equations, but the text was what Baylis promised in his opening paragraph. It was easy to read, light on the science and heavy on the story of how time had been crisscrossing worlds of past and present since it began. There was stuff about the planets and the stars, the light years theory of accessing the future, and simple, almost too simple, explanations as to why the past was accessible too. He was weighing up the idea that time existed in parallels when he heard the announcement that the Leeds train was due in five minutes at platform three. Something must have gone wrong in the system because the voice was clear and precise. As if to prove his point, the next bit of information that came over the station speaker system was completely indecipherable. He finished his coffee and wandered over to the barrier, watched as the train came into view, slowed as it approached, then came to a stop. The door opened and people piled out. Quite a few had passed without him seeing anyone who looked like the picture on the book cover. Where was he? Just then Ian saw him getting out of a carriage at the far end of the platform. He was a big man with his white hair tied back in a ponytail, a wild beard, dark glasses, wearing a long grey coat with a thick jumper underneath, jeans, and black Doc Martens. He had a large backpack slung over one shoulder. Ian was impressed, particularly by the Docs. He'd wanted a pair for the last year, but Nora wouldn't let him spend £150 on them. She was right, but it didn't stop the longing!

He smiled as Baylis came through the barrier. "Professor Baylis, I'm Ian Chambers."

Baylis smiled and his whole face lit up and it made Ian feel that whatever happened, this man could cope. Or was that just wishful thinking.

"Yes, I'm sure you are." Ian's hand disappeared in his. "Roly. Have you got a car?"

"Yes."

"Good, let's get moving, I want you to take me to the place you first experienced it. We'll talk on the way."

"Sounds good to me." He led the way out of the station.

Baylis was finding it difficult in the small car. He'd pushed his seat back as far as it would go but his long legs and body looked awkward and uncomfortable, and his torso, too big for the seat, was overflowing onto the driver's side. He didn't moan about it though and had listened intently as Ian talked, then held his hand up and said to give him a moment. He was now curling his beard between his fingers and looking into the distance. A couple of times he had made a sound then answered it with a deeper rumble in his throat. It was like an intermittent inner body debate. Then there was only his breathing. He'd been like this for the last fifteen minutes and it was beginning to be unsettling.

"Where were you when Walter struggled with the man and the gun went off? The location of your psychical world, not his."

233

"I was at home, in my writing room. There was a thunderstorm."

"And the same was happening there?"

"Yes, a storm." He thought for a moment as Baylis watched him closely and waited. "It wasn't as frightening as the other times. I didn't feel threatened. I was in control, knew what I was doing." He then told him about the one he had last night when he'd broken down. "That was the same, but in the Lookout, it was terrifying."

Baylis smiled. "It would be!" He shifted in the seat and tried to find a bit more space but failed and settled again. "I think from what you've just told me that it is as you thought it was." He stopped for a moment, flicked his eyes towards the side window and then back again, squeezed them shut and then opened them. "You somehow entered into a shared moment of parallel time." He smiled and nodded. "Ascertaining that is what occurred is the relatively easy bit." He paused. "The WHY is far, far trickier!"

"I thought it might be."

Baylis breathed in and blew out a panting sigh. "It's a bit complex but I'll try and keep it simple. Why it happened is that, by chance, when you entered the look-out, you were drawn from one parallel timeline into another, the present to the past, by an alliance of causes; the violent storm, your precise position and location, exact same hour, minute and second of the night, were what ignited an explosion of synchronicity that fractured the line of separation between the two times. It created a symbiotic manifestation that fused you and Walter into a single entity. A little like the movement of tectonic plates creating a fault line between continents that brings about an earthquake. In timelines it is a rare thing and once you are there extremely difficult to return to your own time before the fracture repairs itself. For you to have dragged yourself out of that state and back to the present, there would have been a powerful emotional pull from your life here. You must have fought hard to get back to it. However, you still retained a connection, hence the face in the mirror and outside the window and even the other moments in Walter's life that transmuted into your subconscious. My theory is that transference of oneself to another body can so impact the physical states of both bodies, that what is perceived to exist does not in reality exist in a manifested form, but floats as a force in a bubble of time and space, to land where it finds complete empathy, and therefore…"

Ian was lost. "What? I don't understand a word of that. Is there a quick and simple way of saying it?"

Baylis chuckled then cleared his throat.

"All right, in simple terms, if you don't return from one of these visits it means that what would have happened to Walter, will happen to you instead. In short, your death would ensure his life and the balance of reality for both of you would have changed irrevocably, affecting not only his time but yours too."

"Fuck!" Ian glanced at him in horror, then back to the road, just managing to avoid hitting the rear end of a braking lorry. "Fuck!" He felt that his heart was beating so fast it was going to explode. Perhaps that would be for the best, messy but at least it would mean he'd miss the shit storm that was, according to Baylis, almost upon him.

Baylis didn't seem to notice the near miss or Ian's reaction. He watched him closely, impassive, still.

Ian was hit by a stunning fear of mortality. It flashed a stream of memories of when he was a child and was terrified of dying after his aunt was killed in a car crash. It had taken him years to get over it. There was a long pause. Baylis moved his head slightly nearer and studied him.

Ian glanced at him again. "What?"

Baylis shook his head and leaned back in the seat his eyes still on Ian.

"Can I do anything to stop it happening to me?"

After a moment and a long silent breath, Baylis nodded. "Let me see the Lookout first."

Not that helpful or positive. "Have you experienced this before with anyone else?"

"Not exactly the same but similar."

"What happened to them?"

"I managed to get them back."

"How did you do that?"

"It won't help you. Everybody is different. The thing you should focus on is that I have had some success."

"Some. That's not the best odds."

"Better than none."

Ian tried to stop the ripples of panic. "I'm going to die in the past and disappear from the present?"

"In the worst-case scenario yes." He said it far too lightly.

"And in the best case, I don't, but end up barking mad

with someone else's life running repeats in my head."

Baylis smiled and shook his head. "Not necessarily."

Ian ignored the reassuring whisper of only partial insanity. "I have no control over what happens?"

"I didn't say that." Baylis gently laid his hand on Ian's arm and there was an instant tingling warmth. The ripples of panic dissipated to a hollowness in the pit of his stomach, then that too disappeared. He felt almost instantly calm.

"Give me a moment to think about it. Try to relax and keep positive." Baylis removed his hand, closed his eyes, and within a minute was breathing deeply. With the magic touch gone and that last little bit of advice, Ian's sense of ease shattered again.

Positive. For fuck's sake! The man had just given him a death sentence. He didn't look like he was coming up with any sort of solution and Ian almost slapped him awake but the big man gave a loud single snore and grunted in his sleep. Perhaps he was a narcoleptic psychopath and his killing kicks were psychological games and insanity. He was certainly well on the way there with him…

Suddenly the blare of a horn as he drifted across the road and came close to colliding with a large van changed his focus. He had to concentrate on his driving. He couldn't kill Baylis before the man told him how to escape his potential fate. And, of course, he needed to be alive to hear it too.

So, he had to make sure he got them safely to the beach. Suddenly, as a portent of doom, the skies darkened, there was a loud clap of thunder, a flash of lightning and the rain came down in a torrent. And, worst of all, he now desperately needed a pee. He'd meant to go before leaving the station, but Baylis had set the pace and given him no time and then in the horror of his lack of a future he'd forgotten, but now it was there with a vengeance. The less he tried to think about it, the more urgent the need. He searched frantically for somewhere to stop before it was too late. Just as he thought he'd have to let it happen and fuck the embarrassment, he saw a pull-in on the other side of the road and, narrowly missing a motorbike and sidecar that swerved around him, he reached it, opened the door and tried to get out with his seat belt still on.

"Bastard!"

He snapped it off, stood, hidden by the open door, struggled with his zip, and released himself just as he could hold it back no longer. For a moment getting soaked and even the proximity of dying was secondary to the pleasure of emptying his bladder, while, inside the car, Baylis pondered his fate in a state of deep sleep.

CHAPTER NINETEEN

Lucy was in the hotel's spa, in the sauna, on her own. It was hot but she poured more water over the stones anyway and gasped as the wave of heat hit her. It would ease in a moment as she got used to it. It was good for her skin and might get rid of the last bit of tension in her neck, back and shoulders. The sex and the walking over the last couple of days had helped too. She was feeling good and was enjoying spending time with Mark. It was fun to be with him. She didn't let herself see it before. She just wanted to be in control and for everything to be on her terms. Mark adored her and was happy to go along with it but it must have hurt or pissed him off at times when she was particularly snappy. He had reacted occasionally. It was only when she said or did something thoughtless, harsh or cruel, that, in her opinion, was down to something he'd done or said, but to his thinking was clearly not. It was unfair and childish. The only positive was that it never lasted long. He wasn't stupid. He was a simple soul but a genuine one. What a cow she was! He was easy to be with and now, after she allowed herself to accept and embrace who he was, they laughed a lot, mainly at silly jokes, the way people behaved and the nicknames they gave them.

She lay down on the wooden slats, the towel taking the edge off the heat, and closed her eyes. It was good being on her own for an hour or two to get things to balance. Mark was in the gym and probably sharing as much of his muscle and tone as he could get away with and still look cool. She knew a lot more about his world than she had before they'd got to the Lakes and had, surprisingly, told him about herself too. Not to the extent of the secret life with Ian though. He was still just her best friend and she deliberately avoided talking about him, particularly after Marky's throwaway about them sleeping together.

She was feeling drowsy. She'd probably had more sex in the last seventy-two hours than she'd had in the previous three months. It was always on offer. Mark was insatiable. He didn't care where or when: in the bed, the shower, the bath, and a couple of times up against trees and once in a boat that was tied up at the edge of the lake. The only time he wasn't up for it was when he was asleep or talking about his family, or his hopes and dreams of opening a bar in somewhere hot when he was about forty. That was a nasty moment for her. She would be getting old then and if the sex carried on in the same way, worn out. How long could she just enjoy the moment and not long for the stimulus of art and literature, to talk to someone who understood about the lonely frustration and fear of inadequacy of creating poetry and prose and the intellectual debate and discourse that had always been a part of her life. Mark did try, but his passions were for different things and his world sat happily within comfortable boundaries, whereas she was always stretching the parameters. It wasn't her fault or his. She knew that the relationship with him wouldn't last.

Suddenly, back it came! Would it have lasted with Ian? No, of course it fucking well wouldn't! It should never have started. They had too much to lose. And they had now lost it all. Never again! Shocked that her mind had flipped so easily, she decided to move and perhaps swim in the pool. She was at the door when it opened and through the mist she saw Mark.

"Hi, babe, there's no one around, thought we could have a little love bump in the sauna. Be another thing off my list. What do you think?"

It made her laugh. Just what she needed, a love bump to banish the bastard.

"Sounds good to me."

* * *

Ian and Baylis were struggling through the howling winds on the beach and heading towards the look-out, just visible in the dim light of the darkening skies. The rain had eased but it didn't look as though it would last as the clouds rolled and twisted together into a mass of solid black. It was almost impossible to hear each other but Baylis' booming voice managed to break through.

"Makes you feel like Nature has decided that the time is right to punish us for our multitude of sins against the Earth. It is magnificent in its anger and fury!"

Ian, desperate to get out of it before the threatening storm arrived but terrified of going into the place where he knew his nemesis awaited him, felt the exuberance and energy in the big man as he picked up speed, his long legs striding out. He was soon ahead. Ian tried to keep up and felt like a small child running after his dad. He almost reached out and took Baylis' hand to feel his strength and envelop himself in the protection of this totally insane and brilliant weirdo, who, he hoped and prayed, would keep him in this world of the living. The list of promises and pledges he was making to balance his mistakes and philandering would, if he was still around, keep him busy until he died a natural death. Hopefully many years away.

A massive burst of thunder ripped and roared, long crackling staccato stabs of fire that seemed to hang endlessly across the dark. Ian had his head down to protect himself from the knifepoint shards of rain that had been released again by the cloud burst and whipped to full force by the tempest like wind. He didn't see Baylis stop and smacked hard into his back. The professor's face was turned up and Ian imagined that he was howling and laughing his derision at Zeus, and the god's pathetic attempts to keep him from his quest. He wasn't. He'd had enough. Zeus too and more thunder and lightning were thrown at the insignificants on the beach. Baylis turned to Ian, distracting him, and leaned close to his ear.

"Let's make a run for it, this is not my idea of having fun."

He set off at a quick pace and Ian, hoping he might show his mastery in this at least, took off after him. He had twenty years on the man and was lighter and smaller. He pounded forward, passing Baylis but, too pleased with himself and not looking where he was going, tripped in a deep dip in the sand and went flying, He had to suffer the ignominy of being pulled to his feet and having twisted his ankle, helped along to the Lookout.

"You need to be more careful. You could have hurt yourself."

"What, more than being stabbed and left lifeless in a different time?"

Baylis thought for a moment. "No, that would be a bit more of a bugger, wouldn't it?" He laughed.

"What's so funny? It's not happening to you."

"With a bit of luck we might manage to avoid that for you too." Not quite as positive a promise as Ian had would have liked.

They were standing at the rubble and rubbish-filled entrance to the look-out.

Ian took a step back. He didn't want to go in. "After you."

Baylis smiled at him then bent and twisted his bulk inside.

The Lookout seemed even smaller with Baylis in it. He was standing in the centre, where the attack had happened, eyes closed, perfectly still, waiting, prepared. Ian, however, was feeling rumblings of death and anticipating the blackness covering him and the pain starting as the knife was driven in. His senses were acute. He could almost taste the rancid smells of dog shit, vomit, and rotting food. And it was freezing. That was good though, wasn't it? Proved he wasn't slipping away. He glanced out through the slits in the wall. Nothing had changed except the storm seemed to be dying down. Baylis had been in this state for ten minutes and Ian was on the point of sneaking out and leaving him there when he opened his eyes.

"There is a strange force here."

Ian didn't think sarcasm would help so bit back the "Really, that's a surprise!" that had almost slipped out.

"What are you feeling?"

"Apart from being shit scared and terrified of not seeing my family again?"

Baylis smiled at him. He was enjoying this, the bastard.

"It's bloody freezing."

"What else?" A hint of irritation. "Fading light, weakness, dizziness, loss of hearing..."

Ian interrupted before he could stop himself. "What?"

Baylis wasn't amused and glared at him.

"Sorry. None of that. Sight is good too and breathing is fine. Last time it wasn't and it felt like there was a huge weight crushing me."

"How long were you in here before it happened?"

"Almost immediately. I noticed that the outside was changing then I was out of it and in this other place."

"The second time was the same?"

"Yes."

"And nothing like this at the other times and places?"

"No."

Baylis was still. He closed his eyes again and breathed deeply. "I'd like to try regression through hypnotherapy."

Ian, after a moment, realised what he meant. "Take me back to a past life?" Then another thought. "To see if I was, am, Walter?"

"It might help. At the very least it will give me a better insight into what, if anything, has influenced your memories and induced those of others."

Ian was confused again but didn't think more questions would help. "Do you want to do it now? It mightn't be the best place. Don't I need to relax? That's not going to happen here."

"No." He looked at Ian for a moment. "I'm tied up for the next couple of days. Would you be happy to come to my clinic?"

"Yes, but I thought this was pretty urgent. What if it happens again before then? That might be the end of everything. Can't we do it now? We could go back to my place."

"Nothing will happen today and perhaps the fissure between times I was telling you about has closed and the time for your transference has passed, although you must still be prepared."

"How, stay awake so I don't dream and let my subconscious kidnap me? And if that happened, would Nora wake up to a corpse or wouldn't I be there at all, or George, or even her?"

"Stop rambling. That's not going to help!" Just what he needed, a sensitive, caring therapist! "It's all right to sleep. Let it happen naturally. When you resist and then give in, as you will, you are at your most vulnerable." He put his arm around Ian. "I'll do my best for you. Now, there's nothing more for us here. Take me back to the station. There is something niggling at the back of my mind and I need help to see it clearly. The answer will be in my research and particularly my archive for *Time*. I will try and move my commitments and fit you in the day after tomorrow."

"How likely is it that I could take his place if I go back before I see you again?"

"I don't know. It depends…" He suddenly stopped, then, like he did in the car on the way there, made the sound in his throat that was answered by another and a nod of agreement. He turned to Ian. "There is a chance that Walter could change the end point of his fate and if that is the case then you might not be the one who is the recipient of the transfer."

"What the fuck do you mean by that?"

Baylis moved towards the entrance and struggled through.

"I don't understand what you're telling me now. I might not have to take his place? What does that mean? How many of us are down there waiting to see who gets the shitty stick? Bit arbitrary, isn't it? Does Walter just point the finger and it's done?"

Baylis had gone.

"Fuck." Ian followed him, and in the panic to get out, cracked his head against the top of the entrance. He hardly noticed it and ran to catch up with the man now moving fast across the beach. The storm had gone, and the sky was lighter. Perhaps that was a good sign.

Baylis glanced at him. "Your head's bleeding."

Ian felt it then. "Hit it on the way out."

Baylis reached into his coat pocket and pulled out a pack of tissues, gave them to him, then upped his pace. Ian stopped and held the tissue to his head. There wasn't as much blood as he thought there would be. He held the tissue in place and hurried after Baylis.

Baylis didn't speak on the way to the station, just looked as though he was asleep. He didn't respond when Ian had tried to ask him how regression worked and if he had used it before with any success. Either he was deeply unconscious or ignoring him. Either was possible. Perhaps he was communing with a different world. One in which he didn't have to talk to writers whose fiction seemed to be rapidly replacing any sense of their reality. Or he was bored by it all now that he hadn't been able to accompany Ian through the fracture of time. That would have given old Walter a bit of a start. A Gandalf-like figure popping in out of the future. Would Walter know who Gandalf was? Then he remembered that Tolkien had written *The Hobbit* before the Second World War so there was a good chance he might have done. Would a copper at that time, by nature a pragmatist, have read fantasy anyway? Mix all that in with morbid thoughts of disappearing from all he knew and loved, murdered by an unknown attacker and a momentary thought of Lucy sending texts to Nora, telling her everything – not that it would matter if she did after he slipped into a time warp – and his concentration level was not all it should be. He nearly took them into a ditch taking a corner too fast. That gave him a rush of adrenaline and reality and the remainder of the journey was safe and uneventful. All he let his mind explore was the sifting of negatives to see how big the pile of positive outcomes might be. The one positive was that his head had stopped bleeding. Must have been Roly's magic tissue. It had started to ache now instead.

Baylis woke immediately they arrived at the station, looked at his watch. "Ten minutes. I should make that one. I'll call you tomorrow. Do something tonight to take your mind off things. Try to keep positive and don't worry. I still have some tricks up my sleeve."

Back to Gandalf again! Easy for him to say.

"What if I need to talk to you…" The door slammed and he was gone. "All right, I won't."

He decided instead to WhatsApp Nora.

Hi, sweetheart, just dropped the mad professor at the station. Are you at Rose's? Ask her if George could stay over. Be good if we can just be the two of us tonight. There's a lot to tell you and hopefully it's not as dark as I thought. I'll pick you up in about an hour. Love you xxx

She must have had the phone in her hand. The response came back in about a minute.

Already thought that one through and Rose is cool with it. George would swap us for her and Daniel any day, so that's not a problem. Let's get a takeaway on the way back. Love U2 x

He could play that game as well as she could. Or thought he did anyway.

Gr8 x

Piss off, smartarse!

That was that then. Why did he bother? He never won those little games, always let them go on too long. Not this time though. He wouldn't reply. That would show her! It didn't.

God, he was exhausted.

Carefully, he pulled away from the drop offs area and eased his way into the traffic.

They picked up the curry on the way home. Nora didn't want to start on anything deep and difficult until they'd eaten. They both needed calm and focus. Food, wine for him and a half pint of Guinness for Nora would do that. Just the one for Nora though.

After the meal they cleared up the cartons and stuck the plates in the dishwasher. He poured out another glass of wine for himself and, after a bit of thought, a coconut water with melon juice for Nora, then they went into the living room and sat on the sofa, one at each end, facing each other. Those seemed to be their new combat positions, or perhaps, 'keeping out of reach until the words had finished bouncing across the divide' positions. Nora took a sip of her drink, grimaced and put it down. She smiled at Ian. "Sorry, it's too healthy."

"I'll get you something else."

"No, it's fine. Thank you."

It was all unreal. His own personal Armageddon was about to be unleashed and they were being cautiously casual and polite. "Shall I start?"

Nora slid her legs over so they were alongside his on the cushions. "Yes, just the facts."

"All right." He didn't see how he could make it more fantastical and inflated than it was already. So, he began.

It took him an hour and a half to tell the whole tale from meeting Alex to dropping off Baylis at the station. He missed out the odd bits of bile floating around for Sally Ryan and her book. He had enriched some bits, without, he hoped, Nora noticing. It was a constant of his to never let the whole truth get in the way of a good story. And it had become more instinctive now than deliberate.

When he stopped, he let it settle and give her time to consider. She looked at him for a couple of minutes, her eyes locked on his. But he couldn't tell anything from them. Usually, he could take a guess! But this was like they were in a blinking contest and he struggled not to be the first to give in. He failed.

"Fuck me!"

That surprised him. Not her normal reaction. Not that she didn't use the word, but the relish this time was unusual. He bit back his obvious and witty response to that and just waited. She was calm and still. "Do you believe everything he told you?"

It was time for honesty and a straight answer.

"Yes."

"Sure?"

"Well, obviously the bit about the possibility that my moment of danger had passed and the time gap had disappeared again was a positive, as well as the chance that, if it hadn't, it might not be me who took Walter's place in the mortality swap." He couldn't stop the next flip and laughed. "Good concept for a game show. Mortality Morph, the game of life and death, the winner lives, the loser dies! Big online audience of weirdoes and dark web groupies for that one."

"Just follow it through…"

"He seemed to know what he was talking about. He'd gone through it with others who'd had a similar experience. There are a lot of theories out there, particularly his, that would point to proof of the possibilities of there being parallels of time. I think I should go along with him for now and see what the regression brings up. And, in the meantime, I could go to the *Chronicle* and check out murders of policemen that fitted date and place. Walter and Billy. Even during the war, I'm sure that would have been reported."

Nora smiled at him.

"What?"

"I agree with you."

"You do?"

"Yes, I think you should do exactly that and try to keep an open mind about it all."

"Nothing to add to it?"

"No. I wanted you to find your own way not just listen to me banging on and you did. I'm proud of you."

She swung her legs over his and wriggled on her bottom towards him until she was sitting on his lap. It was uncomfortable but he wasn't going to let on. She kissed him, gently then with more intent and passion. Then, just as he was getting warmed up, she moved away.

"What was that for?"

"Sometimes I remember how much I love you. I don't believe that you are going to disappear into a black hole but if you did, I'd really miss you, so just in case, it did happen, I wanted you to know."

Was she taking the piss? He checked and her eyes said she meant it. He tried to pull her back but she slid awkwardly off the sofa, almost dragging his erection with her. He tried not to cry out and managed to reduce it to a whimper instead.

"Sorry, I'd forgotten about your bits. Need a pee badly and then I'm going to bed. If you come up before I go to sleep, you might get lucky."

It wasn't anything that rocked the world but as a warm, gentle connection, it was perfect and they reached a slow and satisfying release, not together, but close enough. It was in the way their bodies fitted together afterwards as they lay in each other's arms, not saying anything, just letting sleep gently come, that gave the most pleasure and said that this, for now, in this moment, was all they needed. As Nora started to breathe more deeply, he kissed her eyes and felt the tears.

"What is it?' He didn't want to break the silence but had to know.

'I love you. I know I can be an old bag and you sometimes deserve it but underneath, you are all I want, you, Georgie, and the lump. And I will fight to the death if anything threatens to take that away." Then, almost as though the words had scattered the last touches of wakefulness, she was asleep.

"I love you too, sweetheart." Then within a minute or two, with, for once, a calm and uncluttered mind, he was sleeping too.

CHAPTER TWENTY

Walter and Cate had just made love. As they lay wrapped in each other's arms she felt the change in rhythm of his breathing and knew he was asleep. She was close to it too, but a momentous truth had washed warmly into her thoughts and kept her awake. Tonight, here in this bed, with the man she loved, she had conceived. She knew beyond a doubt that she was pregnant.

* * *

Something was holding him so he couldn't move his arms or his legs or feel the rest of his body and slowly he was dragged downwards and the light above him dissolved to a pinpoint and then he opened his mouth into a scream that died as he disappeared completely into the endless blackness.

In the bed next to Nora, Ian shook and twisted, then lay still. She didn't wake up.

* * *

Her hands were slipping. She tried to hold on but couldn't stop him dropping through. She watched, helpless and horrified, as twisting and turning, his silhouette slowly sank into a swirling black sea. For a moment there was turbulence then the surface was calm and flat.

The scream woke Mark and he shot up in the bed. "What the fuck…?" Then he realised that it was coming from Lucy. "Luce, what is it?" He wrapped his arms around her. "It's all right, babe, I'm here." She struggled but he held her tightly until she stopped. Slowly he released her and moved his head away so he could see her face. She looked distraught.

"He's dead."

"Who is?"

"Ian."

Jesus, he hadn't expected that.

"No, he's not. It was a bad dream."

"Was it? It felt real. I tried to save him but couldn't hold on to him. It was my fault." Her eyes filled with tears as she went through it again. Then, in moments, the memory was gone and only a feeling of despair was left. She tried to bring back the images but failed. "I can't remember it now."

Mark kissed her head and held her tightly. "Don't worry, I won't let anything happen to you… or your mate Ian." He laughed. "They're tricky bastards sometimes, aren't they? I had one the other night where the boss asked me to give him a massage and when I did he tried to kiss me. I had to nut him. I know that didn't happen. Same with Ian. It was probably because he looked pissed off with you last time you saw him. Don't know why I remember that dream so clearly though."

Lucy laughed through her tears. "You fancy him?"

"Don't even joke about that, he'd kill me if he knew. He's real homo… what's it…?"

"Phobic."

"Yes, that's it." He started to move down the bed. "Want me to give you something else to think about?"

Oh, God, sex again, she was still raw from last night's couplings. "I'm a bit sore. Just…"

"Trust me, I've got a plan."

He disappeared under the duvet. Lucy was thinking that she'd pull him up, then she felt the warmth of his breath and his tongue gently touching her. "Oh, all right, but gently…"

Soon Ian and the dream were no longer part of the story.

* * *

Baylis was in his large book and paper filled study. It was 3.30 and he had woken half an hour ago after three hours' sleep. Before he dragged himself, exhausted, into bed, he had gone through his archive and not found what he was looking for. It was something that he had taken from Abraham Wexler's book *A Confusing Fracture of Time*. Wexler was Chair of Criminal and Selective Psychology at Columbia University. They had been on various international panels discussing Criminal Psychology but also shared a passion for Time and its Parallels. Both academics had, on their theories for this, been reviewed, rejected, and sometimes reviled by the pragmatists and logicians within their peer group who would accept only the credibility of light years travel to the future and, despite the increasing depth of evidence that the two men had uncovered, refused to even debate the possibility of transference to the past.

He and Wexler hadn't always agreed and had appeared many times on podcasts and TV shows to argue and insult and once, in a rare moment of levity, even struggle to gain control by arm-wrestling. Baylis had won that one but afterward conceded that they both might be right. The strangest thing about the way they were perceived was the respect, praise, and credibility that was there for the brilliant and life-changing aspects of their academic work in psychology, and the equally vociferous derision for their theories on the enigmas of time. They were friends and often shared experiences and case histories and occasionally teamed up if something was of interest to both. Perhaps he would call him tomorrow about this one.

He suddenly felt alone and briefly considered it would be good to have someone here now to talk it over with, but there wasn't. His work and domestic life were very clearly defined and separate. He could always phone his wife, Ruby, who when he fell in love with her, twenty-five years ago, was one of his PhD students. She had a sharp and clear insight and often gave him a pragmatic viewpoint that balanced his more eclectic and creative one. She wouldn't, however, appreciate her sleep being broken on a working day. They lived in different places. He was in Leeds and she was in Edinburgh, where she practiced as a barrister. Every weekend they met at one or the other's house. He enjoyed going to hers because it took away the ineluctable pull of work that was always there when he was at home, and he could relax; and she wasn't always on edge that he had things to do that couldn't wait.

So, getting up in the middle of the night, was something that he often did when wrestling with a particularly tricky case. There was no-one there to disturb. A couple of hours of good sleep refreshed and realigned his mind and often removed barriers that had blocked the simplest of pathways that had, before, seemed insurmountable.

This morning it was proving to be tricky and he was ploughing through a bit of a swamp of possibilities. He couldn't even find the signed copy he had of Wexler's book with the inscription *Time will Tell, Abe.* Then it flashed into his head that he had used the particular quote he was looking for in a TED Talk he'd given the previous year, on Transference of Self in a Capsule of Coincidence. It was a title he often used that guaranteed an audience because it always created confusion and vigorous conflicting debate. He started going through the boxes of files that all had some sort of chaotic order, if not in subject matter, then date batches of three months. He found the correct batch and started speed reading the thick files. They were all on a database too. Every three months he paid one of his postgrads to bring it up to date. Sometimes though he wanted to touch, see, and smell the paper of his jumble and notes. Only he could make sense of the scribbles. They were almost indecipherable to even the most agile graphologist, so he made audio versions too. It was what the post grads worked from and if there was a question it was simple to answer it without having to search out his notes again. But he didn't want his voice taking up space now and so this way was better for that and the tactile sensitivity that tonight he wanted to experience.

He flicked through the pages until he found the talk and identified the quote he wanted.

One of the most difficult concepts in understanding transference of self is the way in which it can sometimes change the focus of fate between dimensions. It is created by a fracture in the line between times when the balance of who is the recipient of the transference of self and who is the donator, changes. In that instance the recipient can transfer the fate of that self to another if the reason for rejection is strong enough; the life of the donator and the recipient will both then remain active if their fates are passed to another that is more vulnerable. This transaction again relies upon the speed of transference and the accessibility to the open fracture in the divide between past and present and the two parallels create an equilibrium. An awareness of the potential fates of both the original donor and recipient, by an outside, or out of time, emotional force that is in some way allied to them, can readjust and effect that outcome. Those connectors who share their consciousness can create a channel through which the one in danger of being lost in the wrong dimension can return to their own time.

Yes! He was elated. It had sparked and cleared his head. It might be confusing to some but had a crystal clarity for him. Now he could begin work on a rescue.

He took a large sheet of paper from a roll and put it onto a table with pebbles at each of the four corners to keep the curls flat, chose a red marker pen, thought for a moment, then started to write down a series of equations, numbered geometrics, meteorological and astral chart reference points and figures. Some of it was done at great speed and some after long moments of contemplation and scribbling on a notepad.

* * *

When Ian woke at nine, he was on his own. He had no recollection of any dreams, nothing that had left him feeling raw and vulnerable. Where was Nora? He listened for a moment but there were only the sounds of the old house rattling in the wind.

"Nora?"

Nothing. He got up, had a pee, then went to the top of the stairs. "Nora?" He shouted it this time. He pulled on tracksuit bottoms, a T-shirt and, because it was freezing, a thick hoodie too, and went looking for her. She hadn't said she was going anywhere. She'd left a note on the kitchen table.

Thought you needed to sleep, so didn't wake you. Got the bus, had to get into town early for a pedicure at Magic Stones. I'd forgotten about it and only remembered when I was in the bath at seven. It was on the calendar that you never look at. Get yourself organized and ring the Chronicle. I love you. See you later. Rose is picking me up on the way back from school this afternoon. Date nights are good to get the balance right xx

She was right about the date night and the calendar. He didn't know where it 'lived'! It didn't matter, did it?

He found it on the fridge. How many times had he opened the door and not seen it in front of him? There was a big and colourful picture of Winnie the Pooh on this month's page. How could he have missed it?

That meandering didn't stay with him for long as the need for food ejected it. He was starving, so he had toast with poached eggs and mushrooms. He felt great this morning, his head was brighter and, although he was still tired, not exhausted like he had been for the last week. And he didn't feel so doom laden about his trip to the past after seeing Baylis coupled with the memory of last night and Nora. It was like they had found a part of each other again that had gone missing. He knew though that he could easily catapult himself back into the darkness. He'd fight it hard though if he felt it was happening.

He rang the Chronicle and made an appointment for twelve to meet the archivist. He didn't think they'd be big enough to have their own, but what did he know? Still, they sounded helpful when he gave them a brief outline of what he was looking for and the time span of the issues he wanted to see.

He wondered whether he should send off the book to Janey now, without Nora's take on it. No, that would not be a good move. His idea of a brilliant ending might be delusional. Better to be slapped down by Nora than Janey. He still had a bit of time. It was sensible to wait.

He thought he'd see if he could find anything online about the murder before he went, then decided to do the fire instead, ready for tonight, and, in a rush of domesticity, to give the bathroom a clean and surprise Nora. Warming to this theme, he cleared up the breakfast things and, after leaving the kitchen almost spotless, went upstairs.

He arrived at the Chronicle offices in Bridlington at a quarter to twelve. It was in an old building that was having some major work done to the outside. He made his way through the arch of scaffolding that led to the front door. It had already been renovated and was simple but expensive with a series of call buttons. He pressed the one for Reception. After a second ring a male voice said, "Who is it?"

"Ian Chambers, I made an appointment for twelve with the archivist."

"Who?" A long pause and a deep voice mumbled something. "Oh, that's you, is it, Lenny? 'Archivist' threw me a bit there. Come up the stairs to the first floor. The reception desk is on the right, through the double doors."

"Thanks." He said it to himself as the voice had gone. The door buzzed and he pushed it open. So, what did Lenny normally do? Heavy stuff from the sound of his rumbling voice.

In front of him there was a wide and wonky original wooden staircase in need of serious attention. He went up the creaking steps and found his way to reception. There was a young man, talking on a mobile, behind the desk and next to him a very small, nattily dressed man with a strange wig and long fingernails on one hand. Two small men in two days. Perhaps he was being prepared for a world in which he would be shrunk to fit.

"Mr Chambers, I'm Lenny Dixon." He had a deep Geordie voice that didn't fit his size and delicate features. He could have been anything from late fifties to early seventies.

"Hello, thanks for this."

"It's the best part of my job, usually I just do the hatched, matched, dispatched, but I love the history, so this is the fun bit." Ian was fascinated by his hair. Although it was attached and unmoving, it seemed to belong to someone who had a much bigger head than he had. "Come on, then. Follow me to the bowels." He took off with quick tiny steps, like a miniature Poirot. Ian followed him to another staircase at the back of the building. They went down three flights and finally came to a large brightly lit room with floor-to-ceiling shelving and two small desks, each with microfiche and computer pod. There was also a long table with individual lights on bendy arms.

"Bit of a surprise this, isn't it?" Lenny was proud of his kingdom. "Nothing like this, of course, when I started twenty years ago. It was musty and miserable, but I managed to tart it up a bit." In front of one of the lights were two large folders of original copies of the Chronicle, the light hitting them, soft and focused. Lenny stood next to a chair in front of the folders. He took out a pair of new white cotton gloves. "Here you are, pet. Don't want your mucky fingers all over them. I've got you January to March 1943 and marked a couple of items that might be of interest. Haven't got this far back in digitising yet but this is better anyway. You can smell and taste it."

Ian took the gloves. Lenny pointed to a telephone. "Press six if you need help and I'll come running. I close for lunch at one, so I need you out by ten to."

"Sure, thanks."

"My pleasure." He smiled and hurried off. Ian was left there on his own. His stomach was fluttering in anticipation. He sat down, put on the gloves, and opened one of the folders. There were twelve copies for each month. He'd read somewhere, that because of the war, they'd gone from daily to three a week. He took a deep breath and opened the first, dated 1st January-31st February 1943, glanced over the first page of the issue dated Friday 1st January before going to the first marker that Lenny had put in. He'd check those out first, then do a more forensic examination if he found nothing useful.

* * *

Mark and Lucy were heading down the motorway away from the Lake District. He'd had a call from his boss early that morning. He needed Mark to ferry around some important 'clients' from Switzerland who had to be picked up from Heathrow at six tomorrow morning and taken to his mansion in Surrey. He tried to persuade Lucy to come with him but didn't push her too hard. He'd seen a different way to play their relationship game too and, for now, was happy with that!

He was singing loudly along to 'Hey Jude' and Lucy was looking out at the cars and the grey and shadowy landscape they were flying past. There was a little wedge of light at the corner of the sky and the clouds lightened. The day and Lucy's mood brightened again as the sun came out. She was still shaky about her dream, particularly as bits of it were coming back. She desperately wanted to check things were all right with Ian and to make sure that Nora was good with her too. Going with Mark would be the easy option, but she had to face this out. She knew that they needed to be adult about it. So, he'd been a selfish and disloyal little shit. Perhaps after all that happened, he'd have learned his lesson and they might be able to have the sort of relationship that went forward instead of constantly looking back. She did love him. But it was the love of friendship that she really valued. Being with Mark over the last few days and discovering that she could be content with him and not try to force him into being her ideal man had helped put things in perspective. She was going to phone Ian from the station. If he wouldn't see her, she would get the next train to London.

* * *

Baylis had worked through until eleven thirty then slept. He stopped because he'd worked out a possible plan that would help Ian's chances if he were to slip through again. He thought that from the conclusions he'd come to that he was probably safe and that the time had passed, but it didn't hurt to have a backup. And this one was simple and the opposite of some advice he'd already given him. Try and keep awake through the next twenty-four hours. That was the window he had worked out was possible if the fracture were still active. It would start late afternoon. If, after that, Ian was to allow his subconscious to be susceptible to shared memory, it could be fatal for him. Baylis was exhausted and thought he would sleep for a couple of hours then drive across to meet him. It wouldn't help anyone if he crashed the car on his way there. He'd phoned before lying down on the sofa in his study, but Ian hadn't picked up. He'd left a message explaining and asking him to call as soon as he got it.

* * *

Ian had gone through all the paperclip markers that Lenny had put in and although there were quite a few stories about police bravery and bootlegging there was nothing about a Walter or a Billy. Then he started again, this time from the end of March 1943, and worked backwards. He'd found that looking for something specific this way, particularly with newspapers, often picked up on things he'd missed before.

He was getting disheartened and checked his phone to see how long he had left. It was dead. He'd meant to charge it in the car on the way in and forgotten. He looked around the room and saw a clock on the wall. Squinting, he could just make it out. Twenty to one. He'd have to come back after Lenny's lunch, if he'd let him.

Then he found it: page two of the Saturday, March 6th 1943 issue. It took his breath away when he saw the picture of 'his' Walter under the quarter page article headline. He'd missed it because the pages were paperclipped together and he'd turned over two.

Police Sergeant in Life and Death struggle with Nazi Spy dropped by Submarine on South Beach.

Police Sergeant Walter Robbins, 35, was badly

injured in the Look-out Post on North Beach when he and Police Constable Arthur Riley, 48, were attacked by a Nazi spy on Friday the fifth of March. The German was killed by Sergeant Robbins, who was bleeding badly from a stomach wound and armed only with his truncheon. His life was saved by the quick thinking and first aid skills of Constable Riley. Sergeant Robbins and Constable Riley were praised by the Mayor and the Chief Constable of Yorkshire for their bravery. Sergeant Robbins is married but has no children and Constable Riley is married with two sons.

He didn't die. Walter didn't die! That meant he wouldn't either!

He could hardly contain himself. The relief was immense, He felt weak as it washed over him and his muscles and face unclenched and the tightness went.

He didn't see Lenny approach. "Looks like you found what you were looking for. Wish I could say the same."

Ian glanced up, surprised to see him. "Yes, you could say that. Thank you, Lenny." He handed back the gloves and stood up, his legs shaky.

"My pleasure." Lenny said with a smile and a nod of his head. This time the wig did move and he had to adjust it. Ian had to stop himself rushing out. He needed to charge his phone and talk to Nora and Baylis, in that order. He went out, ran up the three flights to reception and made his way down the main staircase. As he opened the door the sky darkened. Then there was a loud clap of close-by thunder followed by a sharp crackle of lightning. Shit, he hoped he'd make the car before the rain started...

As he got through to the edge of scaffolding in front

of the building, he didn't see the plank slip out of the hands of the guy who was passing it from the top level down to the second, nor hear the shout. He just glimpsed the long heavy plank as it bounced off the scaffolding and, almost vertical, slammed into his stomach, the metal edging, half-ripped-off and sharp, tearing through his flesh. Then the plank hit the poles, twisted again, and hit him with huge force on the head. He dropped like a stone, cracked his head on the kerb, and was unconscious by the time a man walking passed reached him and the scaffolders jumped down. They all froze for a moment then Lenny, coming out through the door, saw Ian lying there, and took in the blood and the plank.

"Anybody phoned 999?" Obviously, they hadn't. "Fucking do it now!" His booming voice broke the spell and they all took out their mobiles. "Just one, you wankers." He knelt by Ian, saw the blood pouring, pulled open his coat… "Fuck it!" He pulled off his wig and pressed it hard against the wound.

One of the scaffolders had got through. "They're on the way." He noticed Lenny and the wig and started to laugh.

Lenny glanced at him. "Don't you fucking dare!" He was small but his voice wasn't. It was threatening and aggressive. The scaffolder shook his head, mouthed, 'Sorry', and turned away.

In the distance were the faint sounds of a siren…

CHAPTER TWENTY-ONE

It was late afternoon and getting dark. The rain had eased for now. Walter, starting his shift in a couple of hours, was checking his moustache in the mirror. He had the scissors in his hand and was just about to trim it when he realised the light wasn't good enough. There was a small lamp on the table under the mirror and he switched it on then… "Shit!" immediately off again. He put it back on the table, went across to the window, and pulled the blackout down, then came back, turned the lamp on, and held it up so he could see what he was doing. Carefully he cut across his top lip until his mouth was clear of hairs, snipped another couple from his nostrils, then examined his face turning it one way then the other. 'Not bad for an ageing copper.' He took out his comb and as he tidied the bits sticking up, he noticed a couple of grey hairs and pulled them out. He wasn't going to make it easy for time to stamp him yet. He smiled at his reflection and winked.

"You'll do, Sergeant."

Then he winced at a sudden jab of pain in his leg. It was playing up today, probably all the rain that had been non-stop for weeks. He sat on the chair at the kitchen table and stretched it out then pulled up his trouser leg and rubbed the long deep scar for a couple of minutes then flexed and released the muscle a couple of times. It helped. He checked the time on his pocket watch, got up, stretched his leg again and went to the sink. It had the dishes he'd used in it. He washed them out and put them on the draining board and dried his big old mug. He felt the teapot under the cosy and poured out a half-mugful. It was dark and probably a bit stewed. He didn't mind that, gave it a bit more of a taste. He added a bit of milk from the jug on the worktop then sat in the chair next to the range and put the mug on the floor. He leaned his head back against the antimacassar and closed his eyes. He'd have a couple of minutes.

When he woke up, Cate was standing over him, the mug in her hand. "It's stone cold. I'll make you another."

"Thanks, love! What time is it?"

She checked the clock on the mantelpiece. "You've got another hour before you have to go." She kissed his head, pulled back and studied his face. "You've tidied up your 'tache. Makes you look a bit like Errol Flynn."

"You think so?" He smoothed it with his hand. "Wish I had his other bits."

She looked confused.

"You know, he's supposed to have a huge…"'

Her eyes opened wide. "Don't be rude, Walter Robbins, or you won't get your tea!" She rinsed out the teapot and giggled. "Still, if you ask me, you don't do so badly in that department." She filled the kettle and placed it on the stand over the fire.

"I'm shocked at you, Mrs Robbins." He looks closely at her for moment. She was looking pleased with herself, a smile coming. "You look different. What is it?"

"A secret."

"Tell me."

"No."

"Please."

"What's it worth?"

"Anything you want."

"Really?"

"I'll make the Sunday dinner."

"Promise?"

"Yes."

"Honest?"

"Come on, yes. What is it? Is it good?"

"Yes."

"Catherine?"

Cate smiled and took his hand.

"I saw Elsie at the bus stop. She thinks she might be pregnant again."

"What? Is that it? I don't know how he does it. He was only home for three days. It's not fair that some folks just have to look at each other and the babies come."

Cate suddenly smiled and laughed. "I'll be due first though."

Walter looked at her in shock. "What?"

"I'm having a baby."

"How?"

"Well, you know, you have to put…"

He laughed. "How do you know?"

"Went to the surgery this afternoon. That's why I'm late back."

Walter jumped up and hugged her.

"Cate, that's wonderful! When?"

"It'll be a late summer baby, September probably."

Walter felt the tears and tried to stop them but couldn't. Cate couldn't either.

"I love you," he said, kissing her.

"I love you too, Walt, and I'd rather have you than Errol Flynn and his big bits any day."

After a moment, Cate pulled away. "Don't say anything yet."

"I won't."

You could hear the storm outside even in the small windowless room where Walter and Arthur sat, having a last brew and a warm before going out. They both knew they couldn't hang it out much longer. Walter drained his mug, looked across at Arthur. "You ever feel guilty, Arthur?"

"What about?" He was doing up his jacket.

"Us, being here and not risking our arses at the sharp end?"

"Don't think about it much. Too old anyway. Wouldn't mind a bit of sun, though." He picked up a paper from the floor and looked at the football on the back page. "What made you think about it now? Bad enough going out in shitty weather like this without getting depressed about things we can't do anything about."

Walter took a long breath and sighed.

"Tommy Bourne's missus got a telegram yesterday. *Missing in action presumed dead.* Bloody terrible. Can't even grieve until you know for sure. Cate said she was in an awful state."

The door opened and Dan Pilkington stuck his head around it.

"Time you two weren't here."

Walter picked up the mugs. "On our way, Sarge. We

were just saying how lucky we were to have a nice, cosy number like this."

There was a loud clap of thunder. Pilkington smiled.

"Off you go then. Enjoy."

Walter put his helmet on. "What time's Taff in?"

"Why?"

"We're going to have a break in the hut on North Beach about three. Ask him to drop off a flask of tea ready for us?"

"Cheeky bugger! Now shift yourselves."

Huge crashing waves were battering the shoreline as howling winds and torrential icy rain whipped and twisted. The black sky heaved as the cracking thunder and jagged spasms of lightening bounced and echoed around the cliffs where the beach ran into rock.

It was a hell of a night to brave and battle against this sort of violent storm but Walter and Arthur, dressed in heavy capes and helmets, were almost at the end of the deserted promenade, their bodies leaning into the howling wind, metal-toed-and-heeled boots clicking and sliding on the saturated slabs.

They stopped at steps leading down to the beach, moved their heads together.

Arthur wiped the rain from his face. "I'll see you later, then."

"Unless I get washed away."

He stepped carefully and slowly down onto the steps, hesitated and, as Arthur turned and started towards a small hut edged against the cliff, he shouted to him, his hands cupped around the sides of his mouth. "Arthur. Arthur." It took a moment for Arthur to hear then he stopped, looked back and, seeing Walter wave him over, moved to join him on the step.

"Instead of a quick peek to see if all's as it should be, why don't we raid the Home Guard lad's tea? Stay out of the storm for a bit."

Arthur looked back at the hut then at Walter. "Percy still bring those boxes of Ginger Nuts from the Co-op?"

"So Albert says."

"Why not then, nobody'll miss us. If they do, they'll check the hut first."

"Thought you'd asked if Taff could drop off a flask."

"Won't happen. Dan's got a bit of a grouse on from the look of him. And if he does that'll save for later."

They moved down onto the beach, Walter limping on the uneven sand. It was tough on his leg in the middle of weather like this.

They battled against the wind and rain. Walter glanced at the raging and crashing sea. The noise was almost unbearable.

They were lashed by the wind, rain and spray. Arthur looked towards the outline of the just visible Lookout post. Suddenly he saw a brief flickering beam of light bounce and disappear. He grabbed Walter's arm and pointed towards the light as it flashed again. He shook the rain out of his eyes and squeezed them to focus on the Lookout.

"Looks like they're there after all." He started to pick up speed.

Walter grabbed his arm, stopped him. "No, Dan told me on the way out that they're all on an exercise. There'll be no-one there till about four." It was hard to breath in the raging wind. "There's something up, I can feel it."

"Don't be daft, Walt. You're as bad as that bloody Bott woman, seeing spies all over the place. It'll be someone sheltering or a couple of randy kids."

It was hard forcing their way through the buffeting and blowing but eventually they got to the dark and rough building and moved around it until they got to the door. There was some shelter and for a moment, Walter hesitated, then reached inside his cape, took out a truncheon, held it at head height, then grasped the handle, slippery in the wet, and with difficulty turned it and slowly pushed the door open. Arthur pulled out a torch and switched it on. The beam was dim, the batteries flat or too wet to work well. He shook his head. At least it showed up a bit. He took out his truncheon with his other hand and nodded. Walter slowly pulled open the door.

For a moment they stood in the opening, breathing hard and listening for any sounds that weren't their own. The light from the torch died suddenly and for a moment the dark was absolute, then an explosive zigzag of lightning cracked and sparked directly above the Lookout and reflected on a long, serrated knife blade as it slammed towards Walter, slicing through the cape, uniform, and into his body.

Walter brought the truncheon down hard, grabbed the arm with his free hand, and pulled with all his strength. The knife flew out of the hand and the man fell forward, struggling to keep balanced. Walter and Arthur followed him down and pounded him with their truncheons. They held them in both hands so they didn't lose grip and shouted as the man writhed from the blows, trying to protect himself. They were too much for him. At last he was still. There was a lot of blood. Arthur stopped, breathing heavily. Walter was about to bring the slippery truncheon down again, but Arthur grabbed hold of his arm.

"Walter! Walter!" He had to pull him up onto his knees to stop him. "That's enough, Walt."

Walter's face was contorted and tears streamed down his cheeks. He started to shake then collapsed. Arthur held him then saw the blood spurting out from the knife wound. "Oh, fuck, Walter." He pulled off his cape, held it over the wound, then took off his belt, struggling to pull Walter up, and tied the belt around holding the cape in place. He reached down and touched the knifeman's neck, feeling for a pulse. It was very faint, almost gone. The bastard was just about finished. He could wait!

Arthur picked Walter up and laid him over his shoulder, then glanced once more at the body on the ground and backed out of the door and headed down the beach. In the distance coming along the promenade was the shadow of a van; pinpoint headlights flashed on then off. Arthur stumbling with the weight of Walter, caught the faint moment of light. "Taff, thank fuck!"

CHAPTER TWENTY-TWO

At York station Lucy had tried to get hold of Ian. The message from his mobile was that it was unavailable. She'd left two messages on the house phone. She wasn't going to panic. But she was close to it. She looked at her phone, flicked through her contacts and found Nora. She hesitated a moment then called her. It was busy. She tried again and again. The fifth time it rang, Nora answered, and the world changed.

When Lucy arrived at the hospital in Bridlington, Nora wasn't in the A&E waiting area. There were small groups and singles and an odd couple, two men, one, a giant with long white hair in a ponytail and a bushy beard, the other a very small bald man holding what looked like a mangled hairy scalp in his hand. Strange how Lucy picked all that up on her way to the reception desk, but at times like this her senses were heightened. She was terrified that Ian had died and had to be told to take deep breaths before the nurse was able to understand. Her calm and efficient handling of the panic eased Lucy and she was able to ask where he was. The nurse said that she would find out what was happening. She then pointed to the odd couple. "Those gentlemen are waiting too. The little one came in with him. He was a bit upset because he ruined his wig but that probably kept Mr Chambers alive until the paramedics arrived and took over. I don't know the full story. Why don't you wait with them?"

Lucy was shaking as she got to where they were sitting. The big man gently helped her to sit down, his deep voice soothing as he introduced himself and glanced toward the little man. He looked up at her and said hello. It was as if the large man had channelled his voice through him. If anything, it was deeper and almost, to her, unintelligibly Geordie, whereas the other was slightly posh. The big man took her hand.

"Roly Baylis. All we know is that he's in theatre. We've got Lenny here to thank for keeping him from bleeding out."

Lucy felt like she'd slipped into another dimension. The small man put the wig on the floor then wiped his hands using a large pack of wet wipes. "Always carry them. Don't know what you might pick up."' She noticed he had very long nails on one hand. He saw her react. "I play Spanish classical guitar."

Lucy was losing it. This was unreal. "What happened to Ian?"

"He was hit by a scaffolding plank coming out of the newspaper office. Cut into his belly and knocked him out. I used to be a gymnast and trained as a medic to handle any injuries in the troupe. Long time ago now. Anyway, I was able to help a bit. Ruined a five–hundred-pound wig mind. If it doesn't clean up, I'll want another."

Baylis tapped him on the shoulder. "I'll buy you one. If he comes through this, I might even get you a spare too."

Lenny wasn't sure if he was taking the piss. Lucy knew they were both mad. She looked at Baylis. "Why are you here?"

Lenny laughed. "If you think I'm weird, listen to what Thor's dad has to say…"

* * *

In the look-out, the man's eyes flickered, opened briefly, then rolled back into his head and he died.

* * *

Cate was sitting with Arthur in the hospital waiting room. He had his arm around her and his voice was quiet. "He's a tough one. Got over worse than this."

Cate pulled away from him. "He can't die, Arthur, we both need him."

It took Arthur a moment to realise what she'd said. He took her hand.

"He won't. The nurse I talked to before you got here said it had missed most of the vital bits and looked worse than it was. Close though, and he'll need time to recover."

Cate was unsure. "Are you telling me the truth?"

Arthur hesitated.

"Most of it." She looked hard at him. "Next couple of hours anything could happen. If he gets through that he should be all right. Does he know about the baby?"

"Yes."

"Then he'll fight like hell to stay with you."

Just then she saw a doctor come out of a set of double doors. He looked around, saw Cate and Arthur, and came over. Cate stood up, frightened and shaky. "What is it?"

"Just wanted to let you know that the operation went well, Mrs Robbins, and he's in the recovery ward. Private room. Would you like to sit with him?"

"Yes, please."

Arthur smiled at her. "I'll be here if you need me, love."

Cate nodded and then went with the doctor. Arthur watched until they went through the double doors, then looked around and clasped his hands together.

"I know I don't talk much to you, don't even go to church, so shouldn't just ask when I need something. It's not for me though. Cate and her baby will need him. Just give him a bit of a hand, will you. And, if someone needs to go to keep up the numbers and the lad in the look-out won't do, then you can have me."

He looked around to see if anyone had heard him. The place was still empty. He looked up at the ceiling. "Deal?"

* * *

Baylis had just finished telling Lucy how he'd met Ian when she saw Nora. The other two followed her look. "It's his wife." she said and then all three got up. Lucy turned to them. "Please let me talk to her first." They both nodded and sat down. Lucy felt the tears start as she went towards Nora, who saw her, stopped and waited. She looked wiped out, pale, eyes red and lost. Lucy put her arms around her. Nora slowly pulled away. "Why are you in York?"

"I had a bad feeling. I didn't part on the best of terms with Ian. Mark had to get back to London and I thought

I'd spend a day here and try to sort it out. I didn't really think that anything would have happened to him. How is he?"

"He got through the operation. It was a deep wound but missed all the important bits." She looked over at Lenny. "Without his quick reaction, it might have been different. He managed to control the bleeding. They've just done a brain scan. They're waiting for the consultant to check it out. He's badly concussed." She looked at Lucy for a long moment. "Is it over?"

Lucy's heart bounced in her chest and her eyes gave it away. Nora touched her arm.

"Something went on between you two. I know him too well." She leaned in close to her. "He's a prick and you're a selfish tart!" Then she moved back. "Once this is all over, I might challenge you to a duel but if it ever happens again, I'll kill you both." She took a deep breath. "For now, he needs all the help he can get. We both love him. That's enough for me."

Lucy was stunned. "I'm sorry…"

Nora shook her head. "I don't want to hear." She got up. "I can go and sit with him now. Do you want to come with me?" Her eyes filled with tears. "I don't want to be on my own."

"Are you sure?"

"Yes. I might make you sit outside though."

* * *

Cate was sitting at the side of the bed holding Walter's hand. She was on her own in the room. She watched him closely. "Come on, love, I need you." She pushed back the tears. "I love you so much. I know we had some ups and downs, but I never stopped even when I was horrible to you." Suddenly she was taken over by the tears. She didn't see Walter's eyes flicker, open briefly, close, then open again.

"Cate." She didn't hear him. He said it louder. "Cate."

She suddenly realised and looked up at him and her face lit up.

"Hello, love, you gave me a bit of a scare."

* * *

Nora sat by the bedside. There were monitors and tubes plugged into Ian. She couldn't stop looking at the heart monitor. She missed his eyelids flickering then slowly opening. He watched her, struggling to focus.

"Hello, sweetheart."

Nora snapped her head around. "Shit. Sorry. Oh, fuck I was so scared." She pressed the call nurse button.

Ian watched her. "What happened?"

The nurse rushed in, Lucy behind her.

Nora laughed. "He's back!"

EPILOGUE

Ian, the baby strapped to his chest, Nora, and George walk along the beach. It's hot and sunny. Evie is four months old. Life is good again for the Chambers clan. He and Nora are back on track. His TV series has been picked up, and the book is on a final edit, with Janey still spitting threats but letting slip that she'd have missed him if he'd left her world. Lucy is out of the way in Australia for a year. Enough time to forgive and heal for all of them. People are in the sea and the sand is crowded with families, sandcastle builders, footie and ball players. George sees a football coming towards him and kicks it back to...

...Walter, who then kicks it back to the kids playing football. He smiles at George, waves and sits back down on a rug on the sand next to Cate and the small baby she's breastfeeding.

For a moment Walter and Ian's eyes meet and they smile and nod.

Then each disappears into their own time and their own place.

Printed in Great Britain
by Amazon